FINALLY . . . YES!

D. H. CROSBY

authorHOUSE®

AuthorHouse™
1663 Liberty Drive
Bloomington, IN 47403
www.authorhouse.com
Phone: 1 (800) 839-8640

Published by AuthorHouse 10/04/2017

ISBN: 978-1-5462-0969-0 (sc)
ISBN: 978-1-5462-0968-3 (e)

Library of Congress Control Number: 2017914720

Print information available on the last page.

This is the same author that brought the romance to life in her last three books of the saga

"GM & GS Private Investigation Service"

Enjoy the same amount of suspense and intrigue, humor and family values that a good romance deserves!

PART ONE

CHAPTER ONE

The night had a deafening silence. No sound was a good sound after the day she had had. Dealing with the family of a deceased child was not one of her fortes. It always pierced her heart. As a private eye, she had to report the facts and that was an extra heavy weight tonight ... because it was her own daughter's death date.

She poured herself a rum and coke and flopped down on her plush sofa kicking her heels off. The promise she had made to herself was to never drink. This was the only one she had had in fourteen years so to justify it, she said to herself, "It is okay for this one time. You deserve it Martina."

Throwing it back in one gulp, she sat on her window seat staring out the window of her apartment. She could see the rain pounding the sidewalk. The streetlight was aglow and a halo was forming around the Victorian lantern light fixture.

She had chosen this area of town to settle in ten years ago. She loved the gated community that was drenched in historic beauty and fine dining. An art gallery was nearby and she would visit it tonight. It always calmed her nerves after a case had been closed.

She could walk through it and gaze at the beautiful masterpieces and replace the ugly stench of death with the beauty of the canvasses. Refilling her mind with glorious images of landscapes divines and strolling from one to the other, she smiled. Then she saw him.

He was walking toward her and she turned her back to him. Phillip had always come to check on her after she solved a case. She had to stop doing this. She had worn this fancy Oscar de la Renta dress of mauve and three inch black heels for him. She clutched at her black matching Prada purse.

He knew her every move and that was good. She might even tell him, "Yes" tonight. She secured her long mossy brown hair behind one ear so her shoulder would be exposed to him approaching her on that side.

He stopped and kissed her tiny four leaf clover that was behind her left ear. It was so tiny only he knew it was there because her hair hide it from view during the working day.

"You are late!" She said not turning. She continued to stare at the picture and tilted her head to focus on the countryside. It displayed the most beautiful canvas. A field of lilacs, they were her favorite and he knew it.

"Yes I am indeed … because I had to get these," and she turned. There in his left hand was a bouquet of lilacs and the other hand was grasping her hand to steady her. "If I didn't know better, I'd say you have had a nip, my lady!" grinning and devouring her with his eyes.

Her eyelashes were fluttering to see him better and she extended her neck upward to look at this six foot four gorgeous man of hers. In her heels she was his match but with out the three inch heels she was a mere five foot six. On a good day she would put on five inch heels just to mess with his concentration, and she smiled.

"You are so observant and the flowers are breathtaking," she smelled of them and looked into his eyes. He knew that look and he nearly buckled.

When her eyes were twinkling, she was going to be his tonight. Why would she do that in this crowded room? She knows what is does to me he said to himself. He straightened his suit coat.

She looked at his tugging and placed a hand on his shoulder and said, "Yes, I am all yours!"

He picked her up and kissed her in front of all the art gallery's patrons. They all knew these two and they began clapping as Phillip grabbed her waist. Then he went down on one knee, and reaching into his coat pocket to retrieve the engagement ring that they had picked out months ago.

"Will you, my darling Martina ... put me out of my misery and marry me? I promise you that we will always come here on our anniversaries in the future. Be my wife!"

She waited and looked around at her friends and then to the man that was kneeling on the floor. "Yes, I will marry you on one condition ... that you don't try and change me! Is that clear?"

"Yes, I will have you as you are for the rest of my life," and he arose and sealed the deal with a kiss.

"You have been drinking!" she had kissed him with no reservations as she usually did. Dang! If he wasn't going to have a hard time getting out of here with this erection she had caused. His eyes had widen to survey her erotic appearance.

"Complain! Complain! Yes, I am loose as a goose. Now hold me before I either fall or change my mind!" and she smiled with a ridiculous sideways laugh.

He immediately grabbed her up with that ring on her finger, and carried her past the cheering crowd to his car. He stood her on her feet and opened the door.

"You are not going to blame our engagement on being drunk, and didn't know what you were saying. I've waited four years for you to say yes. Now do I have to ply you with black coffee or not?"

"You can ply with that gun in your pocket Buttercup, if you want to?" and she was running her finger across his lips as he held her waist.

He pulled her to him and she was in no doubt that the word "Buttercup" had triggered a greater need than anything a man-made male enhancement could ever do.

He always showed her that he was not a buttercup, but a ferocious tiger in the bedroom. She had done it on purpose. He was going to let her call him that every day for the rest of their lives in PRIVATE. He would let her slide today. It was her child's death date and he knew it.

Now this date would be their engagement date, so he was going to make it special. He open the car door of his Levante Maserati and helped her in. She immediately reclined the seat. "I want it now!"

4

His eyes dilated and his mouth flew open, "YOU are not going to pull that stunt again. This is my engagement too, and I will take you out for a nice dinner and black coffee! Is that clear? Your Buttercup has spoken!"

"Spoil Sport!" she slurred her words and he knew, too well. No way was she going to have sex in front of the Art Galley no matter what he did. She told him that in the past.

She is baiting me he told himself, but it will not work this time. "I will eat first. Then you will pay the price." He looked over and she was fast asleep.

He drove up the coast to Malibu and he had called ahead for a table at their favorite beach restaurant. Yes, Nobu Malibu. The wonderful sushi was her favorite and the spectacular ocean view was his favorite.

She straightened her mauve attire and freshened her makeup before exiting the car with a whiff of Ciara meeting his nostrils. It was a testament of her quick spray from her purse.

She was going to drive him mad before the dinner was through. She gave him a sweet grin as if to say, "I know it and you know it."

He quickly grasped her elbow and steered her in without her touching him in any way. She was known to let those long fingers delve in his hair and roam across his chest, and he was having none of it. Until she has some coffee, and they are back at her apartment. There she would have free rein of him.

He dined on Maine Lobster with an artichoke salad

just for him, and she had Miso soup with Tofu. Her main course was her favorite Sushi and Sashimi.

Phillip said loudly, "Two black coffees!" as she sipped her water.

Martina said, "You are really showing off, aren't you?"

"Yep and you love it. Don't you? Now keep your shoes on please. I want to take them off at your place and nibble your toes."

She lifted his pant leg with her big toe and ran it up his shin. "I don't listen well. Do I?" smiling and sipping her coffee while peering over the rim of the cup at him.

He sucked in a breath as he grasped his fork to stab at his lobster's tail with a vengeance. "No, you do not. That is a fact. I have grown accustom to it. It will only mean we sit here all night. I truly cannot arise from my seat with the condition you have caused." he arched one eyebrow to emphasize his predicament. "Satisfied?"

She leaned in and stated with her hand squeezing his knee and said, "Not yet." Then she put her shoe on quickly and her hand on her purse because she knew he was going to wave to the waiter and request the check.

On cue he had her out the door, and in the car that the valet brought to the front post haste. He scurried around the car and down the winding road, he drove without saying a word.

He pulled over at a vacant stretch of beach and parked. Then directed for her to get out. She did because that coffee had her wide eyed, and she was ready for him.

He took her by the hand, and they strolled down the beach. He was going to make her beg for his advances. He thought he could until she proved him wrong by inserted her slender hand into his pant's pocket.

She was a master at proving that he had no will power when it came to her. He could handle business meetings, and wheel and deal with powerful people, but this one woman could destroy his best strategic plans.

He was a happy man because this night she had **FINALLY said YES!**" She would be in his bed every night soon. It had taken him four long years for him to convince her that it was her that he wanted. Not one of the rich bimbos that were always at his beck and call.

She was his equal in the bedroom and intellectually. She challenged him every day. When they had met, she was on the police force and dressed in a navy blue business suit. A mere detective working a case. He had bumped into her on the sidewalk while he was going into his office building.

She was embarrassed her badge on her hip had got caught in his suit coat, and he had held her too close to keep her from ripping his expensive Armani suit. Then she punched him because he had moved his hands from her waist to her buttocks. That pushing him away was not something that had not happened to him for many years, and he looked at her and asked, "Do you know who I am?"

"I haven't the foggiest, but if you every touch me again. I will break your fingers! Sir ... one twist and you will never touch another female as you have done me!" glaring at him.

Her hair back then was in a tight bun, but with the

struggle it had spilled onto his shoulder. As she jerked to get her badge free, and that hair smelled of Ciara, her perfume still today.

Now she had her own Private Investigation agency. She still took his breath away as she had done that day. She was right. He had not manhandled another female since their first meeting.

It was only her that had been in his thoughts. Since that day whether he was in a meeting, on a plane, in his car … his thoughts were all of this beautiful woman. He turned her around and kissed her.

She was responding and he was coming undone. "We are not going to make it to your place."

"I know. Now don't wait another minute," she purred in his ear and ran her fingers through his hair, and licked his lips as she stood on her tiptoes.

He reached for the hem of her dress as she unzipped him and he found she had no lacy undies on. His eyes widened.

"You went to the gallery, out to eat, and anyone could have seen my treasure?" and gritted his teeth.

She was moving her hands to better adjust him into her as she wrapped her legs around him.

"I won't do it again again again, I promise," as he lifted her and lifted her until he felt her quiver and his clinched teeth became a grin.

"I needed this to see your face as we make love, and I will make you happy as you make me for the rest of our lives. Oh baby again again, I promise" It was the slow coupling that each savored, and then it intensified as usual it was explosive to the point that neither could breath, but only gasp for air.

He walked her to her door. "Can I come in?" rubbing her buttocks as he held her close.

"If you do, you will be late for work tomorrow. I will be late," gasping for air and closing her eyes.

"I think out engagement spread all over the front of the newspaper will mean, I don't need to be there early at my office. The circus will probably be here any minute so let me in quickly."

He was in her door and had it locked just in the nick of time. The reporters would be kept at bay by the gatekeepers, and he was into her pounding her as they pounded on her door. It was oblivious to them. Nothing mattered outside her front door.

"We will remember our engagement day for years to come. Let us marry today and you can plan a big wedding for later? I cannot bear another day living without you by my side."

He was begging and slaking his desire in unison.

She simply said, "OK OK ... Oh Oh ... Okayyyy ... Sounds good to me!" as she matched him.

CHAPTER TWO

Phillip was grinning as his best friend Sammy came striding through his office door at a rapid pace. "Is it really true? Are you and Martina finally getting married?"

"Nope!" and he kept on writing in the margins of the report not looking up.

"But I ..." he was sad faced. Then he saw Phillip grinning again.

"Confess and leave no details out. You know I love details."

"Sorry if I tell you, then I'd have to kill you," continuing to edit the report which Sammy snatched from his hands.

The grin became a smile and a sigh, "I am a happy man!" and he relaxed over exaggerated slouching for Sammy to see. He slid down in his chair as if he was an unhealthy weakling.

He was trying to display an exhausted look, but he was too happy to be pitiful and smiled widely, placing his head on his hands that lay on his desk.

"What is wrong with you? I've never seen you like

this!" Sammy was getting concerned for his friend's health.

Phillip could hold it in no longer and burst out laughing.

"We got married on our engagement day, and we've been having non-stopped sex for 24 hours. YOU can tell no one and I mean no one … do you hear me? Speak Sammy!"

Sammy was now sitting and acting like someone who had just been punched in the stomach. "You got married and didn't tell your best friend."

"We didn't want the whole paparazzi following us. We are going to have a big wedding and you can be my best man. Okay?" Phillip said and saw a smile finally cross Sammy's face.

"That's more like it. Congratulations! When can I kiss the bride?" Sammy asked eagerly panting like a mad dog.

"Never!" Phillip said and laid his head back down on his desk.

Sammy patted him on the back and left the office saying, "Get some rest. You are going to need your energy for tonight!" Phillip knew Sammy would not say a word and would keep everyone away from him this day. They had been friends since kindergarten and no one messed with the other without a fight ensuing.

Meanwhile Martina was stepping high and in no way tired … only the opposite. She had more energy today at her office and Nancy was about to knock her out.

"Will you pleaseeee sit down! You are really getting on my last nerve. What kind of caffeine concoction did you

11

make this morning with that espresso machine?" Nancy glared at the desk next to hers.

"It is called a dose of happiness," spreading her fingers into air quotation marks as if it was the newest name for her java.

"Ok, give? You can't fool me. Who is the new guy?" Nancy was fishing.

"Nope same old guy. Just a new ring!" and she dangled her engagement ring for the first time to show it off.

Nancy rounded her desk and took a good look at the ring.

"Anyone I know? He has got to be loaded to buy a ring like that! Must be that rich guy that's has had the hots for you for four years … but you treat him like CRAP. Ain't him, is it? Please say NO, because I have gotten use to feeling sorry for him for barking up the wrong tree!" she stood looking at Martina with a puzzled stare.

Martina didn't answer. Had she really treated him badly, and she frowned. Then a big smile came to her face that scared Nancy. She was thinking about how good she had been to that poor pitiful husband of hers, and knew beyond a shadow of doubt that she had made up for any putdowns she may have made prior to yesterday.

She had definitely treated him the best last night, and had been very GOOD to this man that Nancy felt sorry for. She would tell Nancy. She will tell everyone about their engagement, but she would not tell her about her SECRET wedding. No, that was for no one's ears in this office.

She would tell her best friend Nell later. She would tell

no one and have that circus of reporters around her door, day and night. NO Way! She frowned at Nancy and that made Nancy shake.

"Yes! I have accepted his marriage proposal. Now go back to feeling sorry for him," Martina stated as she opened a new folder.

"Poor man! He is a glutton for punishment!" Nancy said and grinned.

Martina did not look up but thought, "Yes I am going to punish him today and tonight. Punish and punish him all I can. Oh crap, now I got to call him!"

"Honey can you meet me at home in about 30 minutes. I have something for you, and it cannot wait till tonight! Hurry! But don't get a ticket ... Buttercup!"

He about broke his neck getting out of the office door, waving to his secretary, and met Martina at the front door.

"What kept you so long?" she purred.

They were undressing as they walked to the bedroom and it could all be gathered for laundry later ... much later. At the moment, all they needed was for skin to touch skin.

"I'll never be able to work another day without looking at the phone waiting for you to call me." Phillip told her.

"Oh Buttercup come home! Oh Yes! You found home base! Each time your batting average is going up up up! One strike at a time. I am never going to be able to solve another case without your help help help!" Martina confessed.

"Buttercup is on the job ... day or night! But only if you promise, NOT to call me Buttercup in public because you know what it does to me. The women will be following me all over the office," he grinned.

"Oh no you didn't say that. I will scratch their eyes out!" she wiggled and squeezed.

"You do that again and I am never going to go back to work," he closed his eyes.

She squeezed and he lay back for her to ravish his body again and again.

"When do you want to get the big wedding over? It must be soon," Phillip emphasized.

"There is no rush. Is there?" Martina asked.

"Yes indeed there is. You are coming home with me and sleep in my bed! That is what a wife does!" he was on all fours on the bed as she stood wrapping her robe around herself and frowning.

"That is not in my near plans, Buttercup!" she got two steps before he swooped her up, and plopped her back in the middle of the bed. Her robe sash had been undone with the expert maneuver of Phillip.

He was kissing Martina's left nipple to emphasize her priorities. First the left, then the right. She was not objecting in any way. He was right. She just had been on her own for so long. Her first husband had been killed in Desert Storm leaving her to raise their daughter alone.

When she was killed in a car accident, there was no home. His house on the hill meant nothing to her. That's why she liked her tiny apartment. It had no family appeal. Just loads of cabinetry which held her work and that was all she wanted for so long. Work was her only companion until Phillip. How could she explain her feelings to him?

He lived in a huge house up on top of the hill in an affluent neighborhood. That was not her cup of tea so to speak, and his friends were not her friends. The women all sneered at her and whispered.

How could she concentrated with him nibbling every inch of her body, and she gave in and set the future plans aside for them to discuss way way down the road.

He on the other hand while showering with her by his side turned and said, "Mother can help you with the planning. She is a master at delegating people to do her work for dinner parties and functions. Just think about it darling," kissing her on the nose.

He had no clue what she was thinking, but her wheels were turning, and he was going to have to hold on tight to her. She stated, "So you think your mother is going to run my life?"

He saw his mistake in suggesting such a thing. It was written across her face that beautiful face was now huffing and puffing. She was scrubbing his skin off.

"Whoa! Wife of mine! It was just a suggestion and I didn't think it through. I am new at this. I've never been married or ever come close. I have a lot to learn," he kissed her shoulder and she began to cry. He had never in four years seen her cry.

"I know you don't understand, but I want to live here right now. That's why I have fought you and did not want to marry without you knowing all of me. Why I am the way I am. You have had four years ... to study me. Do you really think I can live in a big house? With your family? Do you?"

"No, you are right! We need our own house. Here is," pointing to the floor of her apartment, "wonderful for now. I love you and if this is where you want to live for now. So be it

BUT only for now. Agree?" he was smiling and rubbing her erotic places that only he knew where they were.

She was cooing again, "Clear as a bell that we must talk … and talk … here … and here." Two could play at that game and she kissed his navel and then his hip.

16

"We must perfect our negotiating techniques. Don't you agree? We have plenty of time for discussions later!" Martina continued persuading him to her way of thinking.

"Much later! YOU are going to have your way and I will agree to anything, if you don't stop what you are doing," Phillip stated firmly.

"I agree it would be a mistake not to finish this merger," she responded as he settled between her legs. He was going to slip and fall.

That did it! He cut the water off and did a caveman. Yep! Threw her over his shoulder and walked her to the bedroom and laid her gently down. She could see her prize more clearly from this angle. She moistened her lips in anticipation.

"This bed is MY bed from this day forward. On this bed I will make my wife so very very happy. NEITHER of us, will ever want to leave," Phillip had finished his speech.

"I agree. Now stop talking!"

CHAPTER THREE

Phillip's mother was not happy that her son was engaged to a commoner. Cynthia Porter nee Rockafeller was going to put a stop to this nonsense. She was going to call in the ladies to plan an engagement party. That would look good to her son without him realizing her real motive for the party which was to dissolve any future wedding.

This little fiancee` of Phillip's named Martina will run so fast away from their family after she sets her friends to pounce on her. She giggled like a schoolgirl fixing to play a prank on one of her sorority sisters that they all didn't like.

None of the women in her country club would do anything ever without consulting Cynthia for her approval. She was truly the Queen Bee for her woman's league, and had the power to manipulate her pawns anyway she chose.

In waltzes Bartholomew her husband, to everyone else the name was Bart. Cynthia insisted on calling him by his proper name. She proceeded to tell him about the engagement party that she was going to throw for Phillip.

"That's splendid my love. What does Phillip say about it?" Bart inquired.

"He doesn't know yet! I have to get started today," and off she went to the kitchen for her cell phone. Then phoned her friends and continued to set an agenda.

Bart rubbed his chin and yelled, "You had better ask him first, dear. I do think that would be wise," and he walked to the window to see his wife running all over the courtyard arranging this party for Phillip and his betrothed.

Bart was shaking his head because he knew his son was not going to be pleased. That boy had confided in him about what a time he was having to convince his future wife to marry him. "She hates big crowds and the less formal she likes it. She's a good woman father, and I love her very much!"

Phillip had said this and he never said he loved anything, or anyone until now. His father had congratulated him, and they had embraced. Bart remembered it, and it had brought a tear to both their eyes.

He smiled to think how happy his son was of late. This engagement really agreed with him. He said to himself, "I just hope Cynthia doesn't interfere in their happiness."

"Bartholomew! Bartholomew! Call your brother. I want all the men in this family at this elaborate wedding engagement party!" and she flitted by him on her way out the door to get in the Rolls with her personal chauffeur.

"Yes dear! Have a good day!" and he walked back into the house and straight into the den, his sanctuary.

"Oh boy! I must call Phillip and warn him . He can deal with his mother better than I can." He admitted and leaned back in his desk chair. Behind the massive desk were shelves of law books and business periodicals. He punched in Phillip's number on his new jitterbug phone. He hoped to reach his son quickly to stave off World War III.

"Hello father. What do I owe the honor of this call? Is mother alright?" His father never called unless something was wrong or someone was sick.

"Hate to be bearer of bad news, son. Your mother is splendid but in a tizzy, planning your engagement party. I thought you should know. Now I have to call Bridgeston. Her orders, but I will hold off for a day or two encase you can talk some sense into that wife of mine. I SURE can't!" and he laughed.

That was better than growling into the phone which was what he wanted to do. Phillip didn't need to deal with both his parents' bad behavior. Bart relied on his sense of humor. It was what he had done through the years to make peace with his wife and his son.

Bart heard his son smash something, and he hoped it was not a priceless object or else Cynthia would blame it on him and not Phillip. Never Phillip. He could do no wrong in her eyes until today.

"Phillip are you okay, son?" Bart needed to know that Phillip was okay. His voice was in a panic.

"Relax father, I'm fine! I just cannot believe mother would do this without saying a word to my bride. I mean my fiancee`. It is sweet of her, but as I told you Martina doesn't want any hoopla. She will be devastated. Stop mother, if you can. I am on my way!" Phillip was back in his office pacing from one wall to the other.

"She has already left the house on her mission to the club."

Martina was back in her office pouring over potential cases and sharing solutions with Nancy. They liked to pull together as a team before committing to any clients.

"Without a solution, why take a case," Martina always said.

In walks Phillip and she had just left him so something was up. You didn't have to be a P.I. to know that.

He smiled at Nancy and she asked, "May I help you?" as if she didn't know who he was. Martina bristled.

"Back off hussy. I'll handle this client. He has my name written all over his face," she said without taking her eyes off Nancy who was drooling. He was so handsome and Martina was not in the mood.

"Possessive, isn't she?" Phillip said as he rounded her desk and Nancy could see she was not wanted and flew out of the room. "Smart girl not to answer that question!" his eyes were devouring her in those tight navy blue dress pants and the severely cut white shirt she had on. That blouse covered every inch of that voluptuous body and he was so thankful because it was for his own private viewing.

Shaking his head as if to erase this morning of pure delight and regain his focus on why he was there. It was not going to be a task that he was going to enjoy. Her eyes were squinting as if she knew something was up, and she began chewing on the inside of her lip when she was concentrating on solving a case.

She was not going to like what he was about to say.

So he had to choose his words carefully, or all hell was going to break loose. That was one of the things, he loved about her.

She was passionate about everything. Mediocre was not in her vocabulary. She did everything outstanding. This was going to top the Richter scale.

"We have to talk. Can you leave now with me? You don't want to have to explain to Nancy!" Phillip offered and he frowned.

"You mean I didn't do my homework good enough?" she challenged him and came to breath in his cologne, and walked away.

Damn he was hard again. She saw it and grinned. "You know the more I get the more I want, but this is about my mother so please get your purse so we can go."

"Is she okay?' she asked as she strutted to the door with her clutch in hand, and he had to walk slower, and moaned.

"She is fine at the moment." He placed his hand in the small of her back to guide her out and then withdrew it, quickly when he saw Nancy winking at him.

He may need to use both of his hands to restrain Martina, if she saw it. She hadn't so he open the door, and she slid into the car asking, "What is wrong? You must tell me!"

He buckled and swerved out into traffic. She would not test him as his speed increased. She did not want to hear the answer, if it made him drive like a maniac.

"MY mother has done the unthinkable and I know you will be upset. I just got off the phone with father, and no I did not know this this morning, or I would be ravishing you on the roof of this car." That will bide him some time while she digested the memory of their morning interlude.

"Okay let me have it, and pull no punches. Remember I know you inside and out. What has she done that has you in a bunch?" she closed her eyes so she could cope with whatever he was about to say. Yes without his pleading eyes, and that … try and understand look. Accompanied by that phrase, "Honey she is an old woman and she loves me." He did that only once and she had said, "So that is to make up for her atrocious behavior. Right?"

"She has called all her cronies, love. They are at this minute planning us a wedding engagement party," he said it and cringed. It was out and she was not saying a word. Just sitting there quietly, looking out into the traffic as he weaved in and out to make a quicker retreat to her apartment. Her safe place where she spoke her mind, and boy could she speak her mind.

She turned and smiled at him. This was not good. She now was plotting, and he could see her wheels turning.

"Men are pawns in the female chess game of life," he said to himself. "Mere pawns and these two women that he loved to pieces were going to be in checkmate soon, and he would have to referee. He was going to remind both of them, they neither could have all of him that they must share."

Now he was grinning the naive boy child of his mother's making, hadn't a clue what he was in for. His new wife knew. She had investigated a many of these so called goodie-two- shoe mothers of high society. This inside info would serve her well. She had dealt with this kind of woman before effectively.

With her new outlook she stated, "That is marvelous! It is not like she is planning our wedding, Buttercup! We have solved that problem and at the engagement party my dear husband … you can set your mother straight!" she nodded. "Yes you can announcement to all the party attendees that we," she put her hand where his brain was working lately and rubbed it until he said, "No problem that I will do! Only I can't tell you to stop, but I may wreck this car and kill us both. Then mother wins."

He grinned like a Cheshire cat because he was going to sit back, and let them both play their games, and support each the best that he could. All while praying his father and uncle would help with the aftermath.

"You must take me shopping after you find out what the colors will be. She will have a main theme, and I will make you so proud of my attire. We will pick out the jewelry that Momsie will salivate at, wishing your father had bought it for her. Do I make myself clear husband of mine?" Martina stated.

"We are home dear and crystal clear .. love the way your mind works. It is all about ME … Making me proud!" He had to praise her, so she would continue stroking him to ecstasy and back. He had fought too hard to get her to marry him.

Yes she must be in charge and then with his mother, he would be in charge. "OH my my," he said to himself, "I hope this doesn't backfire."

Meanwhile Cynthia was conversing with Vivian and Rosalind about the invitation list and formal place settings. The seating arrangements in the ballroom would be crucial.

Sue Ellen and Marjorie were ordering the the flowers and making out the menus for Cynthia's approval. Chloe and Nicole were selecting the best photographer that everyone gave a five star because he captures the best facial expressions of all his 'Brides and Grooms'.

That was the name of his magazine and it was difficult to commission him for an event. Cynthia was hoping his pictures would help dissolved this fiasco of an engagement and Tyree was the best … so her friends claimed.

Cynthia shrieked, "Oh Tyree! I want you to get the one when she is crying her eyes out, PLEASE! Even if you get no other," and she patted his fake tanned cheek that was only acquired in a high class tanning salon.

"Oh Miss Cynthia! Have no fear Tyree always gets his man … I mean woman!" and he giggled and patted his own back as if to congratulate himself beforehand on a job well-done.

She smiled and crossed her arms, tapping her index finger on her jaw while surveying the room. All her players were in place, and she was delighted until she saw Bartholomew and Bridgeston standing shaking their heads.

She had to break them up. They would be protecting Phillip, and agreeing with him instead of her. She quickly pranced over to her husband and his brother. "What are my two handsome men up to? Don't you think this is a fabulous and a wonderful way to celebrate our son's engagement?" kissing them both on the cheek and not waiting for a response, but flitting on her way to her next task.

"I've got to call Phillip and report Mother's doings to him. I promised him. Do you want to retire to the den away from this noise?" His brother nodded in agreement.

Walking slowly Bart said, "That that wife of mine has bought home an entourage of pests. Mark my word Brigs, she is going to regret this!"

Brigs nodded again. He was a man of few words. Once in the den, Bart inquired if his brother wanted a brandy and he nodded again.

They both sipped and Brigs said, "Call him. He has a right to know what she is up to and let me speak to him when you are finished."

Bart dialed and Phillip answered on the second ring, "Hello Dad?"

"Yes son. It is I. It is a circus here as we thought. Brigs is here to help me assess for you and offer suggestions."

"Thanks to both of you for your help. I have told Martina and she took it well, but she had one request of you father," Phillip was going to play this as Martina wanted.

"And what might that be son?" Brigs saw a puzzled look come across Bart's face. Thank goodness he had him on speaker phone, "She wants you to survey mother's jewelry and pick her out a piece for me to buy her that is not like any mother has. Something that will make all of her friends envious. Can you do that for me and meet me at the Jewelers this afternoon?" Phillip was pleading.

He never begged his father for anything so this was going to be done with haste today. His father's support meant everything to that boy.

The two men were grinning. Bart said, "Your mother will be busy all day, and I will do my deed, and meet you at six o'clock sharp at Tiffany's. Be there with your fiancee`. OK? There is someone that wants to talk to you. Here!"

Motioning for Brigs to come closer to the speaker, "Hello there, my favorite nephew. I do believe you have a winner there. This girl speaks my language. There is nothing that will drop your mother to her knees than a fine piece of jewelry that she can't have. I am going with your father and survey, and make sure he doesn't duplicate anything. You know his eyes are getting bad!" and he laughed as Bart punched his shoulder.

"Six remember. Now GO! I have things to do before I knock your uncle side-winding," and he hung up. He had always hung up before the other person had time to reply.

The two older men began sauntering through the house making their way to Bart's wife wall safe. He had the combination memorized. They did their deed, and Bart said that the jeweler has a list. I have bought some from abroad so it was good that we looked together. Now let's go! Only two hours and the traffic will be bad."

Off they went slowly walking to talk to Cynthia. Telling her that they were going to the golf course for a few rounds. What a lie!

They both never cracked a smile, but once in the limo they were unable to contain their laughter.

Brigs said, "I sure have missed you brother."

Bart replied, "And I, you. Thanks for helping my boy!"

Brigs said, "I love him, too! He is like one of my own!"

"He is my only one and he is spoiled, but I have nothing else to spend my money on."

"Now you will have a daughter-in-law, and I want to help you shower her with gifts. Do you agree?"

"Yes please. Cynthia is a handful. That woman can smell a new diamond creation in the air ... a mile away. Brother pay that jeweler extra to keep his mouth shut that is all I ask. I will tell Phillip it was a wedding gift," Bart said.

Brigs said, "You are a genius. Phillip will be thrilled his uncle did that for him!" grinning at Bart.

"I am taking the prize. I am going to be at the top of his list because I am the one funding the piece... THE piece that Martina will wear at the party!" then he grinned wider and Brigs frowned.

They had always competed to be the best. Top the other all through their lives... even now.

Brigs put his hand on his brother's shoulder, "It's not about US this time! It is about PHILLIP this time!"

"Thanks I needed that! Remind me again, if I get off track,"

Bart grimaced.

CHAPTER FOUR

Martina was told by Phillip that his uncle and father were going to meet them, and the jeweler at Tiffany's at six sharp. She smiled and went to dress. She had to look her best, and it was killing him to watch her dress.

Finally he told her, "I will be back in a few. I cannot be here in this apartment with you half-naked. I'm about to lose my mind. This is too important. Don't come near me!" and he ran out the door.

She was nervous about this piece of jewelry, but the look on Phillip's face was priceless when he saw her new black lacy ensemble of Victoria Secret's finest. Push up bustier and matching skimpy garter belt with thigh hose that clung without attachment if you wanted, and thong black panties.

"Yep I have blown his mind. He didn't even want to see what I was going to wear over this getup." She grinned into the mirror, and slid into a pair of black dress slacks and a white turtleneck. Yep, all covered up and she grinned into the mirror as she put in her usual gold hoop earrings. Then sprayed Ciara on her four-leaf clover behind her left ear. Pulling her hair on that side up with

28

a black hair comb with black sequins securing her tresses, and stepping into her five inch black heels.

She text him to take her to the jeweler's, so they would not be late. He opened the door. He was there all this time.

She smiled sweetly and grabbed both his hands. "Go in front of me. Think of your MOTHER, not of me!"

"You sure know how to flatten it, don't you?" he frowned.

"Thank you! You are right. This is important, but I had rather stay home and ..." Phillip begged.

"Focus Buttercup! Focus!" now she was getting horny.

She jumped over to the door handle and said, "Stop it!"

He said, "I didn't say anything," and steered the car onto the freeway.

"I wasn't talking to you," and she began chewing the inside of her lip. "I was talking to myself."

His eyes dilated, "Oh my goodness! We are gonna!"

"No! FOCUS your father and your uncle are waiting for us!" she was talking it out for both of them. "Now tell me about your uncle?"

"He has been there for my father, and always has been there for me. Even though he has three girls. My father said that he always wanted a boy and that he would share me with Uncle Brigs! It made me feel so special" and he peeped at her.

"Don't you dare start crying. It will mess up your make-up and I have told Uncle how fierce you are! Wonder Woman!" and he grinned.

"You are so going to get it when we get home!" she vowed.

"I know and we are here. The valet will park it so sit until I come around!" she always jumped out of the car. Saying," I am strong enough to open my own door. This is the Women's Lib Era," but for him she would act like a lady. "It's a good thing I didn't where my holster and tote my concealed weapon that would have really embarrassed you."

He had her by the arm escorting her in, and whispered in her ear, "If you don't shut up talking dirty, I will whip out my concealed weapon!"

Her eyes dilated, "You wouldn't dare. What would your FATHER say?" and she strolled up to the jewelry counter and began looking. Leaning over so her hair cascaded to one side exposing her four-leaf clover behind her ear. She heard him moan and say, "Hello father! Uncle Brigs! This is my beautiful fiancee …. Martina. Isn't she ….. breathtaking?"

Both men agreed and kissed her cheek. She never took her eyes off Phillip, and he never took his eyes off of Martina.

They were escorted to the private viewing room, and cases were brought out. The list was provided, and it had checks by the jewelry that Cynthia had already purchased.

"What do you think Uncle? Which would make mother's toes curl? MY girl doesn't usually like jewelry. For our engagement party, she has agreed to wear a piece that you two select for her. Right, Honey?" eying her up and down and he moaned again.

Martina nodded. It was all so expensive, and she didn't like any of it, but for Phillip she would do this. It was her idea because she had seen many of her clients fight over such baubles. She just hoped that she wouldn't live to regret it.

Uncle Brigs chose the necklace, and it was adjusted to fit perfectly. The diamond dropped into her cleavage and Phillip closed his eyes and said, "Take a link out of it. Don't dislodge that cluster on either side." No way could he let it, hang there.

Bart put a hand on his son's shoulder, "Have no fear, son. If they do, they will have to answer to me," and he grinned at the jeweler who quickly reassured him. "And the price?"

"A quarter of a million, sir," the man said after writing the measurements down.

"Done!" said Bart. "Keep it in your safe and bring it to the party and have your men place it, and guard it that night."

"Yes, sir. We will follow your instructions and we appreciate your business," the man bowed.

Martina began to rise from the chair and Bart said, "Have a seat my dear. That was from Brigs. Now can you bring the matching earrings. They are my present to you and Phillip."

The clusters were the same as the necklace clusters, and the man handed each to Phillip to put on her ears. He was having a time because the cleavage was exposing a tip of lace, and no one knew what that lace looked like but him.

Finally he got one in her pierced lobe and the four-leaf looked so inviting. "Can I get some help, please!"

The manager placed the second and they all viewed them.

"Perfect," Bart said. "How much?'

"Quarter of a million, sir" the clerk said.

"Done, "Bart said and smiled at Martina whom he thought was going to faint. "Son catch her!" and she did.

Phillip picked her up and toted her to the car and kissed her neck all the way there, and left the men talking and agreeing that their purchases were equal.

They would not be bickering over who spent the most tonight. Both agreed again which was rare. These purchases were their secret. They both loved that boy, and now this girl was warming their hearts because they saw first hand how much Phillip loved Martina.

"He made a good choice! Don't you think?" Bart asked.

"I think she … she is lovely! For the third time today, I have agreed with my brother. What a concept!" Brigs admitted.

"Let's go get liquored up on the way home. So they will think, we HAVE been golfing. The limo has a bar. Voila! Put on the golfer shoes, too! I put them in here earlier today! Dang we now got to stop, and walk around on some DIRT!"

"Back yard has some of that. Anything else we forgot?"

"Nope, that about covers it. Just like old times covering for each other. I'll take a hug!" Brigs said.

"I agree again. Dang it! I need one too!"

Martina came to before they got to the car, "What happened?" holding her head up and her arms were around Phillip's neck. He was so strong.

She jumped down, "Where is your father and uncle?" she was quickly remembering what happened.

"They must think I am a gold digger. The price on those things blew my mind. My head exploded," she was hitting Phillip on his bicep.

"Why didn't you tell me about the prices before we left home?" she demanded.

"You wouldn't have gone! Simple as that, but you made two old men very happy!" he grinned.

"And you are, you are not happy?" she asked with her lips pouting.

"I am more horny then happy. In about an hour, I am going to be more happy than horny," and he was stepping on the gas.

She said, "Slow down. You are making my head swim again. She was sweating and undoing her blouse.

"Whoa! You can't do that!"

"I can do anything I want to do!"

"Cover yourself. I AM driving over here!"

"Well, stop driving. Pull over and get me some ice so I won't faint again."

He pull in a drive thru and ordered, "Two cups of ice."

Then he backed up again, "Make that four cups of ice. I got a hot wife."

"I see, sir. You are a lucky man," the speaker said.

"See now! I got to go in and punch the dud. Satisfied?"

"Not yet!" and she grinned.

That moved him on down the road with the ice, and he hadn't wasted any time going inside that joint.

"You are so smart my wife. You saved me a trip to the jailhouse and I will NEVER get home with you rubbing ice all over that … that … that black bra!"

"Oh hell you didn't just do that! Stop! Stop Martina! Don't cool that thing off! "He slammed on brakes after pulling off the road. "You just had to do it! Didn't you?"

"Yep! Only way to get you to stop!" She had him hard as a rock and she was wet all over from the ice. There she sat in her sexy as hell underwear dripping wet. Cars swooping by.

She looks at him and ask, "Do I have to undress you too?"

"You just fainted. I don't want to hurt you. I am beyond hurting myself," he was drooling but in control until she kissed him and lowered her seat. The seat was so soft and when both seats were reclined the SUV was spacious … equal to any queen size bed.

She unhooked the garter belt and bra, and slid out of her wet from ice panties.

He had his clothes off in no time flat, but left the tee shirt on encase someone came by. The windows were dark tinted and no one could see in, but they could see out.

"Honey please! I'm so hot!"

The bustier was still on, and her nipples were ice cold in his mouth. Then he was inside her cold legs. What was in the center was yes … an inferno. "Oh my goodness. Why haven't we tried ice before?" he asked.

She was having no more talking and rubbed ice on

his buttocks that made him spring forward … right where she wanted him.

"I'm in heaven.. baby. oh oh I can't wait!"

"Then go!" She was pulling his hair and moaning as he lunged. Then they were limp. Only she had fainted again. He was rubbing ice on her. She came to saying, "Do it again."

They fell asleep for an hour and he jerked awake. She was still asleep, and had on only the bustier and stockings. She was gorgeous and he wanted her again badly. He covered her and dressed, and drove them home. Thankful no patrolman had stopped and shined a light in on his wife.

He never thought he could care so much for another human being. Why had she fainted twice in one night? Hot she was as if she had a fever. Their lovemaking was so hot that it burned through his core just thinking about it. The ice made it hotter. Was she sick and he didn't even know it?

He sat in front of their apartment and mulled over tonight. Maybe it was so emotional for her, and that is why she fainted. Now he was tormenting himself, and he wrapped his suit coat around her. It was so large that it wrapped around her twice. He lifted her and locked the car up while pressing the apartment door open.

She was safe at home now. Beginning to wake up because she had started nuzzling his neck, and wrapping her arms and legs around him.

"Honey we are home. Just relax, and sleep if you can."

"You don't want me?" she looked up.

"Far from it but you have fainted twice, and I can't take a chance on you doing it again. I am scared of losing you," and he held her. He was trembling and she felt his fear.

"You are going to the doctor tomorrow," he said.

"Okay," and she fell back asleep.

He got up and walked to the window staring at the lantern streetlight. He had counted the days since they had been married. She had always been healthy. We have not missed a night without … "That's it!"

He ran to their bedroom to wake her and then backed out the door. "Don't get your hopes up fool!" he berated himself. He had always wanted a child and at forty-five, it was time.

He had dodged the bullet several times when younger.

Party girls do not make good mothers, but his wife … his wife… was built for it and had been a super mom. She may not want any more because of the pain from her daughter's death. She shied away from any children and would have them move to a different section, if she saw one in the restaurant.

He was pacing by now and rehearsing a speech to convince her to have his child, if the doctor confirmed his suspicion. He had it down pat by the time she awoke. He was grinning like a opossum, and she hid her head under the cover and asked, "What is wrong with you?"

He was never in a happy mood in the morning. Always a grouch and sneered at her, if she tried to arouse him for work. This morning something was amiss.

"You haven't been to sleep, have you?" she was a good

detective, and had weighed the possibilities carefully. That was the only conclusion that she could come up with.

"You are so right, my love. I have been too excited! Haven't slept a wink! " he stated firmly and raised his chin and straightened his business suit adjusting his tie.

She peered out from under the covers again. "Do you have an early meeting?" Then she let one of her black stocking legs come on top of the comforter of black and white paisley. She grasped the middle of the cover as she rose. The black bustier had pressed her naked breast over the top of the spread as she stood. Her hair was in disarray, but she stuffed some behind her left ear and it was perfect.

Her eyes were fixed on him. He had not moved. Then she dropped the cover and he was still standing in the same spot. So she walked swaying her hips and licking her lips all the way to the bathroom.

He was swallowing his pride and went to the door. It was locked. "What in the world? If you faint again, I will have to break the door down! Open it and open it now or down it comes."

She was brushing her teeth when she heard the word faint.

"What are you talking about faint? "She open the door still in last night's attire. "I fainted at the cost of the jewelry that's all. Why wouldn't I? I was in shock!" and she glared at him and he took her in his arms and felt of her bare buttocks and pulled them tight against his manhood.

"What about after we had sex in the car?" He was kissing her four-leaf clover.

"I did not. I went to sleep," she pushed on his chest to see his eyes.

"No you were out cold. When you are asleep, I can easily awaken you. You are going to the doctor today! So get dressed. I have you a ten o'clock appointment. Hop to it WOMAN!" and he popped her on the buttocks and immediately kissed it. He didn't mean to disturb the baby.

"You have lost your mind!" she frowned.

"Yes Madam. I have over my beautiful wife."

"And what is my doctor's name because I don't have one?" she crossed her arms. Still she had not dressed, and he was loving her stance, and started grinning.

"Dorothy Malone OB-GYN ten AM so hurry!" he was smiling and knelt to kiss her bare tummy as she was gasping.

It had never occurred to her because she was never regular. She hugged his head to her abdomen and squealed. "It can't be. I will go just to prove you wrong. You snake!"

"That\'s Mr. Snake to you. Call me any names you want to as long as you call me Buttercup ... only at night," and he grinned and exhaled the breath that he had been holding.

She was going to go.

Dr. Malone confirmed that they indeed were going to have a baby, and gave an expected due date. Phillip caught Martina as the news had hit her hard, and she fainted again.

"Doctor what am I to do? This is the third time. Twice yesterday!" She was limp in his arms.

"She's pregnant deal with it. That's what some women

do. Put her head between her legs and a cool washcloth on her forehead. Kiss her as much as possible. If all else fails, use ammonia. Congratulations."

Dr. Malone patted Phillip on his back.

CHAPTER FIVE

"**O**h my frigging God," said her partner.

Martina had to tell Nancy that she was pregnant, but swore her to secrecy. "The Winston case is complete, and the retainer was deposited. They have given me the fee remainder BUT that husband of mine will not let me drive! He says I might faint behind the wheel. I am so pissed!"

"He's right you know," Nancy said putting a book up to reflect any blows that might come her way. Her boss had no one to boss her around until this Phillip. Nancy was beginning to like the chap.

"So you, all of a sudden you decide to take his side. You are my friend, confidante, not to mention my partner. This is mutiny. Wait until this baby is born ... then I will pay you both back. I just don't feel like it today!" Martina marched into her office and shut the door shouting, "Dang it! I can't even lock my own door at home or here." He had removed the locks. She stretched out on the tiny sofa because she was so tired, and went to sleep.

Nancy was typing up a report when IN came a world

wind named Phillip, "What's happened Nancy? I can't get her on her phone!"

"She's fine Buttercup. See for yourself!" and she pointed to Martina's office. "But be quiet. I have had enough excitement for one day." He flung the door open and eased it back shut,

and tiptoed to Nancy's desk.

Nancy frowned from behind her eyeglasses that had dropped to the bridge of her nose, "Am I going to have to put up with this for nine months Buttercup?"

His spine spasm was intensely painful at this moment and his teeth were grinding. It happened every time Nancy said his wife's word of endearment. It was sacred. "Yes but for only eight months. If she needs anything ... anything at all ... call me. The name is Phillip!" and he winked.

Nancy waved to him as he left, "Will do ... Sugar!" and laughed shaking her head from left to right as she continued to type. She had two boys Michael and Tyson.

Their father was no Phillip. All he wanted was her paycheck and could careless whether she fainted or not. He was a gambler and he had stepped over Nancy when she went into labor with the last boy.

He had to get out the door fast, and place his bet at the racetrack. That was the final straw. Her neighbor had taken Michael to her house, and she had taken the taxicab to the hospital. Tyson never knew his father because she went to stay with her sister when she left the hospital. Nancy raised her boys by herself.

Her sister Bessie did babysit, and she took courses at night to get her degree in criminal justice. Police work didn't appeal to her, but she clerked there in the department until she met that lady lying on the couch. They teamed up and now had a lucrative agency. It was the best match for both of them.

Martina had told her about her daughter, and told her how much she missed her. One day she asked if she could dote on her two boys.

Nancy said, "Help yourself. Dote away!" and their bond was set in stone. If someone messed with Martina, they would have Nancy to contend with, and it wouldn't be pretty.

Brigs had arrived home and told his girls Emily, Imogene, and Elizabeth about the party. They hugged him. All three asked simultaneously, "Can we have a new dress daddy?'

"Of course you can. Mother will take you shopping soon."

His wife Katherine entered at that precise moment as if her radar had zeroed in on the word "Shopping." "Did I hear you right that YOU want ME to go shopping? For what my dear husband?" and she was beaming with anticipation.

"Cynthia is giving Phillip an engagement party! Bart said I was to deliver a special invitation for you and the girls. So do your magic on the girls. I want them to be dressed in the finest, my sweetheart," and Brigs kissed Katherine's hand.

"You must outshine Cynthia. Bart and I insist. She is trying to break up that couple, and they are a perfect match. Bart and I will see to it that that doesn't happen.

Are you up to taking her down a notch or two?" Brigs asked.

Katherine's right eyebrow twitched, "I will make you proud Bridgeton Alexander Porter. Give Trevor and Madeline a call dear, they need to fly over for this soiree. Don't you agree my dear?"

His eyes were twinkling, "I'll run it by Bartholomew. The last I heard, they were not traveling anymore for any reason.

I love my cousin and miss him terribly. That kidnapping situation was really bad. Can't blame them, if they don't come. We should plan a trip over to North Carolina one of these days. What do you say?"

"Sounds delightful to me, but let's get through with this party first. I will have alot to tell Madeline about by then," and she called for the girls to come to dinner. She wanted to discuss where they wanted to begin their shopping spree.

Emily the eldest girl was thin as a rail because she never ate. She was in classical ballet classes at a prestigious school. They had recently visited the Kodak Theatre in Los Angeles, and Emily could not get it out of her mind.

Katherine encouraged her to eat her dinner. "If you don't eat, Eliot will have nothing to hold onto at the school prom. Besides you want to look healthy at the party. If we can't find your size, your father will be disappointed."

Emily replied, "You are so wise mama. I want daddy to be well pleased, so he will want to fund my ballerina dreams. I WILL eat more. I promise. As for Eliot, no worries. He's clingy and going nowhere. I want a lavender dress mama please, and a long one. So no bird leg jokes, will I hear."

Eliot was everyone's target at school because his family had money. The girls flocked to him. He only had eyes for his ballerina Emily. He didn't have to worry about Emily's motives because her family equaled his family financially.

Imogene was obese. She was continuously eating. She was worried also about the dress fitting, but mama would have it altered. "I want pink pastel. I want to fade into the back-

ground and listen to the ensemble. I am hoping that they have one." She was a flutist and loved music dearly. She would play for the family at least once a week. She had no beau in sight. Mama was playing matchmaker at church and one of the choir boys named Anthony had talked to her about music, but no dating had occurred.

Elizabeth which was called Beth, except at home. Her mother insisted, "all my girls were given special names and your father loves to hear those names." Elizabeth, like her sisters wanted her daddy, to be pleased in every way.

Father held the purse-strings to her dressage lessons and she was in love with her horse, Moonbeam. "I want a black and beige dress, mama. The colors of my riding outfit. Okay Daddy?" smiling sweetly knowing not to look in her mama's direction. That would be the colors her mother would have to pick. The gosh awful party dress would be of those colors, if he said yes."

Beth was the perfect body size for a frilly dress. The boy that trained the horses thought so too. He was two years older than her. She had to fight Cameron off at the stable every riding day. He wanted to adjust more than her horse's girth. She had slapped him twice. If daddy hears of it, he will be fired. She had told him that, but he was not a good listener.

"Mother what color do you want your dress to be?" Brigs twisted his handlebar mustache which made his wife blush.

"Whatever color my husband wants me to wear. What color dear?" Katherine batted her eyelashes at him. She could read his mind. Yes I will curl your mustache later. She was becoming impatient waiting for him to answer.

"Sapphire ... to match your eyes, my dear," he grinned.

"And match my OLD jewelry. Yes, that is wise. The girls dresses will cost a fortune. Why would I want any more.

I have enough Brigs!" She turned, "We will start tomorrow girls. We shall leave no store unturned."

The girls all giggled and made plans after being excused from the dinner table.

Brigs and Katherine sat staring at one another.

He said, "Do you honestly think I would let you go to Cynthia's party with last year's jewelry," and he took a box from his coat pocket.

She swooned, and touched her hand to her mouth to stifle a whimper. He came around and kissed her crown and placed the box in her hand.

It was the most beautiful sapphire necklace. It was designed like no other, and she had seen them all. She even searched for all this year's new sapphire creations on the internet. This was not on the market yet.

"Oh Brigs! You are amazing darling. Yes … I will curl your toes tonight when the girls are asleep, and it will reach all the way to those handlebars," she cooed.

He smiled and lead her to their bedroom safe.

Cynthia phoned Katherine to see if Brigs had delivered the personal invitation that her husband Bart had given. She was not going to let them come, and she was furious with Bart.

"Of course we will be there. Brigs loves his nephew as if he were his own," Katherine was stabbing and twisting the knife in her sister-in-law's back.

Katherine had always known that Cynthia disliked the closeness of Phillip's relationship with his uncle. He would do anything for that boy even support her son's decision to marry this nobody.

Cynthia frown then quickly smiled as Bart came into the room. "Yes dear, I am so glad. Give the girls my best, and we will see you all on Saturday around two. Don't be late!" and she hung up before Katherine could respond.

Katherine stared at the phone and looked at Brigs, "She hung up on me! You, my darling are right. She has set her claws out for you and me. This means we must be really early Saturday. I can snoop around and see what she has up her sleeve. We will thwart her evil plan."

She slammed the phone down and marched to Brigs who was already in bed reading a book.

"I told you," and he turned the page.

He saw Katherine's wheels were turning, "Calm down dear. Bart and I can handle it. You need not to worry. Come to bed and do your magic."

"You are right I have a capable husband, and Bart can handle his own wife. It is Phillip and that poor girl Martina that needs us all to buffer for them against this witch."

"Now Now Katherine. Calling Cynthia that is not going to help, even though it is accurate. I don't want the girls to repeat you saying that. OK?"

"NO, I would never teach them such language. Can I say fool?" she had changed into her red negligee and was putting lotion on her hands.

Those hands were making him agree with anything she wanted to say. He kissed her neck, put his book away turning the bedside lamp off. "Of course, my love. Fool it is!"

Martina awoke from her nap with Nancy and Phillip staring at her. She looked around the office. "You two are annoying!"

"I know but it is closing time and ... I AM ...leaving. Didn't want to leave you without Sugar here," and she walked out the front door to go home for the day. Shaking her head, "Eight months of this. Lord help me!" Nancy mumbled.

Phillip smiled at his pregnant wife . He had been on cloud nine since the doctor had told him, he was going to be a father. He had spent the day with his father. He had to talk to him. He had told him early that they WERE married and that he was going to announce it at the party.

His father had agreed earlier that day. That the party was the place to announce it. Bart had told his son this bit of info would not be wise to say until then. He didn't want his wife to have "a heart attack" and it was going to hit Cynthia hard.

"Your mother is up to no good, and you know it. It will be very hard on her with the surprise we have for her. The strong support you have son will be enough to send her into shock," Bart said pacing in the den..

"You are right father. I know she loves me, but she has never liked to share. When she sees how happy Martina makes me, she will come around. Not to mention when she sees Martina wearing maternity clothes THAT will be the day that you nor I will have to worry. Just keep the hospital number on speed dial!"

They both were laughing wholeheartedly and it echoed from the den. The father patted his son on the back after a big fatherly hug.

Cynthia walked in, "Here you two are. I heard you laughing so I must have missed something? Do share with me, I need a good laugh," and she looked from her son to her husband.

Bart walked to the bar. He had already fixed his wife's favorite martini. Handing it to her and sitting beside her on the sofa, "It was a crude man's joke, dear. Your delicate ears does not need to hear such things!" He sipped his brandy.

Phillip was still standing and said he had to pick Martina up from her office not elaborating on why she was not driving.

He kissed his mother's cheek and flew to his car not looking back. His mother would have tried to delay him from leaving on time.

CHAPTER SIX

Nancy arrived home and found Tyson her sixteen year old boy, helping his little brother Michael that was now twelve with his homework. She had a bag of groceries and Tyson lifted them from her arms and sat them on the counter.

"I would have gotten them out of the car, Mom. All you had to do was call me on my phone." He was looking into the bag for junk food and finding none.

"You, young folks think that phones will do everything. Well they won't. When I was little, there was no such thing as a cell phone. "She continued putting the items away in the pantry and refrigerator.

"I knew when my mother was coming home. I watched out the window for her. Saved her a heap of money every month, too!" looking from one boy to the other.

She had posted this month's phone bill on the front of the refrigerator door.

Pointing to it she asked, "Who is this ------?" rattling off the phone number that had been called a hundred times this month exceeding the cap on her minutes.

Tyson gulped and his eyes dilated, "It's my girlfriend,

Amanda. I'll get a job and pay you back." He knew all the time his mother would not let him do that.

"Okay sounds good to me," and she walked to her bedroom and shut the door. Tyson looked at Michael.

"She is pissed at you, brother!" Michael said and continued with his homework. If he didn't finish, his mother would be mad at him.

Besides he was not into girls, and it was no skin off his back, if his brother got into trouble. His older brother was always getting the praise for his school grades and now .... he was grinning at Tyson.

"You had better wipe that grin off before I knock it off!" Tyson stated standing over Michael way too close.

"OK! OK! Sure hope you don't have to get a job after school. Who is going to help me with my schoolwork?" Michael asked.

"You! That's who!" Tyson knew he would still help him, but he should not have smiled because mom is not in a good mood. He'd not have both of them mad at him at the same time.

Amanda lived in a nearby town, and that was why he called so much. He wanted to talk to her every day since he meet her at a rival football game.

She was special not like the girls at his school. They wore their outfits way too revealing. Amanda didn't. She was fully covered, but what he did see was dynamite. She spoke in a soft voice, and it melted his heart, and other things.

They could talk about anything for hours, and he was guilty of running up his mom's phone bill. He'd have to call Amanda in a few minutes, and tell her his predicament.

He was outside on the steps sitting, and she answered. "I was getting worried about you Ty." She was fishing for the reason so he might as well be up front with her.

"I've been having a discussion with my mom about the high phone bill. Going to have to get a part-time job, I guess," Tyson was waiting for her response while looking up and down the street.

"That's easy for me to help. I can solve this for you, Ty."

Tyson was looking at an unknown car that was driving slowly up the road and said, "How?"

"I can CALL you. We have unlimited minutes. So don't do that, you have to focus on your studies. That is ... if you are going to the same college as I am. We will be together then every day ... all day!" Amanda said sweetly.

The car speed up and shots were fired.

Tyson quoted, "B840C2 Write it!" he repeated it twice to Amanda. He had given her the license plate number of the car that had shot him. It was another 'drive by shooting'.

His mother had always taught him to do that. "Get the plate number. Write it down" that echoed through his mind over and over until he lost consciousness.

Tyson dropped the phone and Amanda was yelling into it, "I got it! I got it! Ty! Ty!" as Nancy got to her son. He had been shot and was bleeding profusely from the shoulder. She hear the girl screaming on the phone.

Nancy applied heavy pressure to the gunshot wound

and calmly told Michael, "Call 919 on your CELL phone, then put it to my ear."

Michael was shaking and did as his mother said. He picked up Tyson's phone and told the girl that Ty would call her later.

The ambulance arrived and Michael was the little man that got his mother's purse and locked the front door.

They followed the ambulance to the hospital emergency room, and ran inside to be escorted to a private room. The police were present because it was reported to them by the hospital. It was now a crime scene.

The investigation started now.

"I want to see my son," Nancy said and she phoned Martina. She said, "Now sit down and call Sugar to the phone."

She told Phillip what had happened, "I can't take care of her and my boy at the same time. She will be hysterical. She loves him big time. KEEP her there until I call you. Sugar, do you here me?"

"Yes loud and clear. Will do. Call if you need us," Phillip said. He had a firm grip on Martina who was trying to get the phone away from him. He hung up.

"Okay settle down everything is under control. Nancy wants you to rest here, and not get upset that are her orders. There has been an accident. Tyson is in the hospital, and being well looked after. She is going to call us back in a couple of hours." Martina fainted.

"Nancy I knew this was going to happen," he lifted her and placed her on the bed. He called, "Dr Malone my wife has had a terrible shock. Can you come over and check her out?"

"Bring her to the hospital and I will check her," she said.

Phillip said, "Okay we will be there in a few."

When Martina awakens that is where she is going anyways. So might as well get it over. Nancy had no one and her sister was in another state now. She and Martina always depended on each other.

He had watched their friendship for the last four years. His wife would no more stay put, nor would he. She was like one of the family. His worry now was for Nancy's kid, and his unborn child.

As he was gathering some things for Martina, he saw the News Bulletin flash across the screen THAT brought him to a screeching halt. Frozen to the spot, he saw a bloody Tyson being put into the ambulance. Martina is going to freak out, he said to himself. He turned the TV off and continued grabbing her up, and putting her into the car.

She was nuzzling his neck and saying, "I love this car."

She fell back asleep, and as he drove to the emergency room he called in a favor from his father.

"You know the head of the hospital Dad. I need you to have him put Martina & Nancy in a private room. You've seen the news by now. It is a three ring circus at the emergency room. Reporters everywhere trying to get their story."

"Don't go to the ER, son. Go in the front door and I will handle it. I'll meet you there," Bart said.

"Thanks, Dad!" and he hung up. It was always dad that he called in an emergency, not FATHER.

Martina awoke when they got to the entrance of the hospital, and got out. The valet parked the car and Phillip escorted his wife in telling her, "Father wants us to meet him," never elaborating on why.

When inside the private room, Nancy and Michael came in. The front of Nancy's clothes were splattered with blood stains. Michael ran to Martina, and she held him. Phillip held Nancy.

Nancy said, "They have taken him into surgery. It will be a while before I can see him. The doctor said he would come here to this room when the surgery was over. Thank you all for coming."

Bart was outside the door talking to the administrator.

Phillip wanted to go outside with them and find out details, but Martina and Nancy were talking. Michael had climbed into his lap to tell him what he saw. Phillip was giving the boy precious time to ventilate his feelings. Never did he take his eyes off his wife, just nodded for Michael to continue.

Dr Malone was told what room they were in, and she dropped by to see Martina.

"I was just in the neighborhood and thought I'd stop by, and say hello," Dr. Malone was one smooth operator. She knew if Nancy needed her, Martina would not be examined. This was not about her, it was about her friend. Still she needed to reassure her husband that all was well.

She spoke privately with Phillip to relieve his mind that if something happened to the boy in surgery, the doctors would let her know first and she would come back and see Martina.

Phillip returned and kissed the top of Martina's head, and played some board games with Michael. The nurses had brought the games in because the surgery was going to last approximately five hours.

Soon Michael fell asleep in the recliner and Nancy wrapped a blanket over him. Michael had given Phillip, Tyson's girlfriend's number. "Tell her, he is okay. Mom won't let me use her phone. I left mine at home. I was in a hurry."

Phillip spoke to the girl called Amanda. She was crying and she told him the license plate number that Tyson had recited to her. Immediately he left the room, and found the police officer that was on TV. It was crucial INFO that they needed to find this maniac that had shot Tyson..

The officer phoned the license plate in, and an APB had been sent out. They located the vehicle owner's residence. It had been reported stolen a week ago. So a manhunt ensued to find this vehicle. The attempted murderer was driving that car unless it had been ditched.

Martina was holding up good. No more fainting spells and Nancy was thankful. She told Martina, "Girl you got to stay healthy BECAUSE I may be out of work for awhile."

Phillip assured her that he would pitch in, and work would be fine. "You know I am good at taking care of her by now. Don't you worry about anything right now. It will all be handled."

"I know you are a good man and Martina is a stubborn woman. Thank goodness! She **FINALLY said YES!** Sugar" and he saw a tear fall, then Nancy looked away.

Martina was on the other side of the room in a recliner beside Michael. She had not heard what her handsome husband had said to Nancy, but Nancy was smiling at her.

Nancy stated to Phillip, "I could not handle this without the two of you," she rose and went to the ladies restroom. He knew she needed to cry it out, now that Michael was asleep.

He stood by Martina's chair as they watched the local TV ... Breaking News Bulletin. Phillip stood so it would block what was being broadcast from Nancy when she came back.

It said the suspect was in custody and being transported to the city jail under heavy escort. They flashed a picture of Tyson as the victim of a drive by shooting, and reported that he was in surgery and his condition was unknown at this time.

Phillip flipped the channel. "You okay over there." He asked Martina. She nodded, "I'm fine. Our prayers must be on Tyson. He is a good boy. This coward could not have known him. Why these gangs have to shoot innocent people? Yes, I saw the bandana on his head. It was a CRYP!" now she began pacing.

"Probably an initiation that required them to go to the next level. Yes, your wife, I worked with them on the force ... The BLOODs and the CRYPs. I'm very familiar with their activities. That is why Nancy and I got out.

OH MY GOSH. Do you think it was connected to us! By Nancy and my police background? " Martina was frantic.

"No! No! Now calm down. You are reading too much into it. The police will interrogate the suspect and we will get the report. Until then, focus only on Tyson," Phillip said.

Nancy was out of the bathroom and Martina nodded to Phillip that she would not speak of what she suspected.

"Anyone want anything? I am going for a coffee," he left when they said that they were all fine.

He went straight to the police officer that he had talked to earlier Curtis Latham. He was a burly black man about Phillip's age, and he welcomed anything Phillip had to say.

"If not for you man, we would not have been able to capture the suspect. So watsup! How's the boy?"

Phillip relayed Martina's suspicion. Curtis digested this information over a cup of coffee with Phillip.

"So your wife is the infamous Martina Mc Duff. I have heard all good things about her, sir. This is a farfetched idea but at this point in the investigation all things are open to scrutiny. Our staff will handle it and I'll get back with you. I'll give the interrogators this information when I leave here."

"Here's my cell number. Call me if you think of anything else. If you see my number on your phone, I will have an update on the case. I know you will keep it secret. We need no leaks to the media."

He shook Phillip's hand and said, "Take care of the wife and that pretty little lady that's with her.. The boy is lucky that he has you all but I don't see a husband for the woman, Nancy?"

"That's because there isn't one. He flew the coop when the boys were little," Phillip stated sternly.

The officer walked off and into the command center that had been set up within the hospital.

Phillip went back to the surgical waiting room with a black cup of coffee for Nancy and an apple juice for his pregnant wife.

"Sorry honey. Can't have the baby kicking you rapidly with the caffeine intake in these cups. You will thank me later."

He held up his second cup to the ceiling.

Martina said, "I thought you were never coming back."

"Yeah I went by to talk to that police fellow. You will never believe what he asked me?" Phillip sipped.

"What? Share before I put apple juice in your coffee," Martina threatened.

"Okay! Okay! You would do it. I know you!" he sat closer as if it was the news of the year. Phillip put his hand to cover his mouth and mumbled.

Martina hit him on his right deltoid.

"Alright! Already! Nancy has an admirer," he spoke softly.

"You are kidding me. WHO?" she was now lowering her voice. "Tell me or I'll take a bit out of you."

"Oh my that sounds like fun," his eyes sparkling.

"That coffee is Johnny Appleseed's any minute," she was tiring.

"Mr. P O L I C E officer. Yeah! Just a guess! I kinda know when a man wants a woman. I've had four years of torture and I hope he has the equal treatment," and he was smiling at her.

"You are not kidding," Martina gasped.

"I got to tell her!" she finally said.

"You do and you will spoil it, and I'll never tell you another secret!" he said.

Phillip gave her stare for stare.

"And you would do that," and Martina finished her apple juice pouting. "I won't say a word."

CHAPTER SEVEN

The interrogation officer filled in Curtis Latham, the primary officer that was investigating the drive by. "Did you find out what went down?"

"Oh Yeah! The boy that did the shooting is a member of the Bloods." Showing Curtis the arresting mugshot, "See the red shirt."

"Yes, I see it and?" Curtis breathed deeply.

"See, the boy Tyson had a blue shirt on that day that he was shot. You said he was sitting on the apartment stoop with a cell phone. It must have reflected light and the Blood boy said to me."

"I shot him before he shot me!" the shooter had confessed.

"Oh man, this boy was an innocent. He didn't know about the gangs. He was talking to his girlfriend on his cell phone sitting on his own porch. What a shame! Thank you for telling me. He is still in surgery. I am going over there when I leave here."

Curtis did just that and spoke with Phillip. "How is the boy?"

"Officer thank you for checking," and shook his

hand. "He is in recovery. Holding his own." Phillip said. They sat in private conference room that the nurse had agreed to let them use.

"How is the mother?" Curtis asked.

"She is holding on, too … barely by a thread. She says it just doesn't make sense. Do you have anything yet that I can tell her?" Phillip asked.

"Tell her… oh heck … I'll tell her, if she will see me?" Curtis hesitated. In walks Nancy into the room still in her bloody clothes.

The same clothes she had worn to work yesterday morning. She had pranced into the agency with a new designer pair of jeans and twirled for Martina to see. Was that only yesterday?

She was so use to buying clothes for the boys and now she had splurged on a new outfit. The blouse was a navy and white checkerboard pattern, and fit her curvy bust smug.

Her makeup was now nonexistent and her hair had come out of her bun. She always was dressed conservatively until yesterday. She had needed a pop of color, and that was her new red shoulder-bag and red shoes. Which at this moment she regretted wearing, they were being scrutinized by one male officer.

There she stood and this police officer was running his eyes all over her.

"Collecting notes? I ain't in no mood to be nice. Tell me now what is the skinny on this case. I am a former police officer myself, so don't try to deter me," Nancy fumed.

Curtis was clearing his throat and Phillip said, "I'll leave you two alone. I have to go check on Martina. That's my wife and she is pregnant, and faints at the drop of a hat. If you need me, either one of you, call me."

He knew they both had his number in their cell phones.

Phillip walked up to Martina, "Are you okay?"

"I am fine. Michael is still asleep. They are going to let Nancy see Tyson in a few minutes. He will be out of recovery and in the ICU for at least three days for observation. Where is she?" Martina said frowning.

Phillip said, "In conference with a police officer. I think, he is hitting on her. Yep! His eyes lit up when she walked in. I told you, mark my words. Nancy, of course cannot see what I saw. She will when this is over. He asked where the father was and I told him that she is a single mother. He must be added to our PARTY LIST. So make a note of it, sweetheart. His name is Curtis Latham."

She patted him on the back. "My little matchmaker, you did good. She needs someone strong because you and I are soon going to have our hands full, "Martina rubbed her belly.

"If Michael wasn't in this room, I would ravish you," Phillip said as he walked to the other side of the room.

She blew him and air kiss, "I know. Go! Leave me be and get me a bottle of water, pleaseeee!" She had a whole pitcher of water beside her. She wanted him to stay busy otherwise he would be smothering her again, thinking she was going to faint.

Curtis was a gentleman and in his uniform so he

spoke to Nancy respectfully, "We have a situation here that I am not suppose to divulge any information. You on the other hand need to know it."

Nancy walked closer to him, "And what might that be, Mr. Officer?"

"Curtis," he said.

"Okay, Curtis. What you got?" Nancy grinned. She knew he was about to explode, but she was going to teach this rookie a lesson.

Curtis thought she is playing me, and it is working. I have to be careful, but I sure don't want to. He had to concentrate more because his body was not cooperating.

Nancy was aware at this moment how she had better back off because she wanted him to put those big burly arms around her ... that had not happened for many years. She plopped down in a lounge chair near the door.

He sat down in the chair facing hers. "The boy that shot your son is in a gang called the BLOODs. He thought your son had a gun in his hand and he was wearing a medium blue shirt. So he says he shot him before your son killed him. They have informed him that it was a cell phone not a gun, and that your son is not in the CRYPs. There is no one out there targeting your family, but since the gangsters may want retaliation. They don't know the true story, I want you to have hour protection. I will assign someone to your house when you leave the hospital, and especially when your son leaves," he looked into her eyes.

"I know about the BLOODs and CRYPs. Neither of my boys will ever where red or blue shirts from this day forward. I accept your offer of protection for my boys safety. Thank you!" Nancy said softly.

She bowed her head, "As a black woman in Los Angeles, I have never feared the gangs for myself, but this is different. It is because my boys may be targeted," and she wept.

That's when Curtis stood and helped Nancy stand, "Ma'am you are not alone any more. I am here. Let's go see your son. I will not ask any questions. I will be beside you. If you allow me, I will go in with you?"

She was standing and he was holding her forearm to steady her. "That would be nice. Thank you!" she didn't want Martina any more stressed than she already was, and Phillip needed to be with her and Michael. That is the only reason, she said yes to this officer.

When they went to the ICU nurses station, they were told they could go right in. He was still holding her forearm.

When she saw Tyson on the ventilator and all the machines hooked up to him, she nearly fainted. The arm got firmer that held her up, and she kept walking closer to Ty's bed.

"It is mama, son. I'm right here. Don't try to talk just rest and get well. I will come as often as they will let me." She was holding his hand and kissing it. "Mama loves you. I'll see you in a few," Nancy stated to Tyson.

Her ten minutes was up and they left.

They walked to the waiting room and sat with Martina, Phillip and Michael. She cried and Martina took her in her arms, "He's going to be fine. We are here for you."

"Curtis is too! So if you need to get some rest go on home. Only thing I ask is you take Michael with you."

Phillip said, "Of course we will. Does he have a key?'

"Don't go near my house! Do you hear me!" she was getting hysterical. "I can't have either of you hurt!" Curtis held her then in front of everyone and he stroked her hair. "Let it out. Let it out! I will explain for you. Now sit and close your eyes as Michael is doing." She immediately sat down, and closed her eyes.

Martina eyes dilated and she looked at Phillip, and his mouth was open. Neither had ever seen Nancy obey anyone, as she was obeying this man's instructions.

Curtis said to Nancy, "We are going to the cafeteria and we will be back." Nancy never moved a muscle. Curtis made sure a guard was at the waiting room door, and that no one was to be allowed into this private room that they had. "NO ONE."

After they got something to eat. They sat in a more vacant part of the dining room. Curtis filled them in. Martina was processing the information. She began to elaborate for Phillip because he hadn't a clue that this was more serious than previously thought.

"That's why she didn't want us to go by her place encase the BLOODS were casing her house. I get it now. I know Nancy and she has never been rude to her Sugar," Martina said. Phillip was pointing to himself.

Curtis was laughing, "YOU are her Sugar."

"Yes. She calls him that because we forbade her to call him by my name for him. Right dear?" Martina smiled.

"I can't wait to hear this," Curtis was all ears.

"You wouldn't dare, Martina?" Phillip chided her.

"The man needs to know. My husband's name is Buttercup!" and Phillip smiled sweetly at Curtis.

"These two women dearly love you Phillip. I will store those names in my memory bank for future negotiating power," Curtis laughed and coughed and straightened.

Phillip could not resist, "I can't wait to hear what names they come up for you, my dear brother. I am a negotiating power player. Time will tell!" Phillip smiled at Martina.

"I told you Martina. I have an eye for these things," and shook his head up and down. "Do you want to ask him or do you want me to?"

Curtis was eating a piece of cake and looked up, "Ask me what?"

Martina said to Phillip, "But your mother is in charge?"

"No, dear. I am in charge," Phillip stated firmly.

Curtis said, "You have peaked my curiosity? What?"

"You are now formally invited to our wedding engagement party in two weeks at two pm. Black tie and …" Pointing to Nancy's door. "And she had better be on your arm."

"I thought you'all were already married?" Curtis looked puzzled … but happy at the same time.

"We are, but his mother doesn't know it yet!" and Martina fainted.

Curtis was in rescue mode. Phillip waved him back and said, "Calm down officer. She's find. Just pregnant! Another SECRET you are privy to! Welcome to the family by the way." and he was carrying Martina back to the room with Nancy.

"Girl you got to stop doing this!" Nancy had a cold washcloth on Martina's forehead in a flash.

"Me and TWINKLE TOES are going to see my son. So don't you two move a muscle and watch Michael for me." Nancy took her two fingers and pointed them to her eyes, and then back to them, "I'm watching you!"

"AYE AYE Captain. Take Twinkle-toes with you now. It's time," Phillip stated looking at his watch.

Curtis held his arm out for Nancy to hold onto and she did. "Twinkle-toes?" he asked.

"Twinkle-toes was all I could come up with? What would you prefer me to call you?" Nancy looked sideways at him and frowned.

The door opened and she visited Tyson and there was no change. The nurse told her that he was given medications to make him rest.

The surgeon can over and informed her,"The ventilator is standard to keep his heart from having to work so hard. The bullet had hit his right shoulder, but also went through his right lung. His vitals are stable. This will be the last visitation for the day. So go home and get some sleep. We will call you, if there is any change."

Nancy grabbed for Curtis forearm and they walked out, and down the corridor when she abruptly stops. "You never answered my question?"

"You can call me anything you want. AS long as you call me," Curtis stated smiling.

"Good answer! MR. WONDERFUL!" Nancy accentuated his new name. She was smiling back at him.

PART TWO

CHAPTER ONE

The party goers were arriving at the country club with engagement presents in hand. One limousine after another appeared down the long driveway with two lanes of valet parking service.

Cynthia had clearly outdone herself. She was seen greeting. Welcoming Hollywood guests and her cronies' families that were intermingled. None of Martina's family were invited and Cynthia was cringing that Martina's partner in her business was invited. She asked her son, "Who has gone and done such a thing... a black couple at MY party?"

Phillip said, "It was I, Mother! Make them welcome as only you can do because her fellow is a police officer. I don't want you to get arrested on my behalf," and he grinned and kissed his mother on her cheek.

He walked away to find Martina in her simple white Vera Wang cocktail dress and those diamonds were sparkling from her cleavage and her earlobes. Everyone had oohed and aahed as he escorted her into the room, and sat her at the main table beside his father.

Bart said, "You look delightful. My son is a lucky

man." His mother had not come close to Martina until she finally took her seat. Her cheeks were blood red. Martina's jewelry was outshining hers and she was furious. She gritted her teeth and smiled at her husband.

"You did this, didn't you?" Cynthia seethed.

"Yes, my dear. I love him more than you love yourself." Bart stood with glass held high, "I would like to propose a toast to the Bride and Groom. Yes … they have ALREADY done the deed. I couldn't be more happier. May they fulfill each others dreams and bring us many grandchildren!" Then glasses were heard clinking throughout the ballroom.

Cynthia sat with her mouth open and for the first time in forty-six years of marriage had nothing to say. Her son was married.

"Dad, Mother is in shock! I can't handle both of them. Martina is my prime concern now," Phillip said anxiously.

Bartholomew Porter nodded to his son and said, "She is fine. I will look after her real close tonight," and rolled his eyes at Cynthia. So her shocked appearance was fake and could gain no sympathy from her husband nor her son.

In walks Nancy and Curtis, they were being escorted to Martina and Phillip's table. Yes. The same table where Cynthia sat. She immediately stood up and went to the bathroom.

Nancy looked ravishing because Martina had footed the bill for her to have a long blue sequined gown delivered and her hair done. Since Tyson was home and healing nicely, she could enjoy tonight. Even if Martina chose blue which was the color she said she would never wear again, she had put it on. A note said:

Tonight you take your life back.
You are fearless!
Love, Mr & Mrs Phillip Porter

Nancy's sister had flown over to help her with the boys. Tyson was enjoying the attention and Michael was happy his brother was okay. Michael even asked Amanda to come over to surprise Tyson with his auntie's permission. She was on her way to their house.

Nancy still had an officer nearby until the trial was over. The officer was sitting right next to her in a black tuxedo and blue bow-tie that matched her dress.

Nancy said, "You did good. I like that tie," and smiled brightly. Martina had loaned Nancy a fancy diamond choker that made Nancy look like a millionairess. "I want my mother-in-law to see my partner is a dynamite dresser. We are a team, sister. I need you to be here to watch my back."

Curtis's response was priceless, "I had help. That's the facts, Ma'am!" nodding at Phillip who nodded back at him. They had quickly become friends since Curtis had admitted he was in it for the long haul. Phillip genuinely liked Curtis because he was making Nancy very happy and that made his Martina very happy.

Nancy said to Martina, "We had better watch these two REAL close. They are dangerous together." Both girls turned and stared at their own date which made the guys squirm in their seats.

Then the band began to play and the bride and groom took the dance floor for the first dance. Phillip swung Martina around and dipped her. Her arms tightened around his neck.

"My dress may fall off!" Her strapless was smug. She was just teasing.

"That's for later, for my eyes only. Have fun darling, this is our night. I have energy that none here has because you can't drink, I shall not either. We have thwarted mother's plan. She can't even look at me. Father is so proud of you."

"He is a sweetheart and your uncle is my protector, also. I am a lucky girl to be loved by you. Four years ago, I never would have believed this was possible. I was a sad woman and now everyday you bring me happiness. I love you!"

He held her erect and grabbed her face and kissed her in front of the whole crowd. Passionately, there was no doubt in anyone's mind watching that she WAS the love of his life.

Curtis and Nancy joined them and were dancing at a proper distance from each other. Nancy said, "Don't even think about it or I will have to slap you silly!" and she laughed.

Bart and Cynthia waltzed around the floor and she batted her eyes at her husband. "You have not WON my darling!"

His response stopped her steps, "Yes, I have

grandmother. Our son would never forgive you, if something happens to his child. Whatever you're planning, you better think twice!"

She stared at him and ran off the dance floor to her cronies. She had to regroup and tell them to stop the plans to poison the girl. It was to look like she had food poisoning, but it was much more lethal. She was frantic to get the plate that had arrived at her son's table and sat upon Martina's plate.

She told the waiter to "get that plate at all cost!" He jerked it out of Martina's hands and Phillip looked at his mother. He knew what his mother was capable of, but no one else had observed the exchange.

The party guests were too busy eating, drinking, and dancing, but Katherine and Brigs saw it.

Katherine marched to Cynthia and under her breath said, "I have seen you do some despicable things in my lifetime, but this was the LOWEST. You had better be glad that waiter got that plate because dear sister-in-law, I would have strangled you, if something happened to my nephew's new wife." Brigs was holding Katherine back.

Bart took Cynthia by the hand to the dance floor and began waltzing to keep the party going. "My dear, you amaze me at your EVILNESS. I doubt Phillip will ever speak to his mother again, and I cannot blame him. You had better be on your best behavior and flood that boy's wife with kindness. It will be years before you have my respect again."

He smiled at the couples passing them, and they danced and he whirled her to the ladies bathroom door because by then she was crying real crocodile tears. She ran inside.

He waited by the ladies room door, and talked to other husbands waiting for their wives to return. He was not leaving her for any reason. Not for one minute of this night, she was going to be by his side.

Phillip knew what his mother had done and did not want Martina to EVER find out. "It was cold darling. The food was cold and we specifically told the caterer to serve only hot things hot, and cold foods cold." He smiled at her.

"Okay! You are the expert at cuisine. I would never have known the difference," and she smiled that beautiful sweet smile back at her husband.

The jeweler's guards were present. With the majority of the people leaving, Phillip asked them to take his wife's jewelry back to the store and said he would collect it later.

Martina smiled and kissed her husband. "You are so thoughtful."

Phillip said, "I have decided we must have a house of our own which will have a safe for your own jewelry. This is my parents house and we do NOT belong here. Your apartment is just right for you and I, but with the baby coming. We need a bigger place. Where would you like your house to be built? Think about it."

She said, "We will talk about it later. We will talk and make love and plan."

He said, "Back up. I like that second thing you said. Let's get out of here."

He picked her up after he shot the garter into the air,

and she had flung the bouquet into the crowd. The white limo took them straight to the airport.

Martina said, "You did not tell me about this and I have not packed any clothes!"

"You don't need any!" and he smiled.

They were on their way to Munich, Germany for their honeymoon. The airplane was one of the Lufthansa planes with an air cabin just for them. Chairs, bed, table, etc.

He assured her, "Eventually you may need some clothes. We will go shopping!" She then grinned.

"You mean to say you are going shopping in a tuxedo and I in my wedding dress?"

"Nope," he said. "We will sit in our beautiful room in front of the computer, and you my dear can order your wardrobe and mine. What do you say? We have robes in this closet on the plane. If you want to get more comfortable," he grinned.

"It's an eleven hour and twenty five minutes for this flight. How many mile highs do you think we can have before we get there?" He was unzipping her dress and she was unbuttoning his shirt.

"I have chosen wisely. When I said yes, I knew you were smart, and would always take care of my sexual needs. Now I am finding out you can take care of everything. You are my hero, Phillip Alexander Porter!"

"And you are the love of my life. How are you feeling? You haven't fainted once."

"I hope that phase of my pregnancy is over. I feel fine," and she let her hands wander all over his chest.

About that time the flight attendant past to see if they needed anything.

"Nope and we don't want to be disturbed," and Martina slid the tiny door closed to their first class adventure.

CHAPTER TWO

Amanda had arrived and Aunt Bessie had welcomed her into the house. Nancy had told her sister that it was okay for the girl to visit, but they must be chaperoned.

Michael had helped Tyson into the living room recliner. There he sat. The shoulder bandages were too big to put a shirt on and the ribs were still taped. "Thank goodness the drainage tube is out," he told Michael earlier.

"Ty you look really really good. I didn't bring flowers because mother said no. She is parking the car," Amanda said.

Auntie Bessie went to the door, "So glad you came, I will have a grown-up to talk to. My sister said that she hated to miss you and Amanda, but she had to go to her best friend's wedding party. Make yourself at home."

Mrs. Thomas was looking around, and finally spoke to Tyson. "My girl has been very worried about you. You look like your picture. Glad you are better," she then went to sit with Bessie.

Michael felt out of place so he was going to his room.

Tyson said, "Bro where you going? I need you here with me," and Michael turned back and smiled.

"Do you two want to play a game and your mother will relax. I will get the monopoly game. Okay?" he left the room.

Amanda sat closer and said, "I am so glad to see for myself you are getting better. I will never forget that night. The number you gave me is what the police said helped get the bad guy. We are a team you and I," she wanted to hold his hand, but her mother was watching.

"You did good, thank you. My mom always said get the license number." He had to touch her hand. It hurt to move still, so he motioned for her to move her chair closer.

"We are going to play Monopoly. You will have to sit closer so you can play my part." He said loud enough for her mother to hear. "I can't roll the dice or pick up the cards yet."

"No problem I will help you!" she said it loud enough for her mother to hear.

Michael came out with the game and a TV tray for them to play on. Michael sat where it blocked her mother's view into the room.

Tyson said, "Thanks Bro. I owe you one, and he held onto Amanda's hand which was rubbing his thigh. Their eyes were locked on each other.

Michael said, "If you two don't start talking Monopoly Ty's going to have more injuries for me to take care of."

He rolled the dice and moved around the board.

He was having to play all three players parts. Tyson was so into Amanda's skirt that Michael jumped up and said, "That does it. I win!"

He began putting the game up and turned to Ty "You

are on your own. You may get killed for real!" and he went to his room.

Amanda said, "He is right. My mother will kill us both but it felt so good," and Tyson closed his eyes and tried to reach further.

Amanda moved just in time. Her mother was coming around the corner and Tyson pulled the pillow onto his lap and smiled. "I thank you for bringing her over Mrs Thomas. That was a nice thing to do."

"We had better be going Amanda. It soon will be dark. Your father young lady, doesn't want us on the road at night," she shook her umbrella out. It had stopped raining.

"I'll call you when we get home," Amanda told Tyson and smiled and rubbing her leg where his hand had been.

"Come back anytime," Aunt Bessie said. "It was nice to meet you, too!" waving to them.

Michael said to Tyson, "You have lost your mind. Are you ready to go to bed. I want my recliner back."

"Yep to both. Isn't she something?" Tyson said.

"Something is right. Something that is going to get you killed. Hey, do you reckon that boy that shot you has a thing for her?" Michael asked.

"No Bro, I was on the phone. He never saw her," Ty said.

"Yeah right!" Michael shook his head.

Curtis was taking his time with getting Nancy home. "That dress is beautiful on you Nancy. I am one lucky man to have been invited to this party." He was driving very slowly back to her house. "Would you like to stop for coffee and talk awhile in a quiet place?" His eyes never left the road.

"Thank you about the dress. It has been noisy. We are both lucky to have friends like Phillip and Martina. They are the real deal. I would love some coffee. What do you have in mind?" Nancy leaned forward to survey his big smile.

"My place is quiet," Curtis said. Still he had not let his eyes veer from the road.

"My home is full of people so you think I would like to see where you live. Is that it?" Nancy knew it wasn't, but she didn't want to go home yet either. He had held her so close on the dance floor. It had been many years since she had trusted a man to get that close to her.

"Exactly! I have seen your place and I want you to know everything about me," he pulled into a driveway of a small brick house on a nice quiet street in a good neighborhood.

"You live here? You sure knew I was going to say yes. What else have you got up your sleeve?" and pulled his arm over and looked up his sleeve. "That's good because I don't see anything." He started laughing and walked around the car and opened the door.

As she was getting out she said, "I know judo and pack a derringer, so don't try any funny stuff," then she started laughing.

"You want to make the coffee so you will know that I've not put anything in it?" he unlocked the front door and she went inside.

"You are now a mind-reader. I like that in a man. Yes,

I would love to fix you a cup. Oh My God look at this kitchen. It is the size of my living room." He showed her where the coffee and filters were.

He said he was going to hang his coat up.

"I like a man that knows how to pick his clothes up. I bet you fold everything neatly, too!" She opened the utensil drawer. Dang, all the kitchen towels were folded neatly to the side of the tray.

"Wow! Where have you been all my life?" she said to herself. He was the perfect package now is the time to snoop. He may have an ex wife from hell.

She made the coffee and peeped into the living room and viewed the pictures on the mantle. None had him and a young woman in them.

He came around the corner, "Looking for something?"

"Yeah, I am." She stood with her hands on her hips of that tight fitting blue sequin dress.

"What? Ask me anything and I will tell you," and he walked close to her and placed his hands around her waist, and lifted her, and kissed her gently on her mouth that was open and waited. She was frozen, "Do you have an ex-wife, girlfriend, children?"

"No to all of those questions," and then he was in for a shock. She put her arms around his neck and almost swallowed his tongue. He was on fire for her and she for him. He rocked her and began unzipping her dress.

It fell from her shoulders to the floor exposing more than he could handle. There she stood in blue lacy under things courtesy of Martina. She had persuaded Nancy to go the whole nine yards, if Curtis made a pass.

Martina said, "Go for it! He is a good man. You deserve a good man."

The coffee timer went off. "I need coffee and a robe before I do something stupid," she said.

"I want you so please do something stupid first," Curtis stated.

She walked to him and kissed him deeply, You are mine Twinkle-toes for one hour. Then I have to go, or my sister will be calling your Brothers in Blue to arrest you!" she climbed into his arms and no more words were needed.

It was an explosion beyond either one's imagination.

She lay panting, and he was still kissing everywhere. "Mr Wonderful are you up for seconds because you keep turning on the right button." They were made for one another and he told her that over and over until he said.

"They are going to have to arrest me. I'm not letting you go!" they did not ever think of calling her sister until six o'clock the next morning.

"Bessie I am getting married and then I'll be home. Kiss the boys!" and she hung up the phone and said. "Now where were we," and Curtis knew exactly where they had left off, and brought her a HOT cup of coffee.

Mr & Mrs Curtis Latham stood in front of the Justice of the Peace. She in a blue sequin gown, and he in a black tuxedo with a blue bow-tie that matched the bride's dress. Smiling they were saying in unison, "I do to you what you do to me for the rest of our lives."

When they arrived home, Michael had not gone to school and Tyson still couldn't. They were both frowning. Aunt Bessie was smiling and hugged Curtis first then Nancy.

"I am sorry boys for not letting you be in the wedding, but I didn't want Curtis to change his mind and they both started smiling. "Good idea, mom!" both said it in unison.

Curtis hugged them both and the happy family began making arrangements to merge the family living arrangement.

"Wait until Martina hears about this!" Nancy said.

"Wait until Phillip hears about this!" Curtis said. The boys were in the mean time setting up the computer cam to make a Skype call to them in Germany. They held up the marriage license to the cam first and Nancy could hear Martina screaming "Come here Phillip quick." He came running from the bathroom half naked.

"Martina tell him the boys are watching him, not to mention me a newly married woman is watching. My husband has got more ..." and Curtis put his hand over her mouth. Martina and Phillip were laughing so hard. Trying to give their congratulations!

Michael was recording everything. He was so smart with the technology that Curtis gave him a high- five. Curtis said, "Phillip I have gained two wonderful boys and all because of you two .. that I met the love of my life. I thank you from the bottom of my heart."

Bessie said, "Next time I come, I want a party. Yes I am single at the moment," and winked at the cam.

"Martina have fun, but don't faint over there because I can't help you partner. I will go back to work when I get off my honeymoon! Michael that's a wrap!" and he cut the cam recording off because Martina was fixing to have a fit and Nancy smiled.

She looked around the room, "Yes I am going back to work tomorrow, but only because Curtis has to work, too! Mr Wonderful and I will take our time planning our honeymoon! Barbados, Bahamas, Jamaica?" rattling off more options all the way to the stove.

"But today I am chained to this kitchen with all these hungry mouths to feed," looking around the room smiling at each of her loved ones.

Curtis stepped forward, "Oh no! Mrs Latham can cook tomorrow. but we are all going to Disneyland today!" and Tyson was frowning because he could only walk short distances. Curtis went to his SUV and rolled a brand new wheelchair into the living room with balloons attached that said, "This kid has got new parents."

"Mom you are not new," Tyson said grinning.

"Curtis makes me feel brand new. Do you like your wheels, son?" Nancy asked as she stepped over to hug Curtis. "You thought of everything."

Then the police officers outside began singing, "Here comes the bride. Here comes the bride. Here comes the bride with Mr Wonderful!" and they handed every one tickets to Disneyland as their wedding present.

They were chest-bumping Curtis and formed a line to kiss the bride. Curtis was expanding his chest to say something negative. Nancy pranced in front of him to calm him, "I'll handle this."

"Guys three days ago, I probably would have kissed everyone of you! But as of today these lips are for no one, but Mr Wonderful!" Curtis was beaming. "That's my wife!"

CHAPTER THREE

Phillip and Martina had arrived at the Munich Airport Franz Josef Straub. Phillip and his father had business trips here and he was a history buff. "Honey! Straub was a Prime Minister of Bavaria. Did you know Munich is its capital?"

"I am American and no nothing about Germany except I LOVE their Lufthansa airplanes. I've never seen anything or read anything to beat it." She snuggled up to him, "and my first mile high!" she was still tingling.

"You mean second," and he grinned. "This is Lufthansa's hub and we are definitely going to try for number four or five on the way back ... maybe I am being overly optimistic."

"Yes dear. You are ... because I intend to get your monies worth at that fancy hotel you have us booked at!" He grabbed her.

"Why would do that in the middle of a crowd?" he said and she immediately felt why he was asking.

"Don't worry! We don't know any of these people. It's okay to get horny. You are on your honeymoon. Relax

Phillip, your MOTHER is not here," she turned her head to laugh.

"Okay honey! You flatten it. Have no fear no constituents will report back that I was having an amazing time until you lowered the boom," he had sad eyes.

She bounced in front of him saying, "The Sofitel Bayerpost will change your mind. I remember in the brochure I was reading about the five star hotel and ALL its ... amenities!"

His eyes brightened again, "Let us hurry darling! I think I have fully recovered. How are you feeling?" and he got down on one knee, and asked the baby the same question.

They were in the lap of luxury in the hotel. It was grand and the room was a chic designer's masterpiece. They fell into the plush bedding after stripping at the bedroom door. "I love you, Mrs Martina Porter."

"I love you, Mr Phillip Porter. We are going to have to think of a baby's name before we leave here. Maybe a German name," and he silenced her talking of such nonsense.

They bathed in the marble tub with jets and after love-making sat on the window seat looking out onto the city of many lighted buildings. They were in the heart of Munich and surrounded by history.

They would explore all that Phillip wanted her to see in the days to come, but for now just being in each others' arms was heavenly without the stresses of their everyday life.

She said, "I don't ever want to leave here." He had

his arms wrapped around her and she leaned back on his chest.

"Me either. Right here is where my wife and child are. No matter what city we are in, YOU are my world. **FINALLY you said YES!** I waited four years to hear those words."

They rested for two days, then went to the Englischer Garten. "It's like Central Park but only larger, Phillip."

"Yes, but what I want you to see is the Japanese tea ceremony at the Japanese Teahouse with a beautiful Japanese garden. All right here." They toured the English garden also.

"I'm exhausted," Martina said. Phillip picked her up and walked with her in his arms back to the tourist group which took them back to their hotel.

Martina napped until suppertime. They ate in one of the restaurants called the Ratskeller Munich. Then they took a taxi to the Olympiastadion where her favorite band was playing. "Cold Play! OMG in concert! You've been planning this for awhile. Confess my dear husband."

"Yes my love. I found out they would be here in June 2017 and I do plan well when I have you as my inspiration."

They enjoyed the concert and went back for her to rest.

"We have two more days and we shall rest. Unless you feel up to seeing the museum," Phillip asked loudly because she was now in the shower.

"Phillip let us have something else to come back and

see next year. Our baby's first pictures can be taken there. Okay?"

"Yes you and … We haven't discussed baby names. I can't believe you have not mentioned it," Phillip winked at her.

She stood there naked in the doorway after taking her shower. "We have been rather busy with other more important things. I will try and concentrate on names!"

He was nibbling on her neck and down her arm.

"Tomorrow! You had better be concentrating, too!" she whispered.

"Oh I am truly concentrating right now," kissing her senseless.

The next day, they laid in bed spouting off baby names. Girls first, then boys. None were what they wanted.

"We have another half of an alphabet to go through," she frowned.

"I think we should save that for tomorrow," he smiled.

"Okay," she was so cooperative. With every thing he said.

"Honey I have got to keep you pregnant all the time. You have been so agreeable. It scares me and delights me at the same time."

"Before I was just a BITCH, is that basically what you are telling me?" Martina asked.

Phillip kept his mouth sealed and walked slowly to the window with his eyes widening.

"It's the hormones honey. This to shall come to pass, and I will be back to my old wonderful self," and she had a fit of laughter at herself.

She held her hands up like Freddie Kruger and came at him, "The detective from hell! The better to eat you alive! Oops different movie," and cracked Phillip up.

"We can make our on movies. I can be Adam and you can be Eve," Phillip said.

"That's it! That's it!" Martina said.

He grabbed himself encase she was going to whack him one. "What? What?"

She said smiling and rubbing his hands, "The names ... I was looking for for our children's names! These are perfect!"

"Adam and Eve ...that does have a certain ... POWERFUL ring to it. Are we planning on two children?" Phillip inquired.

"Yes, one of each. I have my order in. You just have to provide the sperm," she said. Now he was grinning.

Back at home, Cynthia had walked the chalk line. Bart was testing her all week and having her rehearse her speech for the newlyweds. It was humiliating for her, but she did it.

Her husband on the other hand thought this is mild punish-ment for the unforgivable deed she almost accomplished.

He called Brigs and asked him and his wife for dinner while Cynthia sat listening. They agreed to come.

"Cynthia, you are in boot camp and will soon be in the trenches. I'll see how you do," and he walked into his den.

She had rather eat fishing worms than dine with that witchy sister-in-law of hers. She thought, but the alternative would be worst. "Put on your big girl panties and deal with it old girl!" she told herself.

No other of her so-called-friends were speaking to her.

She went and bought a new outfit just to entice her husband. It had always worked. Cynthia looked amazing in a Vera Wang pleated chiffon gown and the color was called quartz. It looked beautiful with Cynthia's pale skin and blonde coif. Her matching the eye shadow perfectly with the hue of the dress, added drama.

The new eyelash extensions helped, also. She just hoped Bartholomew appreciated her extra effort. Of course, he never missed a thing. He liked perfection, and she surely was not that in his eyes right now.

It was going to take a lot of work. She had a tough background. Her father was just like him, and he would ship her off to another boarding school when she messed up... one after another. Each headmistress would try and break her down, to no avail. It had toughen her more and more until now, she had actually no feelings except for Phillip. He was her child and she had given birth to him. It was still an emotional feeling, one that brought a tear to her eyes.

He would forgive her, she told herself. He was what she lived and breathed for. She was going to be strong and let Bartholomew handle this situation. Her dear husband that she had ignored for a long period of time.

"He has stuck by me," she said to herself. Time will tell, if he will again. If she just didn't have to deal with Katherine, she could twist Brigs around her little finger.

She had the chef cook Bart's favorite dinner of roast

with mushroom gravy, new potatoes, and baby carrots. Asparagus with butter drizzled all over it that was grown in their very own vegetable garden. Dessert was a coconut layered cake like his mother use to bake.

This was a simple meal that both the Porter brothers would be nostalgic about. Cynthia was hoping that it would put them in a forgiving mood, but Katherine hated simple food and hated Cynthia.

When they arrived, the two women squared off like two bantam hens. Feisty and both were quarrelsome. Cynthia went straight to the point, "I am at fault Katherine, but I am human. I made a mistake. Let's forgive and have a good fellowship tonight."

This was monumental, Katherine squinted her eyes and peered at Cynthia whom was not known for being apologetic.

"We'll see how it goes. You really need to think about how your mother-in-law treated you. See I remember you running to me begging for me to help you. Think about it Cynthia, you are doing the same thing to Martina," Katherine finished for the first time without being interrupted.

Cynthia looked at the ceiling, and walked toward the dining room. "You are right. I just have never thought of it in that perspective. I'll try and do better, is all I can promise," and they sat at the table waiting for the men to enter.

"That is all I ask. One thing, one good thing that has come out of all this, the brothers are bonding back where they should have been before you and I had a falling out. What was it we were disagreeing about?" they both laughed.

Bart and Brigs were hastening down the hall to see what was happening. Entering the dining room found their wives talking like they use to when they were young and best of friends.

Bartolomew kissed Cynthia on the cheek and sat.

Bridgeston kissed Katherine on the cheek and said, "This is more like it. I'll say grace. Thank you Lord for this miracle. Let's eat!"

Both the brothers commented on the wonderful food.

"Just like mama cooked!" Brigs said.

Bart cringed and Cynthia saw it, "Relax Bartholomew. She is dead and we can enjoy. I do enjoy making you happy!" He was falling right back into her trap and boy was he going to fall tonight.

Katherine said, "I always wanted that cake recipe," smiling at Brigs.

Curtis and Nancy were working and at night rearranging Curtis house. The boys would have the two bedrooms upstairs with their own bathroom. They were all, but Tyson working on that. He was sitting in on the progress. He was walking better and climbed the steps, one step at a time, and he did it finally on his own.

Auntie Bessie said, "I'll just take over your place Nancy. Finish out that lease of yours and I won't have to fork out an extra month's rent for another place. Family means so much to me, the older I get. My kids are all married and you need me with these two. It's nice to be needed."

Nancy said, "Sounds good to me. What about you Curtis? What do you think?" She wanted to include him in everything.

This man was happy with giving up all his freedom, giving up all his house. "Only thing I want is a king-size bed. I can't share, but half of that bed. All else is yours to decide,"

Curtis declared.

"For real? I can do anything?" Nancy asked.

"Okay. I want this wall orange, this one fluorescent green, and ...." she didn't get to finish. Curtis scooped her up while she was still talking, and put her in the passenger seat of the SUV, and drove off. Aunt Bessie was with the boys.

"Where are we going now?" Nancy insisted on knowing.

"To get our bed. OUR big bed for this BIG man," and he smiled at her. "Aunt Bessie is going to be a blessing because I can scoop you up and take you to the beach when WE want to or anywhere your little heart desires."

"Bassett Furniture, I always wanted to visit that motel. She went in and laid down on the first king size bed that she saw.

"Come here and see how you like this one," patting the mattress beside her. "Just like a motel right?"

Nancy said and the clerk patted her foot, "Cool your jets honey. He's going to buy one. We just don't know which one and his appetite is real big"............ a long pause......... for comfort. Your commission will be real big. So move over, Curtis I want to try this one next," and she proceeded to lounge in the next one waiting for her man to join her.

The last one he asked, "Have you made up your mind yet?"

"Nah I'm having too much fun. You said we got to have one today. Honey clerk yahoo! Will you deliver this one tonight?"

The clerk said, "No ma'am. I'm not sure when!"

"I'm sure that the next store will," and she started prancing SLOWLY to the door. Leaving Curtis standing with his mouth open, watching his new wife wheel and deal. Because before she got to the front door, the male manager said, "Why of course we can! Would you like to step into my office." She waved at Curtis, "Come on Mr Wonderful. This man wants HER commission. Let us give it to him," and she smiled at the snobbish clerk. She went in, to sit and wait for Curtis.

"Good job darling! I love shopping with you, "and she gave the man clerk her new address.

"Where are we going next?" Curtis asked.

"I don't know. You are the one that kidnapped me," and she grinned. "We could go back to my place since yours is so full of people."

He flew to her old house before the furniture was delivered.

He was smiling while opening the door for the movers and blowing Nancy an air kiss. "Thank you! I needed that!"

She quivered and said, "Anytime!" as she bent over at

the waist to tie her tennis shoe. Curtis almost grabbed her, but Michael came through.

"What a bed! Never seen one that big before," Michael said.

Nancy was standing in front of Curtis, "I've never seen one that big either. I just had to try it out again and again before I saw if it would fit my backside. I will sleeeeeep so good! Curtis are you okay?" He had closed his eyes and sat down.

"I'll help the guys with the bed arrangement in the room. You just sit there and relax your muscles, and she wiggled on off to the bedroom rearranging until the guys were huffing and puffing.

"You guys want some homemade lemonade? Bessie fix a pitcher for these nice gentlemen." Curtis had recovered.

"Ain't she something. Yep! This cute little spitfire is my new bride. This bed is our first. That is why she is fussing over it," Curtis put his arm around her shoulder claiming his territory.

Michael came through and said, "She makes a fuss over everything!"

Tyson said, "Oh No! You are going to get it, Bro!"

"It's the truth. She is the best mom and wants the best for her boys, "Michael said and kissed Nancy on the cheek.

Her expression had never changed.

"Nice recovery, Bro!" Tyson high- fived Michael.

"I learned from the best," winking at his mother.

CHAPTER FOUR

The Lufthansa plane had landed and Martina had just finished dressing. "I love this air cabin. It is the only way with our little baby between us to play with for eleven hours and twenty five minutes next year!"

"Oh that child of ours will be sleeping most of it, my darling," and he kissed her thoroughly. They walked out prim and proper with his coat hanging across his forearm to cover the damage his wife was doing to his body.

The white limo was waiting to take them to her tiny apartment. He was all smiles and so was she. As they rounded the curve she saw a moving van at Nancy's, "Let's leave them be. I am in no condition to move anything ... but you from left to right and up and down and all around," he closed his eyes that were full of memories.

"I have spoiled you this vacation. It has been mutually satisfying for me, my husband!" and she purred in his ear.

"It's a shame we have to go back to work tomorrow." She added, "But I could never be a lady of leisure. I do love my job. I must call Nancy and see if we have any clients left,"

laughing all the way to the phone.

"Hello newlywed," Martina said.

"Hello newlywed," Nancy said.

"Guess it's over, "Martina said.

"Guess it never began," Nancy said.

"What do you mean, Partner? Martina asked.

"Ho hum someone had to mind the store!" Nancy said sooo pitiful.

"You mean you have been working all week while we played. I mean toured Germany. It is beautiful. You and Curtis must go," Martina said.

"You paying? I love free trips. I'll go and drag Curtis with me. Just kidding! We haven't decided where we want to go, and Curtis has to put in for leave way in advance to the police department's head honcho."

"I saw a van. Don't you have something to tell us?" Martina asked and grinned.

"Yeah, we have two love nests. His is bigger and we have managed to move everything at night. It is perfect. Aunt Bessie will be living in my place for awhile, and I'll have help with the boys because Curtis is a hand full!"

He came around the corner and chest-bumped Phillip and they shook hands like it had been an eternity since they had seen each other. There the girls stood with their phones.

"Man we have missed you' all. Nancy has been ruling the roost. She has it about like she wants it," Curtis said.

"Yeah and he is talking about the bed," and she kissed his puckered lips.

"The man had to have the biggest, baddest bed that I have ever seen," and winked at Curtis.

He pointed to her. "She picked it out!" and he grinned.

"That's my Nancy. The biggest, baddest woman in the detective agency. I'm the sweet, little damsel." Martina put her finger in her mouth like it made her gag to say it.

"Speaking of sickness. Did she faint some?" Nancy asked.

"Not one time ... no not one," Phillip reported happily.

"So it's me that makes you sick," Nancy pointed to herself.

"No way that was just the pregnancy that made me do it." Martina was laughing. "It did happen a lot because I remember you putting a cold wash rag on my forehead. I will do the same with you when you get with child."

Martina was stirring the pot already.

Curtis had turned beet-red. "You wouldn't dare?" looking at Nancy who had her tongue at the roof of her mouth sticking her tongue out at him like a serpent fixing to strike.

It was turning him on and he said, "Okay! We will try again tonight!"

Nancy laughed, "You sir, have two boys at home. You don't need another now. I first got to see how you hold these two's baby. Before I even agree to such a thing ... as old as I am," and she ran both her hands from breasts to hips down her curvy curves causing everyone to laugh.

"I have missed you, girlfriend!" Martina hugged her. "Phillip hasn't made me laugh but once. Too busy making me scream," his eyes got so big. She blew him an air kiss.

He nodded, "Guilty as charged. You, my wife will pay for this. Pay dearly," holding his pillow in his lap.

"I have missed you friend. I need help with this one," Curtis pointed to Nancy.

"I need help with this one." Phillip pointed to Martina. "We are sisters," she said. "We are twins," Nancy said. A white and black bond that no one could break, and many had tried.

Phillip told Martina that they had to go by and see his father. "A courtesy call since they paid for the honeymoon trip," Phillip said. "We will not stay long, I promise."

He waltzed in and his father was ecstatic with glee. He shouted for the maid to go get Cynthia. He hugged his son and his daughter-in-law.

Cynthia came running in and hugged MARTINA before she hugged Phillip. "My dear, I am told you are going to have our first grandchild, and we are so so happy!"

Bart shook his head yes to his son to signify that it was genuine. That is when Phillip hugged his mother. All was forgiven.

This woman that had never been loved as a child. She was now learning to love, more people than her son. Her husband was guiding her. He had taught her a lot about business and upper crust functions, but never truly loved his wife as he did at this moment.

She had always given the air of being better than others, but it was only her coping mechanism. If she rejected others first, then they would never be able to hurt her.

She was putting herself out there to her daughter-in-law

to be hurt. She found a sweet loving girl that hugged her back.

Bart told Cynthia later, "See you now have a daughter to love and do things with. You are not losing your son, but gaining another person to love. She'll love you back ... if you will let her," he felt Cynthia trembling.

"Our grandchild will be raised in a loving family." She kissed her husband and that is something Phillip had never seen. His mother and father showed no outward affection toward each other throughout his childhood.

Martina was observing a quiet withdrawn husband. She would wait and ask him in private what was going on. He said, "We have been traveling and she needs rest so we will say good night for now." They left with his parents waving.

Phillip felt like he had been punched in the stomach, and didn't know why. Then he realized that his mother had meant to harm his wife really bad, and that is interfering with his accepting his mother as she is now. Is she just pretending or is she being genuine as his father has implied.

Time will tell and then he finally smiled at his wife who was making them the most wonderful ham and Swiss cheese sandwich. "Look no sauerkraut!" she said. He laughed.

He had conquered his demons and moved on living his new life. A happy fun filled marriage that took four long years to convince her to become his wife.

FINALLY she said YES!

He vowed nothing and nobody was going to interfere with their happiness.

They ate and started discussing where they wanted to live.

"Do you want to look at houses first? If we can't find what we want, then we can build," she suggested.

"We will have to do it soon because they cannot build this dream house over night," Phillip reminded her.

"It doesn't have to be a big big house Phillip. I will be happier in a small house just one with three bedrooms that's all," she rubbed her tummy.

"Hey that's my job," he said and pounced on her.

"What washing dishes?' she giggled.

"No and what are we going to do in that extra bedroom? I have a few ideas" and he rubbed and rubbed.

"That is not the baby... you are rubbing!" she pointed out.

"I know," He was undressing her in the kitchen.

"I want you to be comfortable as you were in Germany," and he continued. "Beside I like to look at you," and bit her neck.

"The other bedroom could be for a twin," she said.

That got his attention, "What'd you say?'

He had been kissing her stomach and he stood, looking into her eyes.

"I have a family history. You should have known that in the past four years. You have asked, and investigated everything else about me," she said while pulling his shirt out of his pants and unbuttoning it.

"That is true. So do you want a boy and a girl?" he asked unzipping his pants.

"That would be nice. Do you think you can arrange it?" she kissed his navel.

He was ready and she lay back on the sink, "I want all that you got for me and I want it now."

"You are asking for it!" he said sliding between her legs.

"Haven't I always!" and they were home and in the apartment that their love had grown in.

She was proving that it was better at home. In a tiny apartment than across on the other side of the world, in a big fancy palace.

"Oh now that is what I call a homecoming!" he was was salivating and his head went back.

"You are dynamite and I'm exploding again," he was not going to make it to the bed this time.

"Honey don't move. It is too good to waste on walking," she had backed onto the washer and nothing felt better when you were this hot than the feel of cold metal on your back."

"That is it just what I need. Right there, honey. Honey go to the mountain NOW!"

He did and then said, "You are right again Martina. We don't need anything, but a sink and a washer and we can be very very happy for the rest of our lives."

As they showered, "But the babies need, they may need a room apiece and a playroom. We may want a two car garage for that station wagon and the ..." he paused.

She was waiting for his next word and stopped soaping him, "and what?"

"The Ferrari," he said.

"You have a Maserati what do you need that for?" she asked.

"Well you said a boy and he may like a Ferrari, and you said a girl. She probably would like the Maserati. As for you and I ... a station wagon will be plenty of room for us to spread out in. Don't you think?" He was soaping her up.

Martina said, "I think we need to buy buy it NOW ... and test it out before the kids come," she grinned and wiggled.

"You are so smart. I am so glad we thought of it!"

They went the next day after work and looked at three bedroom houses with two door garages. In Curtis and Nancy's neighborhood, Martina found one that she loved.

It was simple and just the right size for a family with two children. She knew Phillip had always lived in a mansion.

She frowned, "It's not big enough for you, is it? I want you to be happy. Please talk it out. Tell me what you like and what you don't like?" she got no response and popped him on his rear.

Her heels were off and she was rubbing her soles. Her first day back, and her dogs were hurting. Her feet had started to swell with this pregnancy as they did with her daughter that had died.

A tear fell from her eyes.

Finally . . . Yes!

He asked, "Are you crying because you think I am going to say no to this house?"

She said, "Lord No! It is my feet!" then she bawled.

He held her, "My feet swelled like this with Gabriella..."

He picked her up, and kissed her, and toted her to the car with her shoes in her hands.

"I think this house is perfect. If you want it, you got it!"

"We will look some more, if you want to?" she insisted.

"NO way, and have your feet hurting more. Then I'll be crying, too! I can't take the tears. Anything that will take the tears away, I will buy today!" and he smiled at her.

"You are a pushover!" she kissed his cheek.

"Yep but you pushed me away for four years and **FINALLY you said YES!**"

CHAPTER FIVE

Sammy said, "So you finally have come back to work with mere earthlings after a Cloud nine for a honeymoon?" He patted Phillip on the back.

Phillip was grinning, "Who told you about the air cabin in the sky?"

Sammy had a frightened look on his face, "I was kidding! I was kidding! Phillip it's no such thing. Right?"

Phillip shook his head up and down and sat down behind his desk and began going through his mail.

Sammy walked around the desk and looked at his friend's face, "You are not lying. I can always tell when you are lying!"

"Why should I lie? It is for real. We took an air cabin to Germany look it up on the internet."

Then he had to mess with the gullible Sammy.

"And it was on Cloud Nine after we took off from LAX and one hour into our flight ... our honeymoon took off into outer space."

Sammy looked at his friend, "That is a good piece of fiction. You are not going to make a fool of your best

friend this time. Last time I fell for your made up capers."
He stomped out of Phillip's office.

His secretary asked, "What in the world is wrong
with Sammy?'

"I told him about my honeymoon and he didn't
believe me."

He shrugged his shoulders and walked to the
breakroom to get his own coffee. Sammy was by the
coffeepot. He was frowning and said to Phillip. "I looked
it up. The air cabin is for real! I'm jealous," and sipped
his coffee.

"You find the neatest things to do. I gotta find
something exciting to do for Rosalind or I am going to
go into outer space all alone."

Phillip said, "Come back to my office and we will
talk. You and Roz just need a vacation. That's all! She
loves you. I'll see what I can do. OK? Relax!"

"Man do I ever! Between the in -laws and the kids,
and the new renovations on the house, we are growling
at each other."

Phillip depended on his friend too much to fill in
when he had to go out of town. He had to make it up to
him because he and Martina had been taking advantage
of their friendship lately. Sammy would do anything for
Phillip.

As Sammy came into the office, Phillip was grinning,
"Oh no! The answer is no!" Sammy said firmly.

"Didn't I say to relax? Sit down. Prop your feet up!"

Sammy sat down and propped his feet up on Phillip's
desk. It made Phillip cringe because he didn't like anyone

to touch his stuff, but he had no IDEA that Sammy would actually do such a thing.

"How you feel now buddy?" Phillip smiled.

"Yes, I do feel much better. Hell yeah! Damn good! Got my feet on the boss's desk and he hasn't strangle me, yet." He quickly removed them. "I didn't get the reaction I was expecting ... sooo ... have you planned my life out, yet?"

"Sammy I can make suggestions. You my friend have to chose one, and make it your own. Let me see. Does Roz love to ski?"

"No nor do I. Tried it! You remember, I broke my right leg?"

"Oh yeah! I do remember you hobbling. How about hiking the Grand Canyon?"

"NO! She hates to sweat. I hate coyotes!" and he shivered.

"Skydiving? Cape Canaveral touring and pilot lessons and adventures?" Phillip was grinning.

"She is scared of heights and I get nosebleeds," Sammy now was shrugging his shoulders. "We are dull people. We like to cook out by the pool and roast marshmallows. Then run back in the house into the cool breeze of the air- conditioning. With kids there's nothing after that, the grandparents kill whatever is left by spending the night."

"OK I see the problem. You need to get away, but not too far away. Otherwise both of you will be worrying about the kids and her parents. I got it you both like the ocean, and Malibu is around the corner. I'll book you a house for a week on the oceanfront."

"Oh my Goodness! That sounds marvelous! I can't wait to tell Roz!" he was almost out the door.

"Sammy come back here and sit down. You cannot tell Roz. You just take a drive one night and take her to the hideaway. The kids will be with her parents anyway. Call them after you get there and tell them you will see them in a week. Roz will say that she didn't have her clothes. You say we will go shopping, we have a whole week. You may not need any!"

and Phillip winked at him.

"You are a GENIUS! That's why you are the boss and I work for you to get these fringe benefits. Dang! I am not one to keep a secret from her. Whoa! I think this has me all stirred up enough to keep my mouth shut!" He crossed his legs and closed his eyes.

"You will thank me! Now don't hurt yourself over there," Phillip said and started reading one of his reports.

"I am just soooo relaxed," Sammy arose from the chair with a totally different attitude and walked to his office with a swagger. He would do more work this week for his boss than he did last week, and Phillip knew it.

Phillip's secretary said, "I want what he had for lunch!"

Sarah was his loyal seasoned employee that is the way Martina spoke of her. "Old is the word dear," he said. She told him he was in good hands with Sarah.

"She is efficient and that is why she is sitting outside my door, AND for no other reason .... than to please you." Martina smiled and said, "Good answer."

"You would not be able to do any detective work over there for snooping in my office every day, if I had a hot young chick over here helping me," and he grinned at the phone that day of their discussion. The memory made him smile at Sarah who was typing away.

Martina had taken herself out of her office, rode her Harley Davidson motorcycle over, and came into his office. Fit to be tied. "So you want a hot young chick in your office, do you? Well here I am! So deal with it!" and boy, did he deal.

Shaking his head, "I have got to get some work done." That he did for the rest of the day until five. Then he was on his way home to that tiny apartment. The one he loves, now.

She was waiting at the door in a silk mauve bathrobe, fresh from a bubble bath. "I have missed you today Buttercup!"

"And I, you!" dropping his briefcase and grabbing the belt to unwrap his prize. Kissing his baby first, then his wife.

"I think this should be our everyday ritual," Phillip said.

"I agreed," Martina said wrapping her legs around him while he closed the bedroom door.

Sammy had secured the keys for the rental beach house and went home. His Roz was decked out in a new dress as he had asked because he was taking her out to eat and a movie. He looked at the in-laws, and said we maybe really late tonight because we are going to that movie afterward. Make your-selves at home, and we will call if we change our plans."

He still had his business suit on, and went around

to open Roz's door, and she got in. "What on earth has gotten into you Sammy?"

"Nothing much! Just a new attitude. I want to bring that loving feeling back again." He kissed her cheek. She almost slapped him. It had been so long since he had opened the door and kissed her even on the cheek was special.

She was going to cry. "Now Roz, if it is going to upset you, I won't do it again." He was playing it cool. She still had not asked where they were going to dinner.

"No honey, you can do it all you want to, but remember my parents are at the house. I don't want you to be disappointed."

"Oh I am not going to be disappointed." He drove up the coast, and entered a driveway that wound around a dune, and around its corner sat the cutest beach house she had ever seen.

"Who lives here Sammy? What are you up to? Sammy?" he helped her out and kissed her like he used to before the kids came, and when they had date nights.

She was giving him back all that he was giving her. He was taking her blouse off. She grabbed his hand, "The people that live here will see us."

"I see you and hopefully all of you. You see me and definitely will all of me. We are the people that live here for a week. Now kiss me anywhere you want!" and he grinned.

"The kids?" she was panting as his hands were rubbing her buttocks and pulling her in.

"Your mother and father will be there for those sweet

abandoned children of ours. They will love this week and darling, they will run out of that door at the end of the week, and won't come back for a long long time to interfere with our child raising!" He licked her lips and kissed her left breast.

"Yes Yes," he unlocked the door and they both were wild animals trying to get their clothes off fast enough.

She stopped and grabbed his face, "Who's paying for all this?"

Sammy smiled and said, "Not me!"

"Good! I'll find out later. Do me!"

Much much later, breathless she said, "Got to be Phillip?"

"Yes Roz. He owed me big time, and I owed you!"

Cynthia was proving to Bart that she was going to follow his advise and ask Martina out to lunch. She rang her office.

Nancy answered, "Why, hi Mrs Porter! What can I do for you. Sugar... I mean Phillip is not here. Yes Martina is. Please hold!" Martina had been in front of her waving her hands no.

Now she faced Nancy who said, "You have to talk to her sometime. Might as well be today!" smiling.

"Now take this phone, before I have to hurt you!" with a sweet smile. Nancy sauntered off to the bathroom, and locked the door. She did not want to be a witness to anything.

Mumbling in the bathroom, "I ain't telling Phillip a lie and Martina can fend for herself. I am not always going to be here always. Yes, I am!," and out the door she flew back to her desk to eavesdrop.

"Yes I would like that. Thank you. Come on over. I'll be waiting," Martina was so glad she had dressed in a loose fitting dress, and wore her sandals with a heel.

She walked by Nancy, "Are you satisfied? Now I got to go to lunch with her and you can do all the work. See what happens when you meddle?"

"I just answered the phone. No big deal. I always answer the phone." She acted like she was the injured party, then frowned knowing that it was not working.

"OK Martina fess up. What is it that you are afraid of?" Nancy said it as she saw it.

"I'm not afraid! OK, so I am scare of her a little. She is Buttercup's mother. She may tear me apart. You know I am delicate," Martina turned so Nancy could not see her smile.

"Delicate my foot. You are a bad ass and you know it. I should be praying that you don't hurt this little old woman. You want me to go with you? So I can protect you?"

Curtis had come in and asked, "Who are you going to protect?"

"You my darling! Protect you from all those conniving jealous women out there. Just trying to take my man," Nancy said. She got her purse and turned to Martina.

"I am so sorry. I can't go with you. I have a previous engagement. I have to protect my husband till death do us part!" strutting out the door holding Curtis's forearm.

Martina shouted, "Traitor!"

Curtis asked Nancy, "What's all that about?"

"I don't don't know must be those hormones working overtime! You know how pregnant women are."

Then they both saw the white limo stop and Mrs. Cynthia Porter got out and went into the agency.

"Mr Wonderful! I am so glad you came when you did or I could have gotten injured refereeing them two. Thank you husband of mine!" She smiled up at him sweetly.

"You mean you are just going to leave Martina without Phillip to protect her? MY! MY!" Curtis shook his head from side to side.

He looked disappointed.

So she took out her cell phone and dialed, "Sugar, I got to go to lunch with Mr Wonderful and your wife is going to lunch with your mother. I thought you might want to know that before they left the office. Bye now!"

Phillip sat staring at his phone. He had a big meeting in ten minutes.

"Hello Dad! I need your help. Mother is taking Martina out to lunch … intercede I can't! I got to take care of business and you know I do. Please I am dying over here."

"Calm down son. I suggested that they go to lunch. I wanted your mother to be a part of her grandchild's pregnancy. That was the happiest time of her life when she was carrying you. Who knows they may go shopping today. Your mother does it so well," and he chuckled.

"But I will go, if it will make you feel better. Relax! It is all good. I will go. I know where they are dining," Bart knew Phillip was not going to trust his mother right away.

"Thanks Dad. I'll talk later!"

Phillip was trembling all over and shook his head and swung his arms, and took a very deep breath. He looked like a prizefighter preparing himself for battle. He opened the door and walked into the board room ... cool as a cucumber.

Smiling and welcoming all to his presentation, and began in a sedate voice that put half of them to sleep. Then he slammed a book on the table, "This the most important thing that I want you all to remember is Porter Law Firm will not back down. This merger is going to strengthen this firm. Its new title will be Porter Brothers & Son Law Firm," pacing.

"My uncle and father have had separate law firms all these years. They have done very well, but the three of us can tackle more and rise even further to the top," he stopped.

"Only with my dedicated employees would I consider such a venture. I have confidence in all of you, and have no fear ... I have made your jobs secure."

The congrats began and Sammy came to him. "I am so glad to hear that last statement because with your fine recommendation of a vacation. I may have a new mouth to feed," he winked.

"Yep Bro! I did a bang up job! All because of you. Roz said to tell you if it's a girl, her name will be Phyllis and if a boy, his name maybe Phil." Sammy shook Phillip's hand.

"You can't! Those are my kids chosen names," Phillip said. "You must name yours after Martina, like Marty and Martin please!" and he began laughing.

"You know me to well Phillip. Yes Roz was on the pill! She may leave without any clothes, but keeps those things in her purse at all times. I can't seem to wipe the smile off my face yet though. That was the BEST vacation, we have ever had. Yes sir, you will have to plan our next one," nodding his head up and down.

"You can't refuse. I run your firm. So you have a year to think of something." Then Sammy turned and left Phillip, whistling all the way down the hall.

The echo of whistling could be heard throughout.

Only a triumphant battle hymn could equal Sammy's whistling.

CHAPTER SIX

Cynthia sat with Martina talking about her pregnancy and drinking ice tea at the vegan restaurant off Cross Creek Road.

It was just the atmosphere that Cynthia wanted to convey a healthy diet.

Martina was really liking the way Cynthia was taking her under her wing, and making her feel supported. "I remember when I was carrying Phillip. I ate healthy and didn't drink or smoke the whole pregnancy. He was perfect at birth, I touched him before the cord was cut, and counted his fingers and toes. I had him natural. No drugs. I am talking too much. Too much coffee!" She laughed hysterically.

She was nervous.

"Talk all you want. I want to know everything about your Phillip. He is the love of my life. I fought him for four years and told him no. This time he convinced me and I **FINALLY said YES!** This baby means so much to me. I lost my daughter. She was in a car wreck." Martina turned her head away and composed herself.

"I want you to know how special your Phillip is, he

propose to me on her death date to make it a happy day for me. He is the best dose of medicine. He is my hero."

Cynthia got out of her chair and came around and hugged her. "Until this moment, I did not know how special you are and my son chose very wisely without anyone helping him."

She kissed Martina's hair and said, "You are my child now. If you will help me, I will be the mother-in-law that I never had. I will be a good one."

"Never had a mama that cared as you do for Phillip. I had to fight for everything. I am rough around the edges, but if you will be patient with me, I think we can make a good team for Phillip and his dad."

Cynthia cried and she never cried. Martina cried and she never cried. These two women were were so different, but emotional so much alike.

"I want there to be no secrets between us. I did a terrible thing, but I did not know you. Please forgive me. I was going to give you food that would make you sick at the party. That was before I learned you were pregnant. I would never harm an innocent baby nor would I ever harm you now that I know you," she turned to see Bart and Phillip listening.

"Phillip tell her … I am a good mother. I will teach her to be a good mother, if she will let me. I had no one, but evil people around me growing up. Rich is not all it is cracked up to be."

"Mother … it is time to go home and we will talk later. You have poured your heart out enough," and Bart lead her to the long white limo and wrapped his arms around Cynthia.

Phillip took Martina in his arms and said, "I never wanted you to know. My mother is begging, not only for your forgiveness, but for mine. I told her I would never forgive her, if she harmed you in any way. She is a broken woman and will do nothing, but love you. It is your choice. Whatever you decide, I stand by you. You are my wife. Let's go home."

Once home Martina was drained. She did not go to work the next day. She went to Nell's. Her best friend's when she was growing up. She told Phillip where she was going and that he need not come. She would be back tonight.

Nell was to be her bridesmaid. She was her best friend throughout school. Only Nell was there for her, others had shunned her. Only Nell had protect her from the cruel jokes at school about her clothes, and about her Spanish family that worked in the fields of a California vineyard.

When her father died from pneumonia, her mother was soon to follow because the sorrow of his death overwhelmed her. One year after to the day, she died.

Nell' s parents took Martina in, and sent her through college. Nell never begrudged her anything that her family did for her friend. That's the kind of open heart that Nell had, and she encouraged Martina to go for the gusto when she got married to her best friend, Tom.

Nell married Tom's best friend … Nash Timberlake.

Nash was a character. He always made Martina and

Tom welcome. They did everything as couples that was family oriented. Both the girls were pregnant at the same time, and had many shopping adventures.

Then Tom was drafted and the sadness reemerged, but she had Gabriella. Nell had Nash, Jr., and they kept busy with the kids.

The day she got the news that Tom had been killed. She took Gabriella to Nell's, and she took her in, and nothing was said for days.

That is what friends, do they take you in. If you have no family, your friends are the ones that pick you up when you are down. They lie down beside you, and listen to your pain, and love you without judgment or suggestions. They let you make your own way. They know ... it takes time.

Gabriella was so happy at her new school and Nash, Jr. treated her like a kid sister. The mothers meshed. Their careers were flourishing and Martina was on the police force when the call came in about a wreck.

She was dispatched to the car wreck without knowing that her child was in the car with Nash, Jr and his grandparents. Nell had let them go to the nearby ice cream parlor.

Gabriella had been killed instantly.

Martina didn't think she would ever recover. She threw herself into her work telling herself that her child did not suffer, and that gave her comfort ... that God needed another angel.

She excelled and made Detective, working long hours

and never looking for another relationship. She told Nell that it, "Isn't WORTH ripping my heart out, again."

So today, she sat in Nell's kitchen and told her what Cynthia had said to her. "I need an outside unbiased opinion."

Nell sipped her coffee and stared out the window at Nash and Junior playing basketball one on one. Her son was sixteen now. She focused on Martina's question, but couldn't answer.

"How do you feel about what she said?" Nell was a psychiatrist now and never answered for the other person. It was always how do you feel? What do you think?

This time Martina was going to shake the daylight's out of her friend. "I am not your patient ... so stop that mumbo- jumbo with me. I value your advice. I am pregnant again, and am so happy with my husband that it terrifies me," she put her hands over her face.

Tears were falling and Nell handed her some Kleenex. "Go on talk it out." Her facial expression was stern so Martina would not think she was weakening on her task to help her.

She continued, "But his mother just told me that she tried to kill me at out engagement party. You were there, you know it was fabulous, and I had no idea this was happening."

Turning to look at Nell, "Then last night I thought about the plate the waiter had snatched from in front of me. Phillip gave me a cock and bull story that the food wasn't hot enough and that it must be served hot ... not cold."

She walked to the mantle and said looking at her and Gabriella's picture, "He knew Nell, but he didn't tell me. I remembered him staring at this mother, and I thought it odd. I was just so happy that I pushed it out of my memory until yesterday."

Nell finally said what Martina wanted to hear, "He loves you beyond anything else in this world. I have no doubt on that account or else, I would tell you. He did not want it to spoil your wedding party nor the surprise trip he had planned for you two. Do not blame him for what his mother did."

She rose and joined Martina at the mantle, "His mother may very well be trying to make amends. Because of the love I see Phillip has for you, she will lose him if she doesn't... Accept her apology, and go on with your life. You are tough and deserve happiness. My happiness will soon be bursting through that door any minute, so hug me!"

Martina hugged her friend and blew her nose. "You are right. I march to my own drummer's beat, but today I needed you, my friend to pound some sense into me. I'll call you later. I know Phillip's probably standing on his head."

"Call him and tell him you are on the way home. Bye love. Drive safely!" Nell smiled.

Off Martina went after waving to the basketball jocks.

Phillip was sweating bullets when she came in and grabbed her, "Please tell me that Nell made you see the light!"

She hung up her coat, and displayed her first new sexy

maternity outfit. She had stopped to change out of the dull outfit that she had left wearing this morning.

That was a mood, she promised herself that would never resurface. "Life is too short. Nothing nor nobody is going to mess with my happiness from this day forward," she told her windshield as she drove home.

"Nell and I did have a good talk. She is your best cheer- leader," and she smiled and put her arms around his neck.

"We have better things to do ... than talk!"

He looked at the outfit and said, "How do I get you out of this?" She demonstrated like a stripper, "You pull this string at the waist and these two at the top ... and voila!" the garment lay on the floor and she stood nude in front of him in only her heels.

"That's my kind of outfit!" he sighed.

"Curtis you will not believe this! Martina didn't come to work today. She said Phillip's mother tried to kill her," Nancy was cooking and stirring up the spaghetti sauce vigorously as he came through the door.

"Okay! I'll go back to work and have her arrested! That woman got on my nerves anyways, the last time I saw her. I can't wait to put her in my police car, but first...I need a kiss!"

Curtis knew Nancy would never be cooking a meal, if Martina was in real trouble. She would be at Martina's side or down at the police department dragging him out to help her. Never would she be at home ... cooking.

"Don't worry that will come another day! Martina forbade me to tell you, but I did it anyway. You Mr

Wonderful and I have no secrets." She kissed him and turned, "Do we?"

She laughed and started on the salad.

"No, wife of mine. Where are the boys?" he was eying the TV room and no one was in there. No noise from upstairs.

"They are at Bessie's for the night! You and I need some alone time. I am horny," and she slapped the salad bowl down to emphasis her point.

"Oh honey! I have a headache. Why didn't you tell me earlier? I could have taken some aspirins," he turned to go to the medicine cabinet.

She had her wooden spoon in her hand and followed him to the bathroom.

He was taking something from a package and she grabbed it. "Viagra are you trying to kill me or yourself?"

"I want it to last all night long!" Curtis said.

"You are so crazy in four hours, you would be in the emergency room saying HELP me! HELP me! Don't cut it off!" and she threatened to hit him with the spoon.

She told him, "Flush it Mister, if you want some! I don't want you dead!"

He flushed and ran out behind her, "I did and I do!"

"OK sit down at that table and I am going to give you some," giving him her Mae West stance.

"Some supper ... Some supper … I am hungry!" she spoke sweetly.

"And you had better be glad! If I wasn't hungry, I would have hit it with my spoon. I need it though to spoon feed my husband."

He was grinning, "You are right! I am hungry, too! Let's eat."

She turned off the stove and threw her apron on the counter.

"OK," and she walked to the bedroom.

PART THREE

CHAPTER ONE

The Law firm was abuzz with the merger details. Everyone was scurrying around trying to organize the new office spaces to accommodate the new members of their team.

Bart had brought a few of his employees, and Brigs had bought a few of his employees, and Phillip kept ALL of his. That was the deal with father and uncle that he would lose none of his staff, if they merged.

They had all agreed. The two older gentlemen wanted Phillip to think he was in charge, but knew they would be counseling him on almost everything.

They were all counselors and that is why they understood each other so well. Each could finish the others sentence where the law was concerned.

Martina's work was giving Phillip business, also. "Gotta help while I can," and would hold her back like she was in labor and giggle at Phillip's hurrying to reach her.

The cases of cheating husbands when evidence was found, Nancy would refer them to the best lawyers I know "Porter Brothers & Son."

"As long as we keep them working defending my

clients, the more pampers my baby will have. I cannot wash diapers this time. This boy is going to be rotten," Martina said.

Nancy asked, "What happened when the doctor told Phillip you were having a boy?"

Martina asked back, "Didn't you feel the earthquake yesterday?"

"Yes in California I am used to it," and she kept on typing.

"That was Phillip. He was jumping around like a kid in a candy store. At forty-six, he can jump pretty high. Yep he moved the earth yesterday .... when we got home," and she burst out laughing at Nancy's facial expression.

Peering over those eyeglasses of hers, "I guess you had better tell him to stop ... because if my dishes get broke again, I'm going to send him the bill!"

"He's good for one a week now so your dishes will be safe."

she frowned. "You know Nancy he is afraid that he will hurt the baby if we have vigorous sex, what must I do?" Martina asked.

"Don't ask me? Ask his mother! You two are so tight these days," Nancy said without looking up.

"Are you jealous? You are the one that said. Be nice Martina. She is Phillip's mother. She means well, and now this! I can't believe it," she pretended crying.

Nancy walked over to her desk, "It's okay I know how to share. Stop that crying before I hit a pregnant woman," and Martina burst out laughing.

"You know I love you best," and then Nancy was laughing.

"You are going to make me call Curtis on you. He said if you go into labor, he will bring the squad car, "she went back to her own desk.

"Relax! We got it all worked out with Sugar for him to take his mother by ambulance," she resumed typing.

"Two more months of this and the nursery is already finished. That is why Mama Porter keeps coming to the new house. She has got the nursery just beautiful. You know I have no decorating skills. Nancy are you asleep over there?" Martina was teasing.

"No, just snoring out loud. Ever since you moved in the neighborhood my boys don't want to stay home. They want to go over to Auntie Martina's house. She has better snack food mama," Nancy was pounding the typewriter keys. "Mama Porter has spoiled them rotten with those fancy cookies!"

"I will be damn you are really jealousy of that old woman. She has won the boys over. This is not about me. It's about Tyson and Michael?" Martina hugged Nancy.

"I'll be alright, but Curtis has been working a lot lately, and I miss my boys. They're growing up and don't need me like they use to. They're always with Curtis doing things." She stands up and says,"Yes I have the right to have a pity party, if I want to. Never had one … so today is the day!"

"Aww It is okay! We can stage an intervention. I'll call Curtis, Phillip and the boys. Want a pizza for supper?" Martina asked.

"I'll eat anything as long as I don't have to cook," Nancy had her eyebrows furrowed. "That salt will make your ankles swell and that ain't good for the baby," Nancy pointed out.

"You want to cook tonight or what?" Martina threatened.

"OK! Good point! I like to look at you with elephant hooves. Mums the word. I won't say one word! Besides its your feet not mine. See you at six thirty, Partner!"

Cynthia came home telling Bartholomew what a beautiful nursery she had created for the grandson. He interrupted her descriptions momentarily.

"Are you talking about Martina and Phillip's nursery? You did let Martina pick everything out? Right? Cynthia tell me you did," Bart said.

"OK I let her pick out a couple of things. She says she knows nothing about decorating. Believe me Bartholomew she knows nothing. I merely guided her through the process and she chose what I liked. It was a marvelous day. I love that girl!" Cynthia stated.

"Of course you do. She is saying all you want to hear. What if she disagrees?" Bart was testing.

She squinted her eyes and said, "You are trying to cause trouble now stop it because I am being very good. Decorating is one of the things, I excel at nicely. Don't take that away from me," she was pleading.

"Stop! It is not me that I am worried about. It is Phillip. He has his hands full at work. The news that the baby is a boy, I grant you has made him step up his game. He is working on two major cases at once. So don't put any more stress on him," Bart said and went to the den for a brandy.

"You need to take one of those cases and you know it. You and Brigs both should be ashamed letting him do all the work. Shame! Shame! Now tell me you will take one. He has a baby on the way. Please do it for me, then!" and she kissed him on the cheek and took her martini that he had fixed her.

"Of course, you are right dear! I will discuss it with him tomorrow."

Brigs was having the same talk from Katherine. Cynthia had phoned her asking for her help to get Brigs to take the other case. That way Phillip would be free to help Martina with the precious little boy that they were expecting.

"Yes dear, you and Cynthia are in cahoots! Phillip wants no help. I have already offered. He has had a practice for awhile mother, and I can't barge in and take over his cases. Really! It's absurd!" Brigs frowned.

Katherine snuggled up to him, "Remember when we had our first child? You couldn't think straight and asked Bart to take over your caseload for a few. He made it special for you and I, and little Emily," she was refreshing his memory and he was in another frame of mind.

"Katherine you know how to hit below the belt, PUN intended. I will handle it and not another word, except about Elizabeth. I heard that she and that stable boy were making out, and I will not have this type behavior. You see to your daughter. I hate to fire him, if it is HER doings!"

He was fuming. She could handle the girls better than he. He could handled Phillip, but not those girls of his.

"Now! Now! Brigs. Don't get your blood pressure up. I will check into it. I haven't been to the stables in awhile, and need to revisit where she was conceived." Katherine knew that would get a rise out of him batting her eyes, "Pun intended!"

She ran quickly because he was in hot pursuit. Any second she would let him catch her. She sat on the bed and smiled waiting for him in anticipation.

Elizabeth had no idea that Cameron was in the loft above her, as she saddled Moonbeam. She felt something tickling her neck. A bug she thought and swatted. Then again. It was hay falling into the front of her scoop necked blouse. It was loose fitting so she could do her chores.

"This straw! You asinine creep! You better get down from there," Elizabeth was spitting mad.

"I thought you would never ask. Don't move. I'll be there soon as I feed your horse." He threw handful of straw into the stable. Covering her but good, and he then jumped down while she was picking it off her. "SO SO Sorry! Let me help!" and he began reaching into her blouse and pulling out straw. Her mouth was open and she was in shock when he grabbed her to him and said, "I think some got back there. You may need to take them off. Could be a spider in the bale."

She freaked out and jumped around while he was feeling her good. "Stop that!"

"I gotta! It's the only way to kill a spider." He had her in his arms and she did not see the kiss coming, and her mouth was open as her head turned. He was kneading her buttocks and she caught herself leaning on him and kissing him back

He was doing crazy things to her body that no one had ever.

That's when he came to his senses. He never thought she would let him, and it scared him. He was pulling back and she was reaching into his jeans.

"You got to stop! I am not prepared to go any further," he said. He had no condoms and her family would kill him.

"Why would you start something and not finish it?" and she put her arms around his neck. He pushed her hard up against the stable wall and said. "Stop and I am sorry. I just meant to scare you, but you ain't scared of nothing. Your father and mother will hear about this ... do you realize I am dying to have you?"

"Doesn't look like it to me! I guess I will have to rape you," she laughed. That's when he said, "Don't ever worry about me touching you again because I won't. You are the type of girl that will get a boy killed. You ain't worth it."

Elizabeth said, "Oh I am worth it!" and began unbuckling her jeans. Took her boots off and stepped out of them. She took her blouse off and shook the straw from it.

Standing in her lacy underwear brushing the straw and then she popped the top of her bikini panties, then reached into get the straw out of the crevices.

He closed his eyes and held himself, "Please stop! I know I asked for this. Just stop!"

He was in pain and she knew it. "What's the problem we are both eighteen, both consenting. Come here let me teach you a thing or two." He couldn't move so she went to him.

Rubbing her naked breast across his arm, "I gotta get all the straw off. Aren't you going to help me."

"Put your clothes on. You don't know what you are doing!"

She jerked away, "You are damn right. I don't know what I am doing? I'm a virgin and everyone talks a big game. People talk about me at school like I am a freak because I haven't got laid," she had tears running down her face.

She was so humiliated. Cameron took her in his arms and said, "It's going to be alright. Put your clothes on." She did. He brushed the straw out of her hair and kissed her gently.

"One day when I can afford it. I am taking you on a date. Would you date me or better than that would your parents let me date you?"

"I make my own choices. Yes, I would go out with you. I didn't mean to go so far today. It is not your fault. I was just going to scare you, but you did not run. You did good. You actually made me want you real bad. That has never happened before, and I scared myself. Thank you for not taking advantage of my stupidity," Elizabeth said.

"Now that you have your clothes on, may I hold you and kiss you one last time. I am sure I am going to get fired, but I know that is a good idea. Otherwise …." she was against him and writhing. He was holding on to her

D. H. Crosby

and feeling the most wonderful desire. She was matching his thrust with their clothes on.

"That's all I can handle. I got to go!" and he walked up the hill to the bunkhouse and showered and met the ranch boss and quit.

Cameron said to himself, "The next time I see her, she will be mine!" and drove his Mustang convertible to a nearby ranch and applied for a job.

He got it because he was good with horses. The man had tried to get him to work for him for years. He settled in and stayed away from all females that came near the stables.

His dreams were only of Elizabeth.

Elizabeth could not stop thinking about Cameron. The following day, she found out that he had quit his job. She was brokenhearted. He had flirted with her everyday for two solid years.

He was not here today, and the stable was empty of forbidden love. She realized today that it was not only a sexual longing, but that she was in love with him. He was the gentlest most patient person with the horses, and with her.

She had watched him break down the wildest stallions and she felt that he was the tamer of her soul. Where was he? She would ask around.

The tack man said he had taken a job over at the ranch down the road. She would give him his space for a month and then she was going to ride over and talk to him. He may have broken in a new filly by then, but she would fight for him.

She continued her chores combing Moonbeam and cleaning his stall. It was not the same, and she patted her horse's neck and closed her eyes. Just so she could conjure up his image.

The horse neighed as if to say, I miss him, too.

Her mother for some reason came to Moonbeam's stall which was very unusual, and they sat on a bale of hay. "What can be the matter with my girl? You look so sad."

"You know me well. What brings you here?" she was curious. Her mother never came out to the dirty old stables. If she wanted to ride it was with Father, and he brought the horse to the house for mother to mount.

"Well father got the word that a boy down here was making advances toward you. Is this true?'

"No mother that is not true. Contrary to the report, I was hitting on him, and he quit and is working on another ranch. He is too good for me. I am in love for the first time with a man that has high morals. What am I to do Mama?"

Her mother held her. "I fell in love with your father in these very stables when we were young. He pursued me and I let him catch me, and the rest is history."

Elizabeth stared at her mother, "Really? Truly? Father and you. Then you understand." She was smiling.

"The difference was it was his family's land and this young man knows your father would kill him, if he put his hands on you. He was wise to leave."

"What must I do to let him know I love him? Will father let him come and court me? He did ask and I had no answer for him yesterday. Help me mother. I need your help," she was crying and hugged Katherine's waist as she did when she was a wee tot.

"I must think what your father will say and get back with you, but you must promise not to do any thing rash. We together will find a respectful solution. That's what mothers do, help their children. I love you Elizabeth." They walked to the house.

Brigs was standing at the window and spied them walking from the stables. He took a large swig of his brandy, then he turned it up. "No time for sipping. I know those two are up to something. They will be cornering me soon. I must fortify myself so I will not be angry in the least. "Self you might as well have another." He poured and belted it back.

CHAPTER TWO

The new ranch crew was not going to make it easy on Cameron. They knew of him and didn't want him to take any position that a family member of theirs could do.

He gritted his teeth and showed that he was sincere in wanting the position. The horse that he was hired to tame and train was a wild black stallion with a prize winning heritage.

Brian the boss man had taken a chance on Cameron. He had heard Brigs bragging on this boy several times in yearly races between their horses.

His men had better buck up and help the boy, or he was going to lower the boom on them all. So he had a meeting at the bunkhouse and they all were listening. No one was saying a word.

Brian stated, "I have my back against the wall with management, and if you guys can't get this grudge match squared away. I have to let the troublemakers go, and hire some new team players. I hate it, but that is the facts?"

There was a rumbling and for once it stuck. He saw several men go over to Cameron and shake his hand, and welcomed him on board. Brian knew it was the brown nosers. He would have his snitches in place for the long haul.

The owner Colten Travis Bingham III wanted this horse to win the big prize. "Brian whatever it takes, DO it! The sky is the limit, and you will be well rewarded. When that wreath of roses is around FANATIC STRETCH's neck, you will be rich." They shook hands and the deal was set in motion.

Brian talked at length with Cameron and laid out the strategies to achieve this goal. He told Brian, "I am honored that you trust me, and I will not let you down. You know I cannot stay at the bunkhouse. They have made it clear that I am not welcome."

"You will stay at my house, and be welcome. That will let them know. If they mess with you, they are messing with me. You okay with that?" Brian shook Cameron's hand.

"Thank you, sir. It's a deal!" and Cameron went to work with FS. That is what he was going to call the horse, FS. This horse's success meant a name for himself. The prestige that may get him an invite to the table of Miss Elizabeth Porter. Her daddy's fine dinner table.

Either he made it, or he'd die trying. She was in his head. After a month working day and night on his new goal, he rounded the corner. There she sat on Moonbeam.

He shook his head to make sure the bright sunshine was not playing tricks on his eyes. The mirage started moving toward him and he held onto the rope in his hand a little tighter.

She had her usual faded jeans and loose top on. The

same outfit she had on the last time, he'd seen her. He closed his eyes and saw her standing in her lacy underwear that image reappeared every night in his dreams.

"Cameron! We need to talk," she was slowly riding toward him. He had not moved and Moonbeam's nose nudged him to be patted, and he did.

"I got to work little lady," Cameron had to get her to see this job was important to him, and yet he didn't want her to leave. "Can you wait a few and let me talk to Brian about a break?" He licked his lips and he knew she would leave, if he didn't hurry. Taking a deep breath to settle his libido, waiting for her answer.

"No problem! I have waited a month for you to settle in, and call me. Another thirty minutes, won't hurt. Where can I wait? These guys are whistling and getting on my last nerve?"

He gritted his teeth and clinched his jaw at the thought of any of these cowhands making her uncomfortable. He couldn't blame them. She was beautiful. They just didn't know how beautiful she was under those baggy clothes.

He did and it was doing a number on his body.

"Get down and walk with me to the office." He tied Moon-beam to the hitching post out front. She got off slowly and he caught her waist, and immediately let go.

He turned toward the door, walked in and saw Brian sitting at his desk. Elizabeth had come into Brian's view.

"Hey Miss Porter, can I help you?" Brian was grinning because his daughter was friends with his neighbor's child.

Brigs' youngest daughter was a looker.

"You sure can! I need a favor. Can you let his man off

for a few hours to take me to lunch. He and I have a few things to discuss about my horse. He trained Moonbeam. Did you know that? I bet not. Anyways, I need his expert advice."

She did not look at Cameron or it would have blown her mission, and set her hormones to raging.

"Sure, Cameron why don't you take the rest of the day off. You deserve it. You have been working nonstop since you came on board. GO! Get!" and he shooed them out of his office.

She got on Moonbeam and said, "Do you think half a day will do it or do you need all night?"

Cameron did not answer and saddled his horse with haste not once did he look at her or answer her provocative question.

Swinging onto his horse, he rode to the pasture and she followed. They galloped like the wind to the stream that bordered the properties. Then he went upstream to the mountain pass, she was swallowing and began to pant to get her breath. She had been to the secluded area only once, and she was terrified that she had pushed him too far.

She saw him flexing his muscles as his shirt strained across his chest, and his cowboy hat hid his eyes. She was afraid to look lower as for herself, her lower self was on fire.

"OMG. I asked for this!" she reprimanded herself.

He had tied the horses to a tree behind the rocks.

"Get off, "he said firmly.

"No. You got to take me off," she smiled.

He grabbed her buttocks, and jerked her up in the air, and held her there. It seemed like forever to her, and she began kicking her feet. That is when he slowly lower her to him, and kissed her trembling lips.

Gently at first and she wanted more. He wanted more.

"You got to marry me or what I am about to do, is not going to mean a thing. I don't want you just one time. Do you have any idea how I feel about you?"

She did not answer. Only rubbed her soft hands inside his cowboy shirt, and felt his curly hair under his hat. She was taking inventory, and listing it on her checklist for future memories. She wanted to memorize everything about him that she did not know before this day.

"I love you, Elizabeth. You've known it for sometime. Haven't you?" he was unable to stop his hands from going under her blouse and feeling her breast. She had no bra on, and her nipples were hardening, burning his hands.

"OH God! You are killing me. Say something!" He held her away from him and looked at her.

"Yes! I will marry you, but I need you now!" and she kissed his neck, and his chest muscles. He was undressing her. Her jeans were halfway down when he realized, she had no panties on, and he stopped.

"You knew this was going to happen didn't you?"

"Yes and I wanted you fast and furious," she made it clear. He was what she wanted.

"Say it," he was out of his clothes and into the hottest moistest place of paradise. He waited.

"I love you too!" he walked two steps and pressed her back against a flat rock and eased further slowly. He had sense enough to know it was going to hurt her. She wrapped her legs around his waist and said, "Do it!" He lunged once and she screamed. He just held her. Her sweetness squeezed him, and she let her hands roam. He could not hurt her again.

She was feeling all of his body parts, and she began to move. He moved too, and told his mind not to work because everything else was working automatically.

He said to himself, "Don't rationalize. Don't think! This is just the beginning. You are a fool, if you think her parents will let you marry her. This maybe the one and only time you can have her."

He went ever so slowly, and she was loving it. She had waited, and this is what people talked about. It was amazing! His hands were rubbing her buttocks, and he was kissing her breasts. It was making her nerves spasm and spasm big time.

"OH Cameron! OH! You are feeling it, aren't you? I want to make it good for you. You! You! Need to help me now. From this first time, I want to learn how to please you. OMG you are pleasing me so so so goooood!"

She was not the sweet little girl he remember, she was taking over his soul, and rocking him as natural as the motion was … it had peaked twice. It just was unbelievable for him. He could not stop. She could not stop until the earthquake shook them, both. They were meld together for all eternity.

"Get dressed! We have to go today to the courthouse. It is the only day! I may have gotten you pregnant. Let's go! If you love me, we can't waste time!"

She washed in the creek. Moonbeam had her saddlebag of toiletries. She was resourceful and had packed enough for two nights. Encase, she was what he wanted.

They got everything they needed, and the license secured in time for the Justice of Peace to marry them. They were both of age, and it had gone off without a hitch.

"Mrs Elizabeth Bennett. I, Cameron Bennett don't have a house or an apartment to take you to. I don't want you to leave my side for another day, what do you suggest?"

"I have told my mother. How much I love you and she knew I was coming to you. She will help us fend off my daddy. She will help her daughter, and we will have an apartment before this day is done. Can you live with that for now or do you have a better idea?"

"I can get an advance from Brian, and see if he has any housing separate from the farm. No cowhands will ever have access to my wife. You know I will be working from sunup until sundown. I'd like to provide for you from day one. If it doesn't pan out, we can go to your plan B. Okay! What does my wife say?"

She kissed him and had people staring, and she didn't care. "So I guess that is my answer?" she said. He grinned and pressed her closer.

"Yep, and we are going to get arrested. If ... we don't get!" licking his ear which got him moving real fast to his old Mustang convertible.

"We could just live in the car," and he grinned at her.

"Okay by me!" and she cuddled up to him and they went back to the ranch adjoining her home.

"While you are talking to Mr. Brian, I am going to call mother before she sends out the police to look for me."

He nodded and went into the office.

"Mama I am married. Yes, I love him with all my heart."

CHAPTER THREE

Martina was sitting in the rocker in the nursery of her new home. She had been taking inventory of all the items her mother -in-law had supplied. She had not realized what thoughtfulness went into this room.

She had a long day at the office so she was going to just sit here until Phillip came home. She wanted him to sit in the other rocker and do an assessment of his mother's handiwork, also.

They together needed to thank her and make her feel appreciated. Martina fell asleep. Phillip had been all over the house, and finally he found her asleep in the rocker.

He kissed her cheek and she reached for him. He stood in front of her. She rose and said, "Where are we, Prince Charming?"

"Honey you have to wake up before I get lost in your fantasy world," he said. He gently shook her and her eyes opened.

"HI there! Wanted you to sit and rock with me," she said.

"Rock you, of course I will after we eat," and he was grinning. She was not fully awake.

"Promises... Promises," she winked. "Sit in that chair," pointing to the other rocker.

"OK but I am starving!" he sat down.

"Have you really seen what your mother has done?" she asked.

"No, really I haven't. Looks like she outdid herself. Do you like it? Anything you want to change?" Phillip asked.

"No Honey. Nothing do I want to change. I just want to do something nice for your mother to let her know she is appreciated, and that we love her for doing this. What do you suggest?" Martina asked.

"Let me talk to father and ask him. He needs to know how you feel. He will be as happy as I am that you feel this way. This boy of ours has already brought this family together and he hasn't even been born." He bent down beside her rocker.

"Martina, you are what this family has needed. Now five years ago, I would not have known what a powerful woman I was fighting for. I did know I was in love with you, but I had no idea how the depth of my love for you would grow," Phillip kissed her hands. Then he kissed her abdomen.

"You present a good case. You sir are a good lawyer. If I ever need one, I think I would hire you. Since I don't need one right at this moment, will you take me to dinner? I pass on cooking."

She stood and kissed him thoroughly.

"You are asking for it!" he said.

"You betcha, but let's eat first. The baby needs to be fed and then we can rock him to sleep," she purred.

The next morning he walked into Bart's office that was adjacent to his. "Father I have some news," Phillip stated.

"Is it good news or bad news?" Bart asked.

"It's good news," he said and took another look at his father who was frowning.

"What is wrong father? You look upset," Phillip indeed had seen the look on his father's face and was concerned.

"It's your uncle that you should be worried about. You may have to defend him in a court of law before this day is over!" Bart said as a matter-of-fact.

Phillip stepped back a step, and his mouth dropped open in horror because his father NEVER joked about Brigs.

He sat in the chair opposite his father, "What has he done?"

"OH he hasn't done anything yet! That's the problem. I maybe wrong but I think he is contemplating murder!" Bart said.

"And you are just sitting here and going to let him do it?"

He turned his head and saw his uncle sitting at his own desk. He looked at his father again.

"OK Tell me what this is all about. Leave nothing out. I need to know everything," Phillip made that very clear.

"Well it seems Elizabeth didn't come home last night. She is OK... so sit back down. She ran off and got married to a boy that use to work in your uncle's stables. Katherine told Brigs that she loves him and is happy. Seems Beth told her mother, but not her father," Bart said.

"So you are saying you don't know which one Uncle Brigs wants to kill first. Am I right?" Phillip relaxed.

"Yes exactly," and Bart continued to frown.

"Aunt Katherine? Beth? Or who is the boy?" Phillip was in the investigative mode.

"Cameron Bennett the stable boy for the last two years. Brigs thought highly of him. Good horse trainer!" Bart added.

"Is he on uncle's property at the moment?" tensely Phillip asked.

"No! Seems he quit a month ago, and went and is working on the ranch next to Brigs's. He couldn't understand at the time why the boy left," Bart said.

"Katherine told Brigs last night not to kill him that Elizabeth went to find the boy. That she is in love with him and one thing led to another, and he did the honorable thing," Bart informed him.

"So why kill him? He sounds like a responsible young man," Phillip said and he turn to see his uncle standing in the doorway.

"Boy, you have lost your mind! He is a thief! A lowdown thief!" Brigs shouted.

Phillip looked at his father, "You are so right father! I may need to brush up on my law books about criminal defense in a murder trial."

"Don't be ridiculous! I am not going to kill him. It's your aunt and that daughter of mine that may meet their demise. With those two, it is a wonder the boy is alive. They can kill a man. I know first hand," Brigs was getting his anger out and the other two said nothing. Just nodded their heads and listened.

"Katherine, my dear wife says Elizabeth had not seen him in a month, and she went to talk to him. Talk my foot! He is such a good boy instead of getting in trouble, he left. I commend him for that. It is the deception of my family that is killing me. Why Elizabeth didn't come to her father that has me baffled?" He was now pacing the office and Bart and Phillip were still in the silent mode.

"She knew better, that is why! She has not come home, and I don't know where she is. I am going to see Brian today. Bart are you coming with me?" Brigs asked.

"No! I am needed here. Someone has to man the office. You and Phillip go," looking at Phillip with pleading eyes.

"OK Father I will go with Uncle Brigs, but only if he tells me there will be no violence," asking his uncle for reassurance.

"Of course, I am not a violent person. At least, I hope not! OK you have my word," and he went mumbling back to his office, and closed the door.

He called Katherine, "Have you heard from her this morning?" he asked his wife.

"Yes dear. She stayed at Brian's in Cameron's room last night. They are married. Remember that dear," Katherine reminded him.

"How could I forget!" and hung up on her.

He called Brian and made an appointment for two o'clock.

He went and told Phillip they would leave the office at one.

"You owe me Father," Phillip said as he left.

"Big time, son." Bart hung his head and started pouring over a case that Phillip was to try this afternoon.

Cameron and Elizabeth had had the most blissful night, and they could not get enough of each other. Brian had told them since they were married, and he had viewed the marriage license for himself that they could stay there. Cameron had signed a contract and Brian's boss would be livid, if he up and ran off without training FANATIC STRETCH.

This horse is more important than his friendship with Bridgeston Porter. He must warn the young couple about the impending appointment with her father. He rang their room.

He had given the boy the day off, and they had not surfaced this morning. Cameron answered and thanked him for the call. If he needed them to speak to Mr. Porter, "Please call back and we will come over. Thank you again sir, for everything!" Cameron hung up.

He looked at his wife who lay naked and had extended her arms, "Come back to bed. You have made me want you some more. More please!"

He laid back down and indulged before he told her that they needed to shower.

"Your father will be here at two to talk to Brian. We need to be dressed. Oh God I don't want either of us to wear clothes in this room ever again, but for today. It is necessary! You have no ring and I cannot wear one."

"What do you mean you cannot wear one?" She stood

over him with her hands on her hips, only in her bra and panties.

"I saw a man get his finger ripped off when it got caught in some machinery that we were running," he looked at his hand.

"I have a solution for that, I will get a wedding ring tattoo this week whenever you want to go with me, and I will buy you a ring the same day. Do you agree that I need my fingers?" and was working his magic with them.

She kissed his left ring finger and licked his knuckles, "Oh yes you need all ten of them. If you get a tattoo ring then I will also. Our rings must match," and she smiled adoringly.

"You have no idea what you are saying. It will hurt like the dickens! I will buy you a ring that will not hurt my beautiful bride's finger. I'll just slip it on, we must tell your father that we are in the process of doing this last wedding rite, okay?" he asked.

"Okay you can tell him anything you want, but I am getting a tattoo ring just like my HUSBAND!" she had made that very clear.

At two o'clock sharp, Brigs and Phillip knocked on Brian's door. "Come on in and have a seat," shaking both men's hands.

Brian was stone-faced and ready. He had been practicing all morning. This was a tense situation for all.

"Where is my daughter?' Brigs inquired sternly.

"With her husband," Brian stated.

"Why did you not call me Brian? We have always

been upfront with one another, and I have considered you a friend all these years," Brigs said.

"We are friends. I was presented a marriage license and I thought you knew. I welcomed your daughter and her husband into my home where he has lived for a month. That is the facts as I know them." He looked Brigs in the eyes not wavering.

Brigs thanked him for being honest with him. "I want to speak to both of them."

"Certainly, I will call them and arrange that right now," Brian got on the phone and did just that.

"They will be here in a few minutes and you can have my office. Phillip would you like to walk down to the stables, and see the next Derby winner. He is something to see."

They walked out of the door to see FANATIC STRETCH.

Phillip wanted to give Elizabeth and her father privacy. The boy could fend for himself. I'll pray for him he said to himself.

Elizabeth in her same faded jeans and top came strolling in with Cameron dressed in his work jeans and plain cowboy shirt.

She ran over and kissed her father, and he hugged her.

"I am sorry. I did not talk to you. We were so much in love, and were proud of ourselves for handling our wedding ourselves just the way we wanted. I love him. Daddy, I saved you a ton of money." She kept rattling on and tears were forming..

Cameron stood there listening and avoiding eye contact with Mr Porter.

"What do you have to say for yourself, son?" Brigs asked looking at the boy without blinking.

"I love your daughter and will make her a good husband. I would have asked you, but I had a fear that you would not say yes. We both agreed it was best to elope, sir." Cameron stood erect and put his arm around Elizabeth's shoulder as she hugged him.

"I am so happy, Daddy!"

"What more can a father want than have his daughter happy. If you make her happy, then you have my blessing! One thing I must insist on is building you a house. You cannot live here! Is that clear?" Brigs twisted his handlebar mustache.

"Yes, Daddy that is clear. I love you, too so much." Elizabeth could not stop smiling looking from one to the other.

"You two go see your mother, and make your plan and dear girl, if you are going to keep this husband of yours. Put on a dress and be the lady of his house," Brigs shook Cameron's hand. **FINALLY ... YES!**

The day was a day of celebration at the Bridgeston Porter's household, but the couple returned to the little room at Brian's. They had decided to stay there until their house was built. Cameron needed to be there for his work and he did not want to be under the same roof as Mr Porter.

"Honey we don't want either your mother or father

hearing us making love," he said and waited for her response.

"You are so wise my husband because I would not be able to keep you from hollering when I do this or when I do that."

He was moaning and teasing her as he picked her up, and kissed, and sucked, and had her squealing.

"I think it is the other way around, but it is the way I like it. You scream my name any time you want to honey!" and he wrestled her to the bed.

"I love you Cameron!"

"I love you Elizabeth!"

CHAPTER FOUR

The next month Martina was waddling, and the high heels were gone. She was still in exercise Pilate classes, but she had made it clear that she was going for Phillip not for herself.

Nancy asked, "You and Sugar still getting it on HUH?" typing faster and waiting for her answer because she knew Martina was fixing to burst.

"Why do you think I am waddling?" and she exaggerated her walk and Nancy's reaction was priceless. The shocked look was still on Nancy's face when in walks Phillip.

Martina's exercise tights had no pockets so she had put her phone in her tights. The cell phone had worked its way down to her crotch, and when in walks Phillip. The phone rang.

He said looking at her crotch, "Is that calling me?"

That's when Nancy jumped up, "That's it! I got to call Curtis to meet me for lunch. I'm getting pregnant because you two are having ...way too much fun!" Throwing her pocketbook over her shoulder and marching to the door,

"Take that call Sugar while I'm gone!" she went out the door mumbling and dialing her cell phone.

Phillip yelled, "Always I will answer my wife's booty call. You have a nice lunch. I know I will!" he was grinning.

"HUH I bet you will. You sex addict!" and Nancy was gone laughing all the way to her car.

"Curtis I'm ready! I'll met you at the house!" Nancy was smiling when she saw the blue light pull up the driveway.

"I got a speed dial on my cell phone, too!" Nancy was out of the shower.

"What took you so long?" she asked.

"Stoplights!" Curtis said.

"Okay, good answer. Come here I got to go back to work, you know!"

"I know and I got to finish an arrest. I told them I had to answer an emergency call first. Come here Emergency," he said.

"I like the sound of that. Curtis this baby we are going to have Middle Name is going to be EMERGENCY!"

"Sounds good good to me me!"

"Wait a minute what did you say?"

"Shut up and give me my baby!"

"Yes ma'am!"

One hour and ten minutes later, Nancy waddled into the office.

"You are late! I' ll dock your pay, if you don't fess up."

"I'm pregnant. Didn't you see me walk in here. You are going to be a Godmother! Now shut up and pass me some ice cream and pickles."

Martina was laughing so hard, "Have you had a pregnancy test, yet?"

Nancy snapped her fingers, "Darn I knew I forgot some-thing. Let me call Curtis!"

"Honey will you do me a big big favor," popping her lips.

"Anything. What?" Curtis was in a professional interview.

"Can you stop by the drugstore? Get a PG kit!" he fainted.

Looking at Martina, "That's a big big man. It's going to take three officers to pick my husband up off that floor," and she resumed her typing.

Martina asked, "Aren't you worried about him?"

"Nah What he had for lunch probably made him relax. He is faking it to get to nap on the medical bed by his office. If he plays it right... he'll wake up by the time he gets off duty," and she filed the report and dipped on her way back to her chair.

"I know my husband like you know your Sugar. Praise the Lord for horny men!" and marched to the restroom.

"Pregnant women have to pee every five minutes!" Nancy put on some lipstick and walked back out.

"Tell me about it!" Martina stated.

"Me ... tell you. I only been pregnant for two hours, and I am suppose to tell you. You honey been pregnant nine months and you just figured that one out. Oh My Oh My Sh.....t!

You may go into labor any minute. What am I to

do?" Nancy was running from one side of the room to the other .. frantic.

"What must I do?" Nancy asked.

Martina passed her a book, "Here read up on it. If you can't figure it out. Call SUGAR!"

"Hell no! He will be worst than me!" Nancy had plopped down into her desk chair exhausted.

"Then call Curtis. He can turn that blue lights on and have us there in a few minutes. So relax!" Martina said.

"Okay," she got up and walked into Martina's office and laid down on the sofa and went to sleep. When she woke, Martina said, "I see Curtis did a bang up job!" Nancy smiled.

About that time a mask man walked into the office and was holding a gun. He grabbed Nancy, and Martina sat frozen.

The man asked, "Where is Martina Porter?" and pointed the gun at Nancy's head.

Martina stood up and all nine months of pregnancy was shining when her water broke.

Nancy hit the man in his balls, and he dropped the gun. Nancy picked it up and waved it at him, "Ain't you done enough damage. Get the HELL out of here!" the man ran so fast that he was jumping over cars.

Martina said, "I know you are in shock. Nancy so put the gun on the desk ... very slowly!"

Nancy said, "I can't. I got to protect us. From whomever." She started giggling hysterically.

Martina called Phillip and asked him to call Curtis

and have him come and get this gun away from Nancy, and by the way "my water broke".

"Why has Nancy got a gun?" Phillip thought it was a joke.

"We had a robbery. The mask man saw my water break and he ran. Nancy picked the gun up and she won't put it down. Now you both be careful!" and a contraction hit her and she screamed at the top of her voice. "Time it Phillip. I'll tell you when it stops," Phillip fell out of his office chair holding the phone. His father came in, picked up the phone said "Hello?"

"Hi there! Can you help my husband to the hospital. I have gone into labor. I got to call Curtis. Bye!"

"Curtis your wife has a gun and is sitting at her desk. Be careful when you come in. I am in labor HELPPPP!!!"

Rubbing his head he said to himself, "This has been one heck of a day!" he got in the squad car and went to her office.

He entered as usual, "Hi Honey!" There his wife sat frozen with a gun in her hand.

"Where'd she get a gun?" Curtis asked Martina.

"We had a masked man try to rob us...my water broke... she hit him in the nuts ... and the rest is history."

"Where is Phillip?" Curtis asked walking over to Nancy.

"Buttercup fell in the floor. His father is bringing him to the hospital. Can you take me now to the hospital!" she was having a contraction and started screaming.

Nancy's eyes were getting bigger and Curtis had his hand on the gun. "Let me shoot her! Let me shoot her, then she'll stop that screaming. She is getting on my nerves."

"Now Honey! She's your best friend," Curtis had the gun and hugged her.

"I know but I was so scared that man ...all that water ... the screaming...I am a wreck! I don't know how you do it Curtis dealing with all this every day! Can you deliver a baby, too!"

He had them in the squad car blue lights going and slammed on break at the ER. He told a fellow officer, "Get a wheelchair. This woman is having a baby!"

Martina waved at Bart and Phillip, "Glad you came. I was worried." Phillip kissed his wife and she screamed. The contractions were getting closer.

Curtis gave the gun to the officer, "There was a robbery. She went into labor. The man got away. Keep it for evidence.

I'll make a report tomorrow. Put WIFE's office on the label!"

The officer said, "Who is the woman sitting in the car?"

"She's my prisoner. I mean, she is my wife. Oh Crap. Honey I am so sorry!"

"It's okay this was a trial run for when you become a father nine months from today!" She was back to normal almost.

Curtis said, "What is our baby's middle name?"

"Emergency," and she grinned looking at the sign over the door.

"You can count on that!" Curtis said.

Phillip was asking about the gun and the robber, "Was that real?" Martina grabbed his necktie, "You are going to ask me about everything else, but our baby that I have carried for nine months?"

She was having a contraction and pulled on that tie until Phillip was blue in the face.

Bart intervened, "Hi honey! Can I have my tie that Phillip is wearing."

"Sure" and she handed it to Bart who loosened it.

"Thanks Dad. I owe you one," Phillip said.

"No, you went with Brigs. We are even," and he smiled at his son. Then he dialed Cynthia.

"Take a taxi honey! I cannot stand any more excitement for one day. DO NOT DRIVE. Cynthia sit down, I will call the taxi myself. Now put on some makeup. Fix your hair and the taxi will be there to get you soon. Love you, too!"

"Phillip does this hospital have a bar. I need a drink!"

"No but I could use one, too! Call Brigs and tell him to bring a flask!Keg!Barrel! Got to go. She is calling me again!"

"Where have you been? Oh father of my child," Martina had no clothes on ... just a sheet. The nurse said, "She stripped everything off."

"That's my wife! She is having my baby!" pointing to himself. He kiss Martina and she grabbed him and screamed, "You did this to me! Count honey Count!"

FINALLY ... YES! The baby was there.

The baby had arrived.

The nurse told the other nurse watch him. He is going to crash any minute.

They didn't even have time to get her into the delivery room.

The doctor asked Phillip, if he wanted to cut the cord.

He hit the floor.

The nurse looked at the other, "I told you to watch him!"

"Well I was kinda busy helping deliver the baby Mrs Gotrocks!"

"I like that word. I think I'll call you that the next time you screw up!" and they smiled at one another as they were weighing, foot-printing the baby, and assisting the doctor with the sutures.

"Someone needs to throw some water on this man or get the ammonia. Geez! Do I have to do everything around here!"

Martina shouted, "Honey! I'm ready!"

Phillip jumped up and said, "I am always! Where are you?"

"Nothing brings a man back to consciousness than the mere mention of having sex. Remember that nurses!" Martina purred. "Over here with our baby BOY! Isn't he the cutest?"

CHAPTER FIVE

The grandmother arrived by taxi and her husband was there to meet her. Cynthia was frantic, "Is he here? Is he here?"

Bart said, "Yes dear. He is here and they are still in the emergency room."

Cynthia grab her husband's arm, "Emergency room?"

"Yes dear. He was in a hurry like you dear. They couldn't get her to the delivery room in time. They are fine! Now have a seat. Phillip will be out in just a few minutes."

"Look at your suit, son. It is a mess!" As Phillip walked near them, Cynthia began to straighten her son's business suit.

She was all about appearances.

Bart said, "Leave him alone mother. He has been threw enough for one day!" He guided her to the elevator and asked Phillip what his wife's room number was?

They went up to the maternity ward and walked down to view the babies. There he was ... Adam Bartholomew Porter.

"Dad we wanted him to be named after a great man.

YOU. We both came up with Adam in Germany, and if we should have a girl next time her name will be Eve. What do you both think?" Phillip was grinning and had red marks around his neck from the necktie than Martina had pulled on.

"Son, who tried to choke you?" Cynthia was concerned. Not waiting for an answer, "He is a gorgeous baby just like you were," she beamed looking through the viewing window.

His father was having a tearful moment that only his son saw, and Phillip hugged him.

"I am honored and my namesake will want for nothing," and Bart went to stand by Cynthia.

"I'm going on into see Martina," Phillip was anxious to see how she was doing.

"Buttercup, isn't he beautiful?" Martina smiled from the plush executive maternity room. It had a table set for two and a champagne bottle on ice.

"Mother and father are looking at him now. He is the most precious gift you have ever given me. Thank you for naming him after father. He was in tears. You made an old man happy but not as happy as his son." Phillip kissed her and laid his head on her abdomen.

"Tell me you are not in pain?" he wanted to do all the right things, but was at a loss.

"I am fine. They gave me something for pain downstairs and I am going to be asleep in a few. You go and get some rest."

"I am going to be in this recliner all night beside you. But first, a glass of bubbly for me. We can take the rest home. I really need it right now." He poured a glass and looked back and she was curled up fast asleep.

His father and mother tiptoed in, and had a glass with him to celebrate the new birth. Bart said, "We will take a taxi back home honey because I need a second glass. You have no idea what I have been through today."

Phillip nodded at his mother, "We will fill you in later!"

Phillip slept all night in the recliner. The nurses came in and out taking vital signs, and tending to Martina.

She said, "Isn't he handsome? Can one of you throw a blanket over him, please. Thank you. I just don't feel like getting up to do it."

"Get some rest, Mrs Porter. He will be okay. The baby will be in around six in the morning, and wake him up. Are you breastfeeding?" She shook her head no. She had tried with Gabriella and it was a disaster. She had decided not to even try this time.

"We want to bottle feed him, but I want to pump my breast milk. I hope I put the thing in my travel bag."

"While you are here, we will provide it and the bottles. So don't worry about that right now. Just get some rest," and Martina did finally.

Nancy and Curtis came the next morning and brought her flowers. "Sugar you look like death warmed over," and he stretched in the recliner. Then jumped straight up to check on Martina. "I'm fine Buttercup!" she said.

Curtis grinned and patted Phillip on the back, "We saw Adam. He is a fine looking boy and healthy eight pounds fourteen ounces. I'd say he is football material!"

He laughed at the evil eyes Martina and Nancy was giving him. Nancy said, "Mr Wonderful you have lost your mind. That boy is going to be Mr Universe."

They all laughed and Martina grabbed a pillow and held on tight. "Don't make me laugh. It hurts to laugh."

Phillip went up and kissed his wife and said, "Stop it now!"

Nancy said, "You had better stop what you are doing! That's how she got in the condition, she is in."

Martina had to ask, "Speaking of condition I am in ...did you take that PG test?"

"Nope, it didn't take! Got to try again," Nancy frowned and looked at Curtis.

Curtis said, "I can hardly wait. It will be about six weeks Phillip before you can try again."

Phillip eyes dilated and he looked at Martina to clarify that.

"Yes, Honey! Curtis is right. You are on lock down until the doctor says it is okay to have sex again." She blew him an air kiss and he caught it and put it in his pocket.

"You never told me about this Martina. We are going to have to talk about this when we get home," Phillip stated.

He began pacing and Nancy said, "Curtis take him to see the baby, and explain the facts of life to Sugar. Now git! Me and Martina got girl talk to do."

The men walked out quickly. Nancy was one that could clear a room fast.

"I saw you was hurting. Push that red button and order

you some DRUGS because when you leave this hospital, I can't get you none," Nancy said and she frowned.

"You are so right! I got a million stitches down under. Phillip doesn't know anything about a baby and taking care of a baby. You are going to have to help me," Martina said.

"I got to run the business for you. His mother and I don't need to have a FIST fight, if I get in her way. She will be there every day telling her son what to do," Nancy nodded her head up and down.

"That's true! She doesn't need to get knocked out by you. She will be helpful. He is a large baby and I don't want to pop any stitches, then Phillip would go ballistic!" Martina stated.

"Yep! Yep! Sugar would have to be put in a straight jacket, if he can't get some in six weeks. But don't worry Curtis can borrow a jacket from his work ... if he has to!" and Nancy winked at Martina.

"Bessie said if you need her for house cleaning or cooking, she is available," Nancy added her sister needs to work.

Her partner and friend had helped problem-solve in thirty minutes, everything that Martina had been worrying about all morning. Now she could relax. The medication was working and she fell asleep.

Nancy walked down to see the baby and tell Sugar that he needed to go get a shower, and a clean suit while his wife was sleeping, "You look a sight!"

Curtis said, "My wife likes to organize everything, and she is right. You looked in the mirror, Bro?"

"Nope, but I don't have to for six weeks!" laughing he waved and got on the elevator. It had a full length mirror and he saw himself. "Wow!" he began walking fast to his car and drove to the house and followed Nancy's instructions.

While shaving he said to the mirror, "Now they can take pictures of me and my son, and my wife, and my mother, and my father!"

He stopped by the gift shop in the hospital and got an album with a baby on the front. Then had them gift wrap it. He purchased also a bouquet of flowers with a balloon that said IT'S A BOY!

Martina began smiling when she saw it. She had showered and had on a black negligee and black nursing bra. The black robe was in the closet.

He was fit to be tied because she had her Ciara perfume on too! She said, "Your mother helped me pick it out and now that I have an ALBUM. I need pictures."

"My mother just wants more grandchildren, that's not fair! Look at you. You can tell her she is torturing her son," and he nuzzled her neck.

"Oh my goodness you smell so good, Buttercup! You shaved and our son will be in a few. We can get our first family pictures with your cell phone. Adam is a lucky little boy to have you for his father!" Martina said staring into his eyes.

"And to have you as his mother. The sexiest mama on this planet!" and Phillip kissed her.

In walks his parents and he straightens his suit coat.

Cynthia said, "Who brought the album? I didn't

think of that!" she was admonishing herself for forgetting one thing.

"I did Mother. I want all of us in the pictures with him. He has the best grandparents!" and he smiled.

They were snapping pictures when there was a knock on the door.

Sammy and Roz came by to congratulated them and brought a present. When Martina opened it, it was an outfit with a beach scene on the front. Also, there was a beach pail and shovel. A card that read:

FOR ADAM'S first ocean visit
BEST FRIENDS FOREVER!

Martina looked at Phillip and he said, "I'll explain later!" and grinned. "Thanks guys!"

Nell and Nash came by later and brought a present. An outfit for Adam that had a basketball player on the front of it, and a miniature nerd basketball inside. A card that read:

START HIM YOUNG playing a sport
WE ARE ALWAYS ON YOUR TEAM!

Martina said, "Thank you this means a lot!" and told Phillip she would explain later!

They had such good friends and as it got late. Martina said. "Phillip aren't you going home. Don't you have to work tomorrow?"

"I am sleeping in that chair." He spread the blanket

and pointed to the recliner. "No way am I leaving here ... with you wearing that hot outfit. I have to stay, and protect your assets! Besides the house is empty without you, and he went over and sat beside her on the bed.

"I could just climb in this bed with you and get a good night's sleep!" and she swatted at him.

"Stop I just had a baby! Don't make me laugh!" and she grabbed her pillow and held it tight to her abdomen.

"Okay, I'll wait another day!" and he marched to the chair. "I took the week off, so I can spend time with my family. I am going to rest up now. Good Night, Darling!"

The nurses were in for vitals and Phillip was snoring. There he was sprawled out. All six foot four in that tiny recliner, and his business suit had wrinkles in its wrinkles. He was even smiling in his sleep.

Martina said, "That's my big baby over there. He won't be sleeping like that tomorrow night," and she smiled.

"You get some rest little mama. Do you need anything? A sleeping pill may be wise, if you have to take care of two babies tomorrow night," the nurse asked.

"Yes I do. Thank you!' Then she rested well.

Phillip jumped up when a crying baby came into the room the next morning. Martina had pumped her breast, and Phillip had been watching and licking his lips. She said, "Honey take the bottle and feed him."

Phillip was shaking and the nurse told him to sit down, and she would bring the baby to him. Martina reminded him, "Honey take your jacket off first, please."

Martina was hurting and rubbing her stomach like

the nurses had showed her to do. Looking at Phillip holding Adam made her smile, and she rubbed harder. It was suppose to help the pain, and slow her bleeding. The nurse checked her and she was hemorrhaging, and she push the red button.

"Get the doctor in here!" The nurse said calmly into the speaker. Phillip was on cloud nine holding his boy, and he did not realize something was wrong.

The Doctor ran in the room and two of his colleagues followed. He started shouting orders, and an IV line was started, and meds injected into the tubing. Her blood pressure was coming back up. Her pulse was coming back down and they were stripping the bed and remaking it. Phillip had not moved just sat feeding the baby.

The nurse turned and showed him how to put Adam on his shoulder to burp the baby. As he patted his boy, his eyes never left Martina's eyes.

He could not believe the amount of blood, she had lost. He didn't even know anything was wrong. "How could I not know something was wrong?" he asked himself.

"She could have bled to death right in front of me," he scared himself. No way am I taking her home today, and he looked at Adam who was laying on his lap smiling.

The nurse came in to get him, and she saw the baby was smiling. She said, "I'll be back. I'll let him finish first."

"Finish what?" Phillip asked because he didn't want any more surprises.

"Having his bowl movement," and she walked out.

"Do it Adam, because she is going to change you, son. I don't know how," Phillip said out loud.

"You will learn, Buttercup. I will show you," Martina said.

"No Honey don't you dare move. You just lie there and rest. That bag of fluids must be replacing what you lost this morning. You scared me to death. Why didn't you say any- thing?" He was talking low because the baby was in his lap, but he had to know.

"I felt weak and my heart was pounding. I couldn't move. It was just one of those things that happens. Adam was a large baby. I have a lot, a lot of stitches down there. I have to heal. I am going to need a lot of help from you when I get home."

"You got it, but you have GOT to tell me when you are in trouble. All this is new to me," he said. The nurse came in and took the sleeping baby away.

He hurried over beside Martina rubbing her forehead, and kissed the top of her head. He was afraid to touch her anywhere else. She had fallen asleep.

He walked out into the hallway and ask the nurse to explain what happened in there. Being a lawyer he wanted all the facts, he knew his wife's right to an explanation. The doctor would be by to see the patient in a few minutes when he finished charting and writing new orders, he was told.

He called his father and asked him to stall his mother from coming until later. He explained their morning. He went into her bathroom and washed up.

He looked into the mirror. "You are a wreck. Two

days being a father, you look like hell!" he said to himself. Then went to get something to eat.

Martina was resting comfortable. He looked under the cover to see, if he saw any blood. There was none and he told the desk where he would be. He ask them to call his cell when the doctor was ready to talk.

CHAPTER SIX

The stables were abuzz with the arrival of FANATIC STRETCH's owner Colten Travis Bingham III. The white limo had a hood ornament of a Longhorn rack and CTB III on the license plate.

He was about Brian's age and he stood six foot six had on faded holey jeans, a brown Henley shirt, ostrich boots and belt with large buckle with CTB etched into it.

No hat sat on that blond mane that was layered to wing back and a woody peak in front. He had azure blue eyes. And his eyes were on FS.

He had made his fortune in oil. Now that all was running smoothly, he wanted to dabble into horse racing. He was competitive with his rich friends, and the stakes were going to be high. This trip was to see for himself the training process of his horse and he intended to mix business with pleasure.

His cousin Nell had invited him to stay with them. Nash her husband had always made him welcome. So he was going to take them up on the offer, instead of going to a empty room on the top floor of some hotel.

He spoke to Brian who was falling all over his feet,

trying to talk a good report referencing this horse's training. He would introduced him to Cameroon who was putting FS through his paces. The horse was snorting and rearing at times because he was so spirited. Cameron patted him on the side of his neck. The horse immediately calmed.

"That's impressive. The last time I saw him, no one could handle him. That young man is doing a good job, he is busy and I'll be around for a few days. I will see him next time. I'll call first," and Colten grinned.

Brian knew he meant for Cameron to stop what he was doing next time, and meet him exactly the time he specified.

He nodded and then he was gone. One thing Colten Travis Bingham III didn't like was to wait on. anything or anybody.

Nell was the opposite of Colten. He was preparing himself to be patient with her dawdling. She had told her cousin,"You need to stop and smell the roses sometime. You are going to miss out on a special treasure one day. Come take a breath at our place away from the maddening crowds and breathe."

"Okay for a couple of days," Colten had hung up.

"Nash, you will not believe it! **FINALLY he said YES!**

"Nell take a breath... breathe. You are up to something because you are never rattled," she looked away.

"You are nervous about something. Okay fess up and tell me, so I will not have to mediate! I can make him welcome, if I know he is not going to upset my wife," Nash was looking at Nell frowning.

"I asked your sister to come at the same time," and she grimaced and closed her eyes for the scolding.

"Good idea. He's single and she's single," and Nash didn't crack a smile.

"Reverse psychology will not work on me. You are furious! I just think they are perfect for one another, and will never meet unless you and I throw them together. If it doesn't work,

you can tell me … I told you so. Okay?"

"I told you so!" he said and walked to the car and opened the door. "Get in!"

Nell said, "How romantic!" Then she looked at Nash's face again. "What are you doing? I have to go back to work."

"You should have thought of that before now. You have to pay the piper!" he swerved into traffic and down the road to their house.

"Nash, I have appointments this afternoon. Take me back oh well I can drive," she got out and he was walking to the house.

"Where are the keys?" she beat on the car door.

"They're in my pocket. Come and get them," she ran at him and hit his back and tripped. He turned and caught her.

"You don't play fair Nell. "he had her in his arms toting her up the steps, and she was not moving. She had her arms crossed across her chest chewing her lip.

"Caveman!" she mumbled.

"Wow That's the nice thing you have said to me all day! If you think I am staying in this house with YOUR cousin and MY sister for a whole week without sex. You are crazy!"

She started taking her clothes off, "Good point dear. Come here I want my keys," and she reached in his pocket.

"More to the left," Nash was grinning.

Nell canceled two appointments saying an emergency came up and by the time she clicked her phone off, he had her begging to fulfill his and her needs.

"You are welcome. If you decide to cancel another appointment. You know where to find me! I'm the one with the wedding ring on his finger, and a ring in his nose for his wife to pull him around for a week only! I refused to be label as a henpecked husband except for one week."

"Yes dear! I could cancel two more appointments!" she said into her cell phone on her way to her car.

His cell phone rung and he answered, "At least I'd die happy. You have the best medicine. Bet you could bring me back to life." he said starting supper for his working wife.

She pulled out into traffic after finishing her day at work, and was on her way to the airport to pick up his sister. She thought how relaxed she was. She had a thoughtful husband. He had the forethought that she usually was a wreck when his sister came, he fixed that. He was chiropractor and had magical hands.

She smiled as Candice dragged her designer carry-on and matching luggage toward her. She was a model of cowgirl fashion today. She had flown from Dallas Ft Worth to LAX and was only going to stay a few days which meant a week.

Nell laughed and hugged her. "How was your flight?"

She wore faded torn low rider jeans and a brown Henley with ostrich skin cowgirl three inch heeled boots and a belt to match.

Her hair was sandy with blonde streaks and layered long down her back. She had azure blue eyes. What a beauty!

"It was good. I slept all the way. What's that brother of mine cooking?" they loaded her bags up and they were on their way home.

"Probably Pot Roast. Isn't that your favorite?" Nell smiled.

"Of course, he is. He loves his sister!" Candice said.

In the meantime, Colten had arrived and Nash welcomed him in, "Come on in. I got to check on the roast. Nell will be off work and home in no time."

No way was he going to tell Colten that his wife was matchmaking. He would run like the wind, and then she would retaliate. Oh my! Maybe I should that sounds like fun. Focus! Nash told himself.

Colten went into the living room and was looking at the pictures over the fireplace of the family, and the last pictures of him with them. Then he saw a gorgeous girl hugging Nash. He had to ask Nell about that one.

"Where's Junior?" Colten decided to walk into the kitchen and get a drink. They always had wine in the refrigerator.

"He's at a basketball game and it is an away game. So he is spending the night with his friend. Yes, we know the parents otherwise your cousin would not agree to it. I trust her judgment," Nash said.

The women were laughing and came in the back door and Colten froze and Candice froze.

Nash said in Nell's ear, "They even dress alike!" and stared into his wife's eyes.

"I know it is frightening how much I have studied these too!" and Nell smiled at him and kissed him.

"Crap! I forgot Colten you don't know my sister. This is Candice. Honey!" Nash said.

"Candice this is Colten, my cousin. We forgot to consult each other," Nell was waving her hands from Nash to herself.

"About the dates each one of you were coming. I'm starved. Can we eat? UMM something smells mighty good. Honey, you have outdone yourself" Nell didn't want either to have time to say no and leave.

Colten had not taken his eyes off Candice. Nor had she taken hers off him.

He held the chair for her to sit. "I like your style of clothes." Everything she had on, matched his.

"Unreal … you must look at a lot of female fashion magazines?" Candice always said what she thought. She eyeballed his Henley. "Your shirt looks better than mine. I have no chest," and she laughed.

Colten was about to lower the boom, but Nell intervened seeing his sneer.

"Colten she wasn't saying you dress like a woman. It was her way of saying that she works for a cowgirl clothing manufacturing company. The style she is wearing is the latest fashion!" Nell hoped that calmed him and he laughed.

"That explains the flat chest and bony legs!" He was paying her back for embarrassing him. Nash's time to intervene.

"Candice here, is a real tomboy! I have teased her all these years about that very thing, but Colten my boy, she can ride like the wind, rope a calve and barrel race with the best of them! Don't let those high heels, fool you!" there he had defended his sister.

She smiled at her brother and ignored Colten. That was something, he was not use to ... being IGNORED.

"How's the roast?" Nash asked looking around the table.

"Perfect as usual!" and Candice licked the gravy off her fork very slowly. Colten sat up straighter, and by the time they had chocolate cake and she did the same with the fork ... even slower. He swallowed harder.

Colten said, "Oh Lordy! I think I will go and get some shut eye." He walked to the car and got his bags and Nash showed him his room.

Nell was showing Candice her room right across from Colten's. There was only one bathroom upstairs.

"Those two will get to know each other real well before the week is over," Nell said and smiled at Nash that was growling.

"Relax we love them both. It's for the best ...wait and see," Nell was convinced their profiles matched.

The next morning, Candice came out of her room to go to the bathroom. She did and sat, then flushed. The man in the shower cursed. "Can't you see I'm taking a shower!"

"Nope! Didn't see a thing!" trying to run around the shower door. The door opened and he grabbed her, bringing her into the shower. She only had on a white long tee shirt, nothing else. The shower nozzle was wetting her down and her nipples were visible.

With no makeup on, she was absolutely breathtaking and he was mesmerized. He was getting aroused just looking at her.

Candice was pushing on his chest for him to free her. Then she said, "My brother is going to kill you. You animal."

She looked into his eyes and felt him growing. She closed her eyes because it had been so long. He was rubbing her back, then her buttocks. She had thoughts of kneeing him.

She had rested her hands on his shoulders now. They were moving all over his back pulling on him to get even closer, and she wrapped one long leg around his waist.

By then he was panting, and she began laughing and said, "This is insane."

"Yes, you are making me crazy," Colten was feeling all those tiny curves that he had spoke of last night negatively, just to put her down. They seem to fit perfectly to his physic today. Too perfect and he said, "You can go now. Just don't ever come in again while I am showering. Or else!"

"Or else what?" her azure eyes were penetrating into his soul. She would not be dismissed like an unruly child.

She was a grown woman, and use to taking what she wanted. No man had ever made her feel like this. She had put many in their place.

"Do you actually think you scare me?" She furrowed her brows, "I have been all over the world and you, my hick friend are a far cry from the man I like. You are crude to say the least. Now get your grabby hands off of me," she was fuming and twisting which was making her tee shirt raise. Skin was touching skin, she opened her mouth, and moaned.

He placed his mouth on hers and sucked the life out of her.

"I want you, but only if you want it, too! Make up your mind? Yes or No." Then they both moaned together and kissed thoroughly.

"Don't," she said and he stopped to draw back. He threw his head back.

"Stop," and she was squeezing him like no woman had. He had had more than his fair share of women. This woman was sucking the life out of him.

He leaned back and told her, "Get off or finish it!"

She began riding him at a slow trot and then a fast gallop until the back stretch and she had lengthened those long legs till they both stopped on the finish line.

Both staring at each other, the shower nozzle still beating down on them. Either could move because the pulsations were still spasmodic and pleasurable for both.

He was the first to close his eyes and lean back and she gasped. Oh Here it comes again. Do something and he grabbed her waist and hung on as he rocked her back and forth until her eyes closed, and her tongue was licking her lips, and she was arching. He was going mad, the more he gave her, the more she wanted.

"Yes Yes," was all she could say and he was not going to be able to stand much longer with this one. His knees were buckling because it was so amazing. He laid her on the tile bench and held her tighter, and it finally stopped …. they were still intertwined.

He started to rise and she pulled his neck down and kissed him. "You can't leave me like this. I need more!" He had nothing until she moved, and it was growing again.

"No way am I leaving you unfulfilled. You have no idea how much I have to give."

They went into his room and locked the door and she took off her wet tee shirt, and he saw the most beautiful well proportioned body. How could he have missed it?

He had prided himself in knowing how the female brain worked, and how the women would camouflage the outward appearance never did it match the inward appearance. Even now it didn't match, but hers was in a good way.

"I got to go Nash knows I never sleep past noon," and she laughed. "He won't kill you today because he is at work. It's been fun, but don't do it again," she was dismissing their interlude. She walked out to her bedroom, blow dried her hair put makeup on, and dressed and out the door in 5 minutes.

He opened his bedroom door just to see where she was going.

In five minutes she looked spectacular. What it took

the normal woman two hours to achieve. "Where are you going?"

"I have a photo shoot. Want to come?" she was running down the steps with a large shoulder bag, and it looked like she was in a hurry.

CHAPTER SEVEN

"**S**ure, give me a second," Colten said.

"Don't have a second. Grab your boots and let's go. I am never late!" He jumped in the Jeep that Candice had pulled up to the door, and she spun off on two wheels.

"Hope this day is not the day, I meet my maker!" he said pulling on his boots and buttoning a plaid cowboy shirt. Her hair was whipping into his face. It smelled like roses. He closed his eyes and remembered what his cousin had told him earlier. To stop and smell the roses! **FINALLY … YES!**

I am doing that. I don't want to miss a thing.

She jumped out. The valet would park it, and ran into the building. It was a modeling agency. He had not run in awhile and definitely had not had that much sex in awhile.

She was not even out of breath. He sat where she pointed, and flew behind the curtain. In exactly five minutes, she was out on the runway striking poses, and three photographers were shooting her pictures.

Later she told him. "It was for three different magazines that is why so many photos."

She looked at him, "Are you hungry?" and the makeup she had on was doing a number on him.

"More than ever!" and he gave her a sideways grin.

"Food, Food?" He was running his eyes all over her and breathing deeply.

That's when she said, "We can't at my cousin's. We can go to my pad." She drove to a penthouse roof apartment and got out.

"You live up here?" he asked. She frowned at his question.

"Do you not know who I am?" she asked.

"Do you know who I am?" he asked.

They walked into a chic modernistic apartment. The kind he had for himself in may cities. "Sure, I do you are Nell's cousin!"

"And owner of this building and that one," he said. Her legs were weakening. She threw her shoulder bag on the sofa. He was the owner. "Don't be ridiculous!" she said.

He pulled his phone out, "Have Simon fix my usual post haste and bring it up!" Colten was looking for her reaction.

"You are a piece of work. I swore I would never date a rich man EVER!" She stomped up the steps and got to the third rung. He had her waist. He turned her and she kicked his shin.

He almost dropped her, "Listen. Calm down. We aren't dating!"

Then she stopped resisting. "Good that makes me happy because I have seen enough in ten years of modeling to know that ... that is a dead end street. As long as I can use you for fun and no ties, I'm yours."

Holding what he wanted in checkmate, her leg between his.

"That sounds fair! I like that. It's a deal," he said.

"One rule when we are together for however long that it is! NO OTHER MEN. When it is over, you walk away and don't look back," he stated.

He said as if they were negotiating in a board meeting. He stared at her and she stared back at him.

She said, "NO OTHER WOMEN and don't look back!" He nodded. "Then I agree. Come quick. We only have two hours before I will be flying to Hong Kong?"

"Oh no. Yes! Don't! Do that, please." She was in the zone. Licking, tasting and nibbling on him as he made his way up the staircase to her loft bedroom.

"We are in the clouds," she said as the evening was nigh and the smog had developed. It was engulfing the skyscraper, whose entire bedroom was of windows that overlooked the city of Los Angeles.

"I am going to take you over the rainbow beyond these clouds," and he did twice. Then it was time for her to go.

She got on the copter on the helipad and was gone telling him, "It's been fun. Let yourself out. Byeee!"

He lay there staring at the sky. He had done this to a thousand other women, but had never had it to happen to him. He felt empty without his new sex object. He didn't think that of her, she's more than that.

Reappearing was the tomboy in his mind's eye. She

was different. "Oh hell! Nell knew I would react like this! She would never introduce us, if Candice wasn't the real thing!

Nell said if you don't slow down and look REALLY look, you may miss out on a treasure. That's when he jumped out of bed and found his phone.

"James bring the car, in about thirty minutes to the roof," He was going back to Nell's and talk, and find out everything about Candice.

If Nash would let him back in the house, Nell's husband was a body fixer. This is his sister, he may want to crack some of my bones. He probably hasn't put two and two together.

He walked in and Nash asked in a stern voice, "Where is my sister?"

"Gone to Hong Kong and I rode to the airport with her. The least I could do!" he said and in walks Nell.

"Don't believe a word he says Nash. Candice hasn't been to the airport in four years. She always leaves off the roof, otherwise the paparazzi is hounding her. So try again, buster."

"Okay CUZ, you got me. I was on the roof when she left. Remember I own the frigging roof!" he was not going to let either one step on him, but he could understand their concern.

He was known for his womanizing.

"Love them and leave them!" Nash was clinching his fists looking at Colten. Then he turned on Nell, "See what you have done Nell!" Nell was staring back at Nash.

"Whoa! Nash I have not left. She was the one that hightailed it out of there. Look at the facts!" Colten said.

Nash looked at Nell and said, "Tell him!"

"Tell me what?" Colten asked. Puzzled that he had missed something."What?'

Nell slowly sat down, "She told me this morning that she was in LOVE for the first time, and that she had to leave. There is no time in my schedule for romance. I don't know where I am going, but I can't stay here. I have this week off to clear my head, and I will be back to work Monday for real. Tell Nash I am okay, and I love both of you! Then she hung up." Nell was teary and she was the one in the family that never cried not even at funerals.

Colten sat with his elbows on both his knees, and hands laced, and chin on his knuckles. Nell saw his jaw clinching.

"She'll be fine Nell. I will find her," Colten said.

Nash jumped up, "Haven't you done enough?" Nell was holding on to Nash while Colten went upstairs to gather his things. He went into the bathroom and saw her pair of thong black undies on the floor. He picked them up and stuffed them in his pocket.

Then down the stairs and out the door. He was on the phone with the apartment building to ask what private helicopter had picked Miss Candice Timberlake off the roof.

"That's confidential, sir!" Colten was fit to be tied.

"Young man do you know with whom you are talking. This is the man that owns that building that you are standing in."

191

"If you were, you'd know, the answer to that question!" and he hung up.

Colten looked at the phone almost snapping it in half.

"The arrogance of that man. Get his name. I like him. Now get me my secretary, James," he demanded.

"Press one on the car phone, sir. She is number one always. I use it to reach you," James said.

"Thanks, I never call myself," and Colten laughed.

"Angie, I want the name of the owner of the helicopter that picked up Miss Timberlake this morning off this roof. Where her destination was and do it in the next hour. Call me back!"

He showered and dressed in an Armani tuxedo and a pale azure blue dress shirt. He had a function that he had to attend The Met Gala in New York at eight PM tonight."

"Angie, what in the world. To hell with privacy laws. I'm above the law at this point. Get me that Nancy at the Private Investigation office to search and find her. I have to go."

He was frowning. This was new to him, he never worried about anyone or anything. Now this woman was occupying his every brain cell, not to mention the other parts that were aching for her.

The Lear jet was on route to NYC. The limo was there and took him to the front door of The Met. He walked in and was greeted.

He went straight to the bar. Drinks were flowing every-where, but he didn't want to get tangled in someone else's web.

He looked across the room and there SHE was in a designer dress that left nothing to the imagination. She was being paraded down the aisle by the designer for photographers of twelve magazines to take pictures.

She was gorgeous. Her make-up was severe and made her look like Cleopatra. They brought out a yellow python and wrapped it around her shoulders. That did it.

He rushed over to her and said, "Take that off of my wife's neck this minute!" They all knew who he was. They did what he said.

Candice said nothing just stood frozen to the spot. He grabbed her hand, but she could not or would not move.

Nell was watching TV of the Met Gala, "Come here Nash quick! You sister is on TV!"

"What has she done now?" Then he saw them unwrapping a python from around her and Colten. He saw him yelling ...

"Get that snake off my wife!" pointing to the men to follow his commands.

"OH my darling ...You did good! Now I don't have to worry myself to death about her. I hereby give unto you my ULCER Colten Bingham III," Nash said and high-fived Nash, Jr.

"Now all I got to do is get you married off, and" he felt a hand slap the back of his head. "Not anytime soon ... your mother said!" and Nash, Sr. looked at Nell and grinned.

FINALLY ... YES!

"They were married and it was a big to do! Super Model Candice Vivian Timberlake married Billionaire tycoon Colten Travis Bingham III in a private ceremony at an undisclosed area of Malibu on Monday June 19, 2017.

She wore a simple Vera Wang white gown with a long veil and no shoes. She held a bouquet of daisies with a azure blue ribbon. The groom wore an Armani black tuxedo with azure blue shirt. All of the wedding party were barefoot in the sand.

The minister that officiated was Trevor Alexander Porter, a relative of the family.

Seven doves were released to symbolize that it only took seven days for him to propose.

The happy couple will reside after their honeymoon in one of the groom's penthouse apartments. Not to be made public at this time the location.

They left on Colten's yacht to Cabo Lucas and staying at the Hotel RIU Palace.

From the top floor room's balcony, they could view the azure blue waters. The color of both their eyes. He was so in love with her that he wanted them to experience everything.

"I have been here before with work and the only thing I want to do is experience you, my husband," Candice said.

"I have been here before for work and the only thing I want to do is experience you, my wife."

They continued to explore each other's body and found where new erotic zones were. He forgot were he was when she explored him. Her long fingers were like velvet, and her legs went on forever.

He was so muscular from hard work, and he told her he would never slow down unless, she made him. "I have never wanted anything or anybody as much ... as I want you."

"You have me forever. Relax and let me guide you through meditation. I am yoga certified. That is why I am so flexible and she showed him a position, he had never tried. "Every time I want you to have a new experience in a different way until we agree which one is best," she laughed "which ones are best. I don't want you to tire of me."

"Never ...One hundred and one different positions have you showed me. How did you get so knowledgeable my wife." He was staring into her eyes. If a man taught her, he was going to kill him soon as they got home.

"Relax from a book. A Yoga book based on the ancient Sumatra teachings. I will let you read it. You are amazing!"

"No you are!" "We are amazing together!"

Martina was home at last. She had had to stay a week. Her blood iron was low from the bleeding, and now all was under control. The baby had stayed because of jaundice, also.

Since they were being well looked after the lawyer went back to work and when they were released he would take a week off.

Phillip smiled at his beautiful Martina," Honey I am so happy you are coming home that hospital recliner has made a ridge in my backside that I may never recover from."

Martina said, "Bring it here and let me rub it!"

Phillip said, "Don't you dare! You cannot do that to me! Now I have to sleep on the couch when we get home!"

"What on earth are you talking about?" she asked.

"If you are going to be patting and rubbing on me. I will not sleep a wink for five weeks," he said.

"Honey you are obsessing over nothing. Okay I will not touch. Are you happy!" and she turned toward the wall to let the hormonal tears flow.

"Okay Okay touch me all you want to," and in walks his mother.

Cynthia looks at her son and says, "Shame on you for making her cry!"

That's when he went around the bed and took her in his arms and kiss the tears away, and his mother went to the nursery.

"You are free to reek havoc on my body. I am being selfish. I just want you so bad," Phillip said.

"You shall have me for the rest of our lives. I need you to touch me, too!" Martina said and his father backed of out the door and knocked.

"Where's your mother?' he asked.

"Nursery, Dad!" and then they were hugging and kissing again.

In walks the doctor, "I thought I told you two NO sex for six weeks."

Phillip smiled at Martina, "You did. WE are practicing how not to ... in here so when we get home ... we won't! Its called desensitization!" Phillip said.

"Oh Okay! Continue. I will review your discharge

orders!" and neither remembered a word that the doctor had said.

The nurse review them again and they listened carefully.

PART FOUR

CHAPTER ONE

The race track was dirt and Cameron was taking FANATIC STRETCH for a slow ride around the track. He was wanting to run, but Cameron was holding him back. Until the last stretch, then he let him do his thing.

The time was getting better with each timed lap. The hardest thing for a spirited horse like FS was to discipline himself, and hold his strength back for the end. Cameron willed him to conserve his energy not burn out in the front stretch. FS was rewarded each time, he followed commands.

Elizabeth sat on the fence and watched them. She loved to watch him train this monster of a horse. She wanted desperately to ride him. Cameron said, "You got to be kidding. I can hardly handle him. If he threw you, he'd break your pretty little neck and then what would I do?"

"Come and see me, and put me back together, like only you know how to do," and she licked her lips.

"Stop! I can't concentrate when you do that. Needless to say the fellows will be teasing me about how tight my jeans are fitting. Damn it. Come here and block their view. Just until it goes away."

"If I come over there, it's going to get worst so I will mosey on back by my lonesome, and wait for you in the shower."

"Okay that did it! Joe put the horse up. I've worked him enough for one day. He chased Elizabeth back to their room. She was a handful. All she wanted was to have him with her day and night.

"Why are you complaining? When the house is done, I'll never see you," she lamented as if their love would be dead.

"I am not complaining in the least as long as we are alone, but these guys are watching us and it is killing me to see their longing for a woman. They can't have you, and they know it.

So they are continuously teasing me and I need to concentrate on FS."

"Brian even commented on how distracted I have become. I told him, I'm on my honeymoon what do you expect. I could take off for a week, and then he'd shut up," Cameron said grinning at her.

"What I could do to you in a week's time? Hold me back, sweet Jesus," he said and she put her arms around his neck.

"Let me hold you back!" and she did.

When he went back up the hill, he was so relaxed that FS looked at him, as if the horse didn't even recognize him.

He looked at the horse and said, "Don't you start on me, too!" they had a more productive lesson today.

"FS don't be jealous of my wife. I love you, too." He burst out laughing at himself after he had FS back in his stable.

"Yes, I love you. You black stallion and I want to see you do well! So that Colten fellow won't sell you. Why am I talking such nonsense." He looked around, no one was near. No one had heard him. "Elizabeth was so hot. It has fried my brain, FS!" Cameron sighed.

Katherine had come to see Elizabeth, "Honey If you are bored come and help me. We can work on some curtain material, table clothes, or napkins for your own house. We have lots to do, and it will keep you busy while Cameron works."

"That's a great idea. I will do just that! He doesn't want me riding my horse by myself though, and I agreed because there are a couple of men that look at me weird and whistle. That's my worst fear," she rummaged threw the swatches of material her mother had said to pick what you like.

"I would love to be back in my old bed, but Cameron wants to take care of our lodging. He's the man. Maybe I can get him to spend the night one time, and see what he says the next day. I will try and let you know later, Mother!" her father drove her back to the ranch.

"Is it okay if Cameron and I spend the night, Daddy?"

"What kind of question is that? Of course you can. This is your home," she kissed him on the cheek and took the samples of materials into her room.

There Cameron sat in the dark room, "I missed you!" and he hugged her to him.

"I wasn't gone long!" she said.

"It seemed like forever. Don't do that again. I will take you for visits. Okay?" he pleaded.

"Really Really will you! Can we go for an overnight because I want you to see what our house is going to look like when it is finished. I got samples and want you to help me decide on the curtains for each room," she said.

"You plan it anyway you want! I will be happy, if you are happy!" and he kissed her until the morning light.

"Yes, we will go for one night. So make your plans," he said. Elizabeth was all smiles.

It was the most, he had seen her smile in along time. He realized at this moment that his wife had been homesick. It had never occurred to him because he didn't have a family. His parents were dead and no siblings but one. A brother that lived in another country.

Bryce lived in Japan where he was stationed in service. He had learned the language and married. He stayed because his Asian wife had family there. He never returned to the USA.

If ever he made enough money, Cameron promised himself to take a trip over there and find Bryce. He would tell Elizabeth when he had the money, and not until.

Saturday came and they went over. Cameron was in awe. The bath in this house was as big as their place at Brian's. No wonder, she is homesick. The dining room table sat twenty people. The tableware had him stumped.

She said just use what you need honey, and leave the rest alone. That's what I have always done. Her mother had taught her from an early age which fork was for salad or shrimp which was a water versus a juice glass and so on. It really didn't matter to her and she held Cameron's hand under the table. That helped his nerves settle.

Brigs asked Cameron how the training was coming along and they talked and talked about horses, and left the women and went into his den.

"This is my room. The only room in the house that the women don't fess over. I have forbid them to come in here. The man's den or some say the man's cave," and he chuckled.

"Cameron I want to show you our room. Good Night Daddy," and she kissed her father's cheek.

Brigs said, "Run along you two, and we will talk again tomorrow! Don't let the bedbugs bite!"

"What did he mean by that," Cameron asked and began itching.

"It was something he use to say when we were little. I think we thought if we moved at night a big bug would tote us off," and she laughed hysterically.

Her sisters Imogene, the musician and Emily, the ballerina said not a word to either Elizabeth or Cameron. They were too jealous. Cameron and his wife walked into her bedroom fit for a princess. All pink and the bathroom was adjacent was as big as Brian's whole kitchen.

"You left all this for me? Dang I think you love me a lot, and she had begun to undress him. Leading him to the bathroom, where she stripped. They went into the bubble bath. She had drawn it while he was in the den with her daddy.

He sank down and today's achy muscles started to

loosen up. The heat of the bath was relaxing. They sat opposite one another and rested their heads on the edge of the tub. The only thing that was touching were their toes...until she started rubbing her big toe up and down on the back of his upper thigh. He began breathing deeply and said, "Don't start or I am going to finish it."

"I sure hope so. No one can hear us and she said, "We can do our thing" and smiled at him.

"Doesn't this bath make you wanna?" She in all her glory, rose. He saw her nipples hard as little pebbles, and she straddled him. "Oh no Honey! We can't!" he said.

"Why not? We are married!" she had him in her in no time. He was moaning and moving. He closed his eyes so he would not see the house, and held her waist. She was making his world come unglued. She went faster and it was feeling so good, but he had to wait for her.

"Come on baby that's it! Get there," and he heard her whimper. That meant for him to go for it, and he thrust with all his might until she collapsed in pulsations which made his become more stronger. She had a grip on him that was more powerful than any time before.

It must be this room because he was going over again, and so was she. She was gasping to "take it again, if you can." It was too good. They were spent. "Honey this is the honey-moon suite from this day forward."

She said, "This is just the beginning. You have not lain naked with me in my bed. It is soft, you will again. I promise."

She dried him and kiss him everywhere. They walked

naked to the bed. She called it their bed now. "It is so soft."

They were feeling the bed. Then she grabbed the wrought iron headboard. And sat on him, he had the hottest wife. She was fitting all of him into her treasure for safe keeping. It was amazing how she was going around, around then up, down.

Until he said. "I can't wait!"

She said, "Please wait I am almost there!" she got faster.

"Oh Baby you did it! Here!Here! It comes. Oh yes!"

Silence followed. They lay spent intertwined.

Smiling. No more words for awhile.

Then he said, "This is my bed from now on."

"Do you think you can handle my wrought iron bed every night!

"As long as you can hang onto that headboard like that we have to buy one just like this for our new house. Or come over for a visit often. You are a wild woman. My woman. We just got to tone it down in public. I don't want anyone looking at my wife the wrong way because I would have to rearrange their face."

"Yes darling you are my one and only! I guess I never thought about it that way. Other people do this. I thought for a few, that it was just us that feel like this. Then I see babies everywhere. Don't worry I am on the pill. I will never forget. Without talking to you first to see, if you want a child?"

"Not right now after the race, if FS wins I will get enough for us to afford a child until then, we need to have fun."

CHAPTER TWO

The brothers were growing up. "Tyson graduates this year Curtis. What am I going to do?" she was already agonizing over him going off to college. He and Amanda had both been accepted at Duke University. Their grades were exceptional and the scholarship was a blessing.

"Well we could move to Durham, NC or we could drive cross country to Durham or fly to Durham ... BUT ...I hope you come to the realization that we have a home here. We both have jobs here. Michael has two more years in school here and would be very unhappy in a new school at his age with all his classmates from first grade here."

"You make valid points as usual. You are a level-headed man THAT is why I married you. You are good looking, too. I love your assets which are all valid points for me to listen to my husband ... BUT ... my heart is breaking," and she started sobbing.

The hiccups came and he put his arms around her. "That's right, cry it out. You have raised him right, and I have taught him good studying skills. So what is really bothering you?"

"You are so good at interrogation. You should be a police officer. OH yeah, you already are. How did I get so lucky? Let me see?" she hiccups. "It was my boy Tyson laying in a hospital bed, and my knight in shining armor came, and took us all to the land of milk and honey. We lived happily ever after UNTI Amanda came along and stole Tyson's heart.

Curtis they are going to that school and get married, and get an apartment, and have babies and I will never see him again. Except every five years when I save up and send them the money to visit his aging mother and her hero!" Nancy stated.

"How long have you been coming up with this hogwash?" Curtis asked.

"I just thought about it today!" ... Hiccup ... Blowing her nose. Then she snuggling under Curtis's arm again which he had removed when she started going off the deep end.

He stood and paced in front of her. "Here's my take on the situation. Tyson has been an excellent student. Buckling down making the grades to get into a prestigious school such a Duke. One that few people get into, and then to get a scholarship, is icing on the cake. He yes ... will go to school with Amanda, but there are hundreds of other girls there that may be prettier or smarter or more conniving than Amanda. So she may NOT be, the girl he marries. We have to support Michael, and make him feel special! Guide him to a scholarship, so we don't have to fund him. Besides we need a flight to a high rise hotel for a week once a year. North Carolina is far enough away for no one at the agency to bother YOU, and far enough away for no one on the force to bother ME. It is a win-win situation ... as I see it!"

"Oh Curtis! You put everything back in order for me. I knew you were a good organizer when I saw those dishtowels in that kitchen drawer FOLDED, the first time I came in this house!" kissing her man.

Martina was bathing the baby, and dressing him in the new outfit NaNa Cynthia had bought for him. She cooed at little Adam and said, "You are going out tonight to your NaNa's house because your mommie and daddy are going on a date.

"Yes son, I am breaking out of jail! How do you like my outfit?" and she began modeling for her son when she felt fingers around her waist pulling her body backwards, and slamming into a six foot four wall of pure muscle.

"I can answer that for my son," Phillip said as he kissed her perfumed neck and whispering into her ear.

She had her hair pulled up in a clasp, so he would have easy access to her neck. He had always like to nibble on her neck.

It had been six weeks and they both had been looking forward to this night of bliss. He said, "We can just start right now and then go out ... please!"

She almost said, yes. Then she remembered Cynthia's face this afternoon. How happy her mother-in-law had been about the baby coming over to visit his grandparents.

"Your mother would be so disappointed. She has been so good to me and you know I could not have made this speedy recovery without her."

"You are right. With the work caseloads I have had, she has redeemed herself. Dad has even praised her and he is looking forward to it, too! He told the whole office today that his namesake was coming over to play with him tonight."

Martina turned and Phillip saw the plunging neckline of her new navy blue dress and her dangling drop diamond earrings. Her breath was quickening, "Don't touch Buttercup. You may burn your hands. I'm on fire for you as it is," and lowered her lashes to dwell on him dressed in a black business suit, white shirt and burgundy tie.

"You look good enough to eat," Martina raised her eyes to Phillip's and they were smoldering. He did not move. She had hypnotized him.

"Let's go darling. Snap out of it and get the baby's bag!" she said and he reacted quickly like a tin solider marching off to war.

They dropped the child off and he sped down the road.

She said, "I didn't think we would ever get here."

They both raced to the door and began stripping their clothes off at their apartment's front door leaving a trail of clothes all the way to their bedroom.

"Oh my goodness Martina you are so wet and you are sure you are healed?" Phillip mumbled.

"Why are you talking?" and he shut up and kissed her swollen breast gently and he could not control her. She had him on his back.

"You have tormented me to the point. I may take

what I want," Martina said smiling because he said that everyday.

"Take it by all means because when you get through, I am taking what is left to the maximum," he responded.

They coupled over and over until neither could breathe.

Then He jumped straight up.

"Can you get pregnant?" he asked panicking.

"Yes! I can't take birth control pills, if I am pumping breast milk. Why? You don't want a little Eve to go with Adam?"

"Good point ... Now where was I?" he stated as he eased back between her legs, and had her moaning and pulling his hair as he kissed her neck.

Three hours later they were dressed and makeup freshened, and picked up the baby, and went back home.

As they walked into the house, Martina said with a gasp and horrified look on her face, "We have had intruders that came in and tore our house apart. Just look what they did!"

Phillip surveyed the damage and agreed, "It is a mess. We did a bang up job. Didn't we, dear!"

"Let's leave it and go upstairs," she said.

"I thought you'd never ask. I have a lot of time to make up for," he stared at her with a twinkle in his eyes.

She crossed her legs and leaned forward on the top step letting her bare breasts fall out of her plunging neckline and said, "Hurry I think I just had an orgasm. It must have been left over. I thought of you rocking me, and it happened,"

He leaped two steps at a time, unzipping his pants and there in the hallway, they finished another encounter of sexual bliss.

"It was worth waiting for, don't you think? Are you okay?"

He was staring at her, "How did I get so lucky? You **FINALLY said YES!** That's how. I am more than okay. I think we should get undressed. What do you say?"

"Maybe a shower first?" she stepped out of her dress and let it fall to the floor. She had nothing else on and like the pied piper, he was following and leaving clothes everywhere.

"I am hiring you a cleaning crew to clean this up tomorrow and all you have to do is take care of Adam. Be in my bed with your legs wide open when I get home, what do you say?" Phillip wasn't watching her face when he said it..

It went from a blissful state to a distortion of rage, "You male chauvinist pig! I have a job, too! We clean up together, buddy. We care for Adam together. YOU can have it in the bed for me when I get home. If you have a brain cell in your head that I haven't fried tonight, you will rethink that statement!"

"Okay. I see your point ... now." He paced in front of her and contemplated his closing statement. "I was hasty and I throw myself at the mercy of the court. I want makeup sex ... is the only reason WHY ... I said such a thing."

Phillip had pleaded his case. She was nude and

grinning, "Good answer! In that case get in your bed Buttercup!"

They checked on Adam together before going to their room.

He was sleeping peacefully and had no clue that his parents had been shouting at one another or maybe he was use to it. Nine months in utero plus six weeks, well accustomed.

They were passionate about everything and neither wanted the other not to express themselves.

The next morning smiling at each other as they began picking up the clothes, and throwing them in laundry bags.

Thirty minutes later they were having breakfast, and off to their jobs.

She drop Adam off at Cynthia's, and went to the agency.

Nancy said, "I see you are in a good mood this morning."

"Uh huh! "Nancy looked at her calendar and began counting on her fingers.

"Just as I thought! Buttercup nailed it last night! I ain't a detective for nothing. Now go take a nap!" and she began typing really fast.

"I don't have the strength to lie, but here's one that you don't know," she kept walking and Nancy stopped typing.

"What? I know everything. What?" she was looking at Martina for an answer.

Martina said with a sad face, "I am ..."

Nancy asked, "You am what?" she was getting concerned.

Martina bit her lip, "I am probably."

Nancy snapped, "You am what? Probably what? I ain't got time for no nonsense!"

"Probably, NO for sure. I am going to have a little girl nine months from last night. I sure did do all in my power. If Phillip's fishes were starving to swim upstream that is, Goodnight!" and she closed her office door and laid down on the sofa smiling at the ceiling.

She heard Nancy screaming, "You have lost your mind. There is no way. You are not going to have another baby before me. I have to call Curtis right now! No I can't do that because someone has to man this office while a certain partner sleeps the day away!" she was pacing.

She smiled and added at Martina's door, "I'm glad it is YOU and not ME! Sleep good girlfriend. You are going to need it. A little girl … I always wanted a little girl to dress up … A little girl!" then she started typing.

Phillip on the other hand was chipper this morning, whistling and once skipping. Even swinging his briefcase as he entered the office, immediately he put on his somber business face.

His father said to his son, "That son of yours had the sweetest smile on his face this morning. Your mother is having the time of her life. She is dressing him to go to the town today to some woman's function. She wants all her cronies to see him." He looked at Phillip and asked, "Are you okay?"

"Just a little tired. The baby kept me up all night,

but that's the breaks," and he went into his office and smiled as he looked out the window. He had not lied to his father. His baby named Martina had kept him up all all all night long.

Now back to work and back to preparing what he was going to surprise her with this afternoon.

He sent her a dozen red roses and Nancy put them in water. She didn't even wake Martina up.

When Martina did open her door, she saw the roses. "My Buttercup is itching for a repeat. You know twins run in my family. If it is two girls will you take one, Nancy? Their daddy is asking for trouble sending roses, but I don't think he has thought about the consequences of his actions! I'm sure not going to tell him. I do need to run an errand. Is it anything you need from uptown?" smiling as she went out not giving Nancy time to answer.

Martina had been in maternity clothes for awhile, and now she was looking for something sexy to wear tonight.

CHAPTER THREE

Katherine and Brigs sat in the theater loge waiting for the curtain to open. Their daughter Emily was the principal ballerina in this night's production of "Swan Lake."

It had taken Emily ten years of dance to achieve this honor. She was excited her parents and Eliot were here to see her hard work and dedication to her craft pay off.

She was holding her own tonight. The applause was increased when her slender arms were extended backwards, and she imitated a swan flapping its wings. Her feet were on pointe, and moving very slowly across the stage. Slowly ever so slowly, she fluttered down to bend forward her arms extended. Then they ceased to move, as if the swan had died.

It took exceptional control. "She did it," her mother shouted and her father stood and was clapping to the ovation.

Brigs finally saw what a beautiful art ... ballet ... really was because he had encourage Katherine to talk their daughter out of this nonsense to be a dancer. "Why can't she study law? or medicine? Why theater?"

Katherine's response had always been, "She loves it Brigs." She would smile and add, "It is a dying art. She will excel … you will see one day!"

Today was the day. He was a proud papa. His oldest girl had accomplished her goal to land the leading role in the Dance Company. He patted Emily's beau, Eliot on the back.

The boy was proud of his girlfriend of four years. Eliot had been there for Emily. She would cry on his shoulder and show him her bleeding feet. She'd grimace with muscle cramps from practicing, forced to repeat and repeat the stance that her instructor demanded of her.

"Practice makes perfect! I'm okay Eliot please hold me." He was there and she was his. Emily had never looked at another boy. Tonight he was going to ask her to MARRY him. He had the ring in his pocket and earlier talked to her father.

"Mr Porter is it okay, if I ask Emily to marry me? Will you give us your blessing?" Katherine's eyes were on her husband and she grabbed his hand. He had just got over blood pressure problems from Elizabeth's quick marriage.

"Does she know, young man?" Brigs asked.

"She does not. We have not discussed marriage. She may not want to, but I had to asked you first my father said to do it the right way," Eliot stated.

"Edward has raised a fine boy. You have my blessing, if my daughter should say yes," Brigs was calm and squeezed Katherine's hand to reassure her that he was okay.

His thought was that Emily had planned to go on to

school to get her Masters in Fine Arts. Which meant she would move away. Eliot was no where in that picture.

If she did want to marry him, then that would be fine. It would mean she would live here near them. Eliot Fairbanks' family was in the realty business and they had many homes for them to choose from.

It would be Emily's choice.

After the curtain call Eliot found Emily back stage and kissed her, "You did great!"

She smiled, "Thanks my love, I'm going to get dressed. Stay with my parents and I'll find you," then she disappeared into the scenery.

Reappearing in a blue pastel sheath matching ballet walking shoes. Her dramatic makeup was still on, and she carried a bouquet of wild flowers on her right arm which she continuously was smelling as she walked.

"Oh daddy, they are beautiful!" she smiled widely.

"Not as beautiful as my girl!" he hugged her. "We are going to celebrate. Are you ready to go?"

She nodded yes and took Eliot's hand following her mother and father out to the limo.

They ate and chatted, and Eliot's eyes never left Emily's.

"Are you okay, honey?" Emily asked Eliot.

"I am fine, just proud to be your fellow," pausing. "I have to talk to you about something important."

"Well talk away," she waved her hands like in the ballet.

Eliot stood up at the table and looked into his suit

pocket finding the tiny box. He went down on one knee after holding one of Emily's hands tightly.

"Emily will you marry me and be my wife. I have loved you for so long I can't remember a day that I didn't. I will make you a good husband. I have already spoken to your father and he has given us his blessing."

"Eliot I take you as my husband, but only if you understand ballet is in my life forever," she was looking at him for his response.

"I would never want half of you, and ballet will be in both our lives for as long as you wish. I take that as a yes."

She nodded, "Yes!" he rose and kissed her in front of the whole restaurant that was clapping.

Imogene had not gone to the ballet. It was no use competing for her parents attention. Both her sisters had always had it. She ate to fill the void. She had all the magazines spread out in front of her.

They were all concerning weight loss. It was so depressing. Then she saw a guaranteed ad that would house you, and provide only health foods, and provide continuous exercising under doctor's supervision for one month.

"I am going to ask my daddy when he gets home from the skinny- minny's ballet." That's what she called Emily was skinny- minny, and she downed the rest of the bag of potato chips. "Lord knows if I will ever eat them again. If daddy says yes, I will be eating carrots. Yuck!" Then she chided herself. She wanted to lose weight, but could not on her own.

She was not her own cheerleader unless it was for

chocolate cake, and mama made the best. "Come on girl. Go get you another slice!"

"Okay, self I will!" she was smiling all the way to the refrigerator when in walks the group, home from the ballet. She frowns and places the cake back into the refrigerator, and walks out without speaking to anyone.

No one noticed because they were too busy talking about how much fun they had had at the restaurant, and about the magnificent performance that Emily had given.

It was a long while before her mother came up to say good- night to her. Her mother had always made time for Imogene.

Katherine asked if she had been practicing. The flute was the last thing on Imogene's mind tonight.

"Mama I have something to ask daddy, but I need to confide in you first," she swallowed hard and was summoning her courage.

"I want to go to this spa and she showed her mother the article. She almost said, "Fat Farm" but caught herself.

"It is the only way I am going to lose some weight and I know it. I am **FINALLY saying YES!**" she hugged her mother.

"Will you help me, mama to convince daddy? Please help me," and she began crying.

"They sat and talked about the pros and cons of staying on site at a spa facility. "I will help you do anything you want to do to make yourself healthy, but you have to do the work. Not for just one day, but for a month. If you do that, Daddy will be on board for anything else, you need to do. Is that something you are willing to commit to Imogene?"

Her mother had helped her with every program in that area, and they had all failed. Brigs had stopped the monies, "No more money Katherine, until she shows me that she is sincere."

Imogene went to the den and talked to her father. He agreed after seeing the tears. Imogene never cried in front of people always in her room behind closed doors. Both her sisters had boyfriends and she wanted one, too. She told her daddy this and that was the motivating fact, why he said yes.

He could see her pain. A father never wants to see their daughter in pain, especially if there is a solution.

"I will look into the spa and see if it legit, and what it's ratings are regarding fitness standards. I will confirm or deny it tomorrow by noon. Sound good?" Brigs asked.

"Oh daddy, thank you! Thank you! You are the best daddy in the world!" and she gave him a quick hug and went down to the kitchen with her mother. "He said yes!" and she fixed her a bowl of chocolate ice cream.

Her mother stared at her.

"It maybe my last and I am going to enjoy. Tomorrow I will buckle down!" and she smiled at her mother's frown.

"You had better hide it from your father or there will be no tomorrow," Katherine whispered to her daughter.

"I know, but I need it. Love you!" and Imogene was out of the kitchen. Sneaking around the den, and up the steps so quickly that she was out of breath.

Looking down at the ice cream, and then into the

mirror. She walked to her bathroom and poured the ice cream down the toilet, and flushed quickly. "Gone is my guilt. I take my life back."

She went to the computer and wrote an email to Anthony, the boy at church that she had been talking to about music.

"I maybe going out of town for a month to visit a family member, but I can still write you from her house. That is if you want me to?" Imogene typed.

Anthony wrote back one word, "Sure"

At seventeen and a half, this was the only boy whom she had ever conversed. Their relationship was purely platonic.

She hoped if she could lose some weight, she could take it to the next level. He was cute. He was neither fat nor skinny, so that is the size she would shoot for. In her mind he was perfect!

Brigs researched the Weight Loss Treatment Center in Los Angeles, and it was legit. He drove her to the location and went in with her.

She met doctors and psychiatrists, and she admitted she had an eating problem. She did not admit to depression or suicidal thoughts. She was weighed and oriented to the facility.

"I want the in-patient program, so I won't have access to my usual foods. I don't like going to a gym with all skinny people. Those are my only two reasons." These were the answers for them, but the real reason was Anthony.

When ask about her sexual activity, she said, "There has been none. No boyfriend. I hope to get one after this!"

The therapist named Rhonda Brink asked, if she was wanting to lose weigh for a boy. She answered, "Yes."

"This program has to be about YOU, doing it for yourself. Not for someone else. No program will work unless it is for yourself. Everything we teach will be about you, taking better care of you. Your choices about eating will be about you, learning how to cook for you. When you go out to eat, to make wise choices for you. When you exercise, it is for you."

When she came out to the waiting room, she was smiling at her father. "This place is all about me," and she hugged him.

"That's my girl! It is all about you, baby. When do you want to start this journey?" Brigs said smiling at his daughter that barely ever smiled. She was radiant.

"Tomorrow is what I told the lady. I have a list of what to bring. I am so happy. Thank you! Thank you!"

As they drove back, Imogene was a chatterbox and she was having quality time with her father which she had never had. Because her mother and two sisters always came first. She was glad it was the two of them. She loved her sisters, but like her therapist said, "It is all about you" and she was going to do that from this day forward.

"Be selfish" was her mantra, she told herself. From now on for a month, then I will re-evaluate. I just hope by then, I don't go back to thinking about everyone else.

She packed her needed items for her one month stay, and her mother and father went with her this time. That was a first. She had both their attentions. She said to herself this is going to work for me. If these two people believe in me, I am going to believe in myself for once.

The month was a struggle just to be away from her home for the first time in her life was scary. She worked on her food preps with young and old people that had her same problem. This made her feel less alone in her battle.

The exercise regimen was brutal, but she kept with it. She wrote her feelings out every day in a journal. The outpouring of her inner emotions was relieving the stress that use to cause her to eat and eat more. Now she would replace it with exercise and more exercise. At the end of the month, she had lost from 200 lbs to 170 lbs.

She begged her father to let her stay one more month. He agreed when he saw the weight she had lost and the happiness it had brought her.

At the end of two months, she was down to 140 lbs. Exactly where she wanted to be. She looked and felt amazing. She had no desire to be any smaller. Emily was 110 and looked like death warmed over, she told herself.

My sisters will not recognize me. She had gone on a shopping trip last week with her mother. Katherine had insisted. "The sweat pants have to go." Imogene smiled and said, "Anything you say, mama!" Her hair had been long and stringy. Her mother had the beautician layer it in a long bob. Short in the back and long in the front. When she shook her head, it fell back into place.

She could not believe this image was her. Then they went to the nail salon and had her first manicure / pedicure. "No colored polish, please mama! So she got the french nail that was perfect for her. She remembered her sisters doing this every month, but she would never go. Katherine said, "You and I will do this from now on, it will be our girls' day out!"

"Yes mama, OUR day to spend together," Imogene said.

She had wrote Anthony that she was coming home this weekend, and he said he would see her at church. When Sunday came. She walked in and sat in her usual place. He did not come, and he did not come. He text her that "There is a dumb girl siting in your seat."

She text him back. "That dumb girl is me!"

"NO way!" He wrote.

"Yes way! Come and sit beside me, that is if you want to!"

He sat down in two seconds and looked at her. Turned his head away, then back at her.

He said, "Hey beautiful what is your name?" Anthony was in shock, but had to be sure.

"Imogene, dummy!" and she smiled.

That's when he grabbed her hand, and held on as if the earth was moving. "I have talked to you every day for two months and you never once told me about this change in you. Why? Why didn't you share this with me?" he looked at her.

"I wanted to see if you like the old me or the new me," Imogene admitted.

"I like both of you, but now you may not want me," he said and looked at the minister that was frowning at them.

"Are you kidding me? I have wanted you for a

boyfriend since I was twelve! I do not want anyone else, silly!" and she looked at him.

His mouth was open and he said, "YOU want me!" pointing to himself. "Oh my goodness. You got me! You are my girl and don't you forget it!" and he squeezed her hand.

Her mother winked at her and her father said, "Ahem ahem" for her to be quiet in church.

She reached into her brand new Coach purse and pulled out a note pad. She wrote: "We can still talk, just write." Her hair falling forward, so only he could see her wink.

When she got home, the last thing on her mine was food!

CHAPTER FOUR

The wedding of the century was being planned. Emily Frances Porter and Eliot John Fairbanks. The ballerina theme was to continue throughout the ceremony.

Katherine had been working with Emily for the past two months that Imogene was gone. She decide to hire Ventura planners to do their magic at the reception.

Three hundred wedding guests converged at **Le Meridien Delfina Santa Monica** hotel on September 16. The altar was staged in the garden area with two huge urns on the either side of the altar. The urns were filled in four layers of flowers tapering to a top pedestal which held a large crystal BALLERINA. The flowers below the ballerina was of the brides favorite of Lilacs, White roses, and a bright, purplish Fuchsia flowers cascading down all four sides of each urn.

The brides bouquet was of these three flowers.

The white caned chairs were arranged in a V with the bridal path in the middle strewn with fuchsia petals. There was a white canopy overhead strung from the trees to cover the entire outdoor wedding party. Throughout the huge canape's edge were tiny rows of crystals hanging at various lengths to the ground. The wedding party was engulfed by this magical cascade of crystal waterfall.

Emily wore a simple Vera Wang white strapless with a flowing silk small train to the floor. She was tall at five feet nine and if she wore three inch heels, she would tower over Eliot. So she chose ballerina walking shoes, instead.

The long veil was attached to crystal and pearls that were interwoven into a tiara style with a tiny diamond teardrop in the middle of her forehead.

Her long mossy hair was piled high and exposed her long gorgeous neck. Both her ears had double piercings and tiny stud diamonds made her green eyes sparkling. Her make- up was dramatic. It was applied the same for any of her dance performances.

She chose not to wear a necklace. "I think that would be too much, mama. Katherine finally agreed with her daughter.

Eliot was six foot and wore a black Armani tuxedo with tails and white shirt and fuchsia bow-tie. He looked like a Greek god to Emily. His curly hair was blonde and he had hazel eyes with a aquiline nose and stern jaw.

He chose Cameron to be his best man. Emily had chosen Elizabeth as her Maid of Honor. Elizabeth wore a fuchsia long strapless flowing gown that took Cameron's breath away. He wore an Armani black tuxedo without tails.

Eliot's knees nearly buckled when he saw his bride walking down the aisle with her father. He closed his eyes and looked at Cameron and it was an unspoken, "I can't believe this."

Officiating was Brigs cousin Trevor Alexander Porter and they were pronounced man and wife and he kissed the bride.

Edward Fairbanks shook Bridgeston Porter's hand, "That daughter of yours is one beautiful bride. Simply stunning!"

Brigs said, "That son of yours is a very handsome groom."

Their wives Katherine and Edith said, "They are going to have beautiful babies. Why don't we go in and find our seat at the dining table. The pictures are done and its on the ninth floor in the ballroom. The elevators will soon be real busy."

The ballroom was set up with white table clothes and a small bouquet of the same three flowers on each table. There were golden cane chairs with gold flatware around the tables' china. One side of the room had the seven layer cake with the same three flowers done in sugar confection on each layer. The top had a groom holding the hand of a Ballerina.

The couple came in and stood while toasts were made and Champagne glasses clinked. They feasted on seafood which was the bride and groom's choice and all had cake.

The bouquet was thrown and Imogene caught it and looked at Anthony who had caught the garter.

Katherine looked at Brigs and he smiled and whispered into her ear. "Mother we soon are going to have that whole house to ourselves."

Katherine said, "Sounds delightful to me!" and Brigs took a large swig of his brandy.

Brigs asked, "Katherine are you okay?"

Katherine said, "I think I have had one too many," and giggled.

"Sit down dear and let me get you some coffee. Oh Waiter!"

Imogene had eaten no cake and very little seafood and Anthony did the same. All he could do was stared at the garter that he had put on his arm.

He said to Imogene, "I hope one day you will wear this garter on your leg for me," and he smiled.

"Anthony are you proposing to me?" Imogene asked and drop her head so her new hairstyle would cover her eyes.

"Look at me, Imogene. I have no ring. but I am asking you to be my wife?" Anthony said.

"You haven't even kissed me, isn't that a little backwards?" Imogene asked.

"Are you saying no?" Anthony looked at the door.

"No, I am saying you may not like the way I kiss or feel. I want to know you like me romantically."

"I have tried to be a gentleman but there comes a time when a man's gotta do what a man's gotta do. Walk with me out that door to the elevator."

Imogene walked out the door with him into the elevator, and he kissed her very soul. She had never been kissed but she did what the movies showed, and grabbed his neck. He could not let go until the elevator stopped, and they were breathless as the doors opened. She **FINALLY said YES!**

He was fighting for control and took her hand, and walked her to the lounge outside, and asked her again.

"Yes, we do have chemistry," and she played it cool. He was the one that was having a big big problem.

"You do realize, I am about to explode?" he asked.

"I haven't the foggiest what you are talking about," she was going to play it naive so he would explain.

"Will you ride home with me?" he was needing to explain a few other things to her.

"I guess it will be okay. Let me find mother and I will get back with you. Just sit here and be comfortable!"

She knew exactly what she was doing and it felt good to be in control. Her new dress was the off one shoulder style with fuchsia flowers. Her new figure was on display, several boys had winked at her, and she had looked for Anthony, to see if he had seen them.

The three inch heels were killing her feet, but this is the way other girls had to pay the price. New blisters on both heels.

She finally found her mother and father, they said it would be fine. She text Anthony to come and get her that it was okay. No way was she walking all the way back there, and having to walk to the car, too.

He text her to go to the front of the hotel, and he would get the car and pick her up there. When he got there two boys were talking to her, and she was laughing. He was not a happy camper when she got in.

Then she took her shoes off, and rested her feet in his lap touching his bulge. All was forgiven. "OMG I may have a wreck any minute!"

"Please don't, mother and father would never let me go out with you again. Let alone marry you. I'll take my feet back, if they are bothering you."

"Don't you dare move those feet. They are mine. You said, Yes. Right?" He was looking at the road and then at her. All he could see was her hair in her eyes, but she was licking her lips. That was unnerving him more.

He sped up and she moved her toes. "You are killing me and we are pulling over." stopping at the rest stop. He did not want to be on the shoulder of the road. Her parents could come by and see them.

"Imogene, do you love me?" Anthony asked.

"Would I say I would marry you, if I didn't?" she asked.

He was kissing her shoulder and feeling of her buttocks and she was for once feeling things, she had never felt before.

"Oh Anthony what is happening here because I have never been with anyone, and you know it!" she was holding him close and not letting this new sensation die.

"I need you!" Please!" he was taking her panties off and rubbing everywhere.

Then he unzipped and began a feeling inside her that was unexplainable to her. He leaned and picked her up. No one had ever pick her up. "You are so strong. What do I do Anthony?"

"Just hold me tight and I will do the rest. Oh S---t. I am not going to do this. if you don't want me to. Just say it!'

She kissed him with all her might as he did the most

wonderful thing. "People say it hurts, but to me it feels so good," that was all he needed to hear. She had hurt for so long not having anyone that this was amazing.

"I want to stay here all night and make love to you, but your parents are going to shoot me, if I don't take you home."

"Don't stop loving me!" She was tearful and her beautiful large breasts were out of the top of her dress and the flowery dress was up to her crotch.

"One more," and he closed his eyes and loved her in a slow not rushed way that had her moving.

"Baby yes!" and then it happened for her and her mouth flew open. He was going slower, and he had himself inside her, and she was wanting more,

"I need all of you Anthony. It is big, I can take it." Then she could speak no more. Just shudders for both of them. That extra made them climaxed at the same time.

"This is what we will do every night after we marry. I love you, Imogene. You and I will learn more about sex, but first we got to get married. You are eighteen right now and I am twenty- one. Do you want to go tonight and get married or tomorrow? Or do you want a big wedding like your sister?"

"I want you and no big wedding. You are my man. You decide," that ought make him happy to be in charge. Her flowery dress was being rubbed. She was rubbing his back.

"I can't let you go! I saw those two chatting you up at the hotel door tonight. That is my biggest fear, you will latch on to someone, and they will hurt you. You have no idea what men are thinking. I say this because I would kill anyone, if they touch you. We need to find a room," he decide for them.

"You know my daddy will have the police out looking for us," she had to say the truth.

"Then I'll take you home. I'll come back for you tomorrow. You are right," he admitted.

"I do think that is wise," and she sat up and put her feet in his lap as he drove her home. He was rubbing her feet, then her legs and upward, and he stopped the car again.

"I'm addicted to you already," and they went around the world again before getting to her house.

She walked in and went to bed happier than she had ever been in her life.

The next morning she did not eat, she went running with her headset on. She was going to get a run in and then talk to Anthony.

He could not get her on the phone, so he was going to her house and see what was going on.

As he rounded the curve, he saw her jogging. She was not noticing that traffic was near her. He turned and followed her to keep someone from running over her. She had her headset on. He saw that was why she was paying him no mind. When the road was straight, he pulled up beside her and finally got her attention.

"Have you lost your mind!" he shouted.

"What a thing to say!" she was shocked.

"Get in," he ordered.

"I will not!" no way was she going to be talked to like that.

"I am sorry!" and a truck almost hit Anthony, so she got in.

"I thought we agreed to get married today and you are out here about to get killed in front of my very eyes! It scared the hell out of me." He really was shaking.

"I forget this is a rural road. It is not like the city. Where I could jog every day, and did for two months. This is what I have to do to keep the weight off. Do you understand how important that is to me?"

"I hoped getting married would be more important. Promise me, if you jog that you don't have your ears plugged up. A car can hit you. Someone could come up behind you and you would never know until they knocked you out, and dragged you into the woods." He had his head in his hands.

"I see why you were upset. I'm okay now take me home so I can get dressed. I have my bag packed," Imogene smiled.

"When we get married will you take me jogging every day, and watch my back side," she was licking those lips again.

"Stop or I cannot come in … I'll just drive around and when you are ready text me!" Anthony said.

She said, "I'll be smelling so goood."

"Get out before I take you down the road and have my way with you," he said and winked.

"I sure hope so!" she said and he drove off.

Her mother met her at the door, "Wasn't that Anthony?"

"Yeah, he wants me to go to lunch with him," she said. "I told him I stunk and needed a shower, then I'd let him know."

"You go and have a good time. He is such a nice boy!" her mother said and went into the kitchen.

Imogene went and showered and put on one of the new outfits her mother had bought her. Her mother loved dresses and this one had a simple scoop neck. It was yellow and periwinkle plaid, and fit like a glove. The length was just above the knee, but would rise mid thigh to tease Anthony.

She had put on her yellow lacy bra and matching panties. She had shaved her legs and put lotion on them, and slipped her feet into yellow calfskin sandal heels. Her mother did coordinate her outfits to a tee. She had packed five gorgeous outfits and one pair sexy baby doll pajamas. Two pair of shoes and two pocketbooks.

"These will hold me until I get a job," she said to herself. She laughed, "Yeah right! A flutist position … sure!"

She'd flip burgers to be with him. OH no! I cannot be around food. She was always saying that mantra.

As soon as mother left for the market, she was going to leave. She had found her birth certificate and had asked Anthony to find his.

She was ready and called him. He had his certificate in the car's glove compartment, he told her.

He could not believe she was his. "You look delicious.

Come here and let me taste." Her perfume sucked him in and his hands were roaming. Her hair smelled like coconut.

"We need to get the show on the road or MY mom may turn back around because she is always forgetting something."

That's when he got everything in the trunk. Her clothes and his clothes, all their belongings were secure.

As they are driving down the road talking and planning where they will live. A large tanker came around the curve and hit them. They were both killed instantly.

Her mother had indeed turned around, she forgot her list. She saw a huge ball of fire go up in the air from a distance. The closer she got. She saw the fire truck, police cars, and then her heart stopped.

She saw them trying to revive her daughter with CPR. She saw a white sheet over a boy on the ground. She knew it was Anthony. The tanker truck had blown up after they had got the two people out of the car, she was told. The firemen were working hard and another firetruck was arriving to put the blaze out. Cars were being rerouted.

It was like a bad movie that was happening in slow motion.

The EMS said, "We knew she was gone, but we had to try for you Mrs Porter. We have called your husband." Everyone knew everyone in these parts.

She was numb unable to move. She sat on the ground and held her Imogene until Brigs got there. Rocking back and forth, as she did when she was a baby.

Everything they had done together since her birth was flashing before Katherine's eyes.

It seemed like years before Brigs got there.

"Okay mother. I'm here. They have to take her now. These men will take good care of her. She turned and there was a coroner and a rehearse, and she fainted.

She was in shocked and the EMS arranged for the ambulance to take her to the hospital because neither parent could drive.

Phillip and Bart met them at the hospital. Katherine had come to and the doctor ordered her a sedative. She was resting in the private room. Bart was talking to Brigs, and Brigs was not listening.

He was feeling overwhelmed with grief and grabbed Bart's hand. "Tell Elizabeth, no tell Cameron first. Then call Eliot so he can tell Emily. I need to stay with Katherine, and we will make the arrangements soon."

Bart said, "We will handle it for you. Call me, if you need anything else." and he hugged his brother and Phillip hugged his uncle.

Brigs and Katherine could not go home and drive down that road where their daughter had died. They left the hospital and went to the Fairmont Miramar Hotel. No way could they go home. It would be a parade of people so until they could come to grips. They would talk with the funeral home by phone. They just wanted to be alone.

Brigs told Bart where they were, "If the the girls want to come here that is fine because they will not want to go home either."

"I will tell them. I am here for you," Bart hung up.

"Phillip I am going to depend on you to look after the business. I got to be there for Brigs and your mother will need to be there for Katherine," and he hung up.

Phillip called Martina and told her.

He called Edward Fairbanks and asked if they had heard from Emily and Eliot. He said they are on their way back from Hawaii. "They will call you when they get here."

He called Cameron and asked how Elizabeth was doing and told them that they could go to the Hotel tomorrow, but don't go tonight."

"You can stay there Cameron, if Elizabeth wants to. Brigs has a tab there. Do not worry about the cost. Brian will let you off work, I have spoken to him," Phillip said.

"Thank you. I'll see what she wants to do," Cameron said.

Phillip went home and hugged his wife a little bit tighter and kissed his child. Then burying his head in Martina's open arms. As she held him tight to her breast, she felt him sobbing.

She herself was having flashbacks of losing her own child and knew first hand what Katherine was feeling this night.

CHAPTER FIVE

The funeral was somber and no dry eyes were at the visitation. Everyone had been touched by this tragedy.

Anthony's parents had a letter from him the day the accident happened that told them how much he loved Imogene and that they were on their way to get married.

The Porters had a similar letter from Imogene. So they were buried side by side in the Porters's family plot.

Cynthia had become a blessing to Katherine and she told her that, "We have had our differences, but I don't know what I would have done with out you." She hugged her and said, "You would have done the same for me. Are you ready to go home yet?"

"I will never be ready. Brigs and I are going to buy a house on the beach far up the coastline, so I will have no reminders. When the girls come home. It will be new and no memories in the new house. I'm having the moving company to come in this week after we sign. As I unpack I will know where I want things, and whom I want to have certain things," Katherine held her head high and Cynthia had sat and listened for once without interrupting.

"Whatever helps you heal, I am glad you and Brigs

came to an agreement. We will only be a couple of miles apart and I will come when you need a friend. I will be there."

Three years ago they were archenemies. Time sometimes changes people for the better or worst.

Elizabeth told Cameron, "I could not have made it through without you."

He held her and they looked out into the pasture at FANATIC STRETCH grazing. She laid back on his chest and he rubbed her growing tummy. She had been to the doctor and it was confirmed that she was pregnant.

Through all the chaos, these two had been given the words that made their hearts sing. She turned and said, "We will be parents and settled in our own home before the baby comes. I want it to be only joy when we do. If it is a girl I want to call her Joy. What do you think?" Elizabeth asked.

"I think you are my joy and our child will be a joy. Any other name would not be as fitting. If a boy. We'll call him Heracles!" and he lifted her and kissed her.

"We most certainly will not?" Elizabeth said. "Cameron, Jr sounds much better!" and was leaving the area quickly because he was running after her. She would let him catch her when they got in the house and in their bedroom.

He was through training FS for the day. His wife was still training him to come hither when she was in need. Boy did she need him after this week. It reinforced, "Never to take a day for granted."

"Love each day as if it was your last day on earth," he said.

"You are going to make that my mantra," Elizabeth was rising to met him in the heat of passion that was so intense that they could not stop.

"Please say it! Oh so good!" she had thrown her head back quivering. He held still, and then began again until they both were sated.

She moaned, "You make everything right again. I love the way you love me."

She kissed him. They had not been intimate like this since before the funeral.

Elizabeth told him, "It is almost sacrilegious to be so happy. They will never have this happiness," referring to Imogene and Anthony.

Cameron told her, "They are together in paradise and their love is eternal."

That had melted her heart and she knew he was right. He had breathed life back into their marriage.

Emily was not as fortunate. Eliot was trying to be strong. His wife did not want to be blissfully happy. They had no sex on the first day only long travel time, and then one painful coupling in Hawaii. "It will get better," Eliot promised.

"This is not what I want you to do to me. It was awful so stay away from me!" Her anger was not a Eliot. It was really about her sister and Anthony. Her anger was at Anthony, if he had not taken her sister away from her, she could be happy.

Imogene had been the one that had put Emily on a

pedestal, and encouraged her when she was down after an intense ballet practice. She had always been at the house. She never went anywhere. She was like Emily's personal sounding board.

Now Emily had no one, and all Eliot wanted to do was have stupid sex. What is wrong with me?" she asked herself.

"No way, can I talk to my mom, Eliot! I am sorry. I am having major problems here," and pointed to her chest.

He was young and immature. He did not understand why she was NOT wanting to have sex. "Is it me, you abhor?"

Emily ran to him and wrapped herself around him. "It is me and I made an appointment with a therapist."

"A sex therapist?" he was fuming and clinching his fists.

"Yes, and SHE will help us, I promise!" Emily kissed him.

"That sounds good to me. Do I get to join in?" he asked and his eyes were widening while he waited for her answer.

"I don't know. If you know what is good for you, you will wipe that smile off your face. How would you like it if I said, I want to have sex with a male therapist? HUH How do you like them apples?"

"I wouldn't! I would crush him with my bare hands!" he was sexually deprived, and not taking the clue that she needed professional help. Then it dawn on him and he held her.

"Whatever it takes to make you love me, again. We will do it, BUT we do it together. Agreed?" Eliot stated.

"Agreed," she stood and let him hold her for a long time.

She said, "I need to practice. I am going to the basement." They were staying with his parents and they had no home of their own. Another angry point, she could not go home. Her mother would tell her when her clothes arrives at the beach.

The ballet exercises settled her nerves and she was exhausted when she showered. Eliot got in with her, he said, "We don't have to do anything. I just want to be with you, and gaze at your beautiful body." He held her.

"You my husband need to be happy. I will make you happy."

"Shh we have forever!" he moaned.

The following week, they went for their first session. The therapist wanted to talk to them together, and get a history.

They were comfortable with their middle aged sex therapist.

Emily said, "Thank goodness, she is not young!"

Eliot said, "Thank God, she is not old!"

They cuddled and talked more this evening than they had in a long while.

Eliot said, "We can stop at any time. You do not need to feel pressured to do this," and he rubbed her aching feet. She was still the principal ballerina and that was pressure in itself.

"I want to continue to learn and make you happy." Emily held his face and said. "I love you."

He was wanting her badly as always. He withdrew when he kissed her, and she bristled.

"Can I just touch you and you can touch me? Nothing more than that," Eliot asked.

"Most married couples don't have to ask. It must be exasperating for you. I just don't know why, I am the way that I am," Emily cried on his shoulder.

She was so strong in all other areas. Well disciplined and compassionate, and highly intelligent. They lay in bed and felt of each others. She would gasp, if he touched her. She had no qualms about touching him.

The weeks went by and a subject had cause a severe reaction from Emily. Her therapist asked if she had ever been raped? She finally said, "Yes … when I was eight. My dance instructor whom is dead now. It was frightening. I never told anyone. Not mother, father nor you," looking at her husband.

He was clinching his jaw, and his fist hit the table. Not violently, but firm enough to release some anger that this is WHY. She would not be intimate with him since the wedding night that had caused her pain.

"Do you associate sex with pain?" her therapist asked. She did not want to go into the graphic details for her patient to relive what had happened to her at an early age. Just admitting it to her therapist and her husband meant, she trusted them BOTH.

"Yes, Eliot would never intentionally hurt me. It is that I know he is expecting me to be sexually active, and

I can't seem to let go. Can you teach me to please him. That is my goal?"

"Eliot how do you feel about that?" the therapist asked.

"I want her to feel comfortable and enjoy sex with me. Whatever it takes, I am okay with it." He smiled at Emily, "She has been my girlfriend for all these years. I have always wanted only her. Maybe I am doing something wrong?"

"These things you two are telling me, are normal for a rape victim to feel. Yes, Emily and yes Eliot, we three can work on making you both enjoy sex. It will require total confidence in me. I will be your teacher. We will have a private room where you can be intimate, and I will be in the room. I will give you instructions, and give you homework assignments. You both are to report your feelings good and bad. We go over what we need to change, and I can give you different assignments as we progress. My goal is for you two to become a loving couple. How does that sound?" both were agreeable.

When leaving Emily was smiling more and she said, "I have had a weight lifted. I feel like she is really going to help us."

Eliot was glowing, "You are the strongest person I have ever known, and we will get through this. You make me want to be strong for you. I will never hurt you, my love." He had a new understanding. He really thought it was her sister's death that was the cause of her withdrawal. Now that he knew this new piece of the puzzle, he could definitely be more patient.

She was looking forward to their visits. The sessions were longer because they talked first. Then undressed and explored each others' erotic zones.

The therapist showed Eliot where Emily's zones were. Then she showed Emily where Eliot's were. She never touched either client, but ask them to do the touching. Eliot could feel Emily responding in a way that was turning him on big time. The assignment was to continue touching without intercourse. "Emily is not ready yet the therapist told Eliot. The wait will be worth it, young man."

By the end of the first month Emily was writhing, and Eliot was becoming more experienced at it each time. He could get her gasping and thrusting to be near him faster. She'd let her head fall back as he slowly felt her, she was not dry as before. Now moist and inviting.

Emily was instructed to knead and gently squeeze him and run her hands up and down his shaft. She did and he was also moist. "This is called foreplay. You two practice and practice. When she wants you to come in ...go slow Eliot and withdraw four or five times and when she says "Help me!"

"Emily you must tell him THIS phrase! If you want him to pleasure you, he will not know because his mind is scattered at that point. Do you both know your assignments," she looked from one to the other.

"Then let nature take its course, and enjoy each other! Bring me a good report card when you make it to the summit. This is the last session. You both have all the necessary tools. If you should need my help, just give me a call. I am so proud of both of my students. Now get dressed."

When they got home they both went to the bedroom, and stripped, and again began the foreplay taught. It was more intense and she was begging, "Help me!" Eliot did as the doctor said and withdrew until Emily was clawing, and raising her pelvis to met him. He grasp her hips and threw his head backwards. He went slowly and started counting until she shuttered. Then her spasms where sucking him in, and he lunged one time.

Emily said "Help me!" and they both were on the magic carpet ride to the stars, and it went on and on. Eliot was amazed at his wife. She was happy with her performance. She called it, "Our dance of love!" and smiled brightly.

When showering Emily said, "Send Doc some flowers!"

Eliot did and the card read:

FINALLY … YES!
Emily & Eliot

CHAPTER SIX

The moving van was arriving any minute. Katherine was on edge, but she had Cynthia by her side and willed herself to relax.

The girls, Emily and Elizabeth would be here this morning to help. Each room's furnishings and its remaining clothes were labeled on the boxes.

The new house had the same amount of rooms and the space was identical. This beach house had no memories. They would make new memories in this beautiful house by the ocean.

Cynthia knew exactly where Katherine wanted everything. Katherine hugged her and thanked her for all she was doing.

Emily came first with Eliot bringing a housewarming gift of white roses. They were her mother's favorite.

Then Elizabeth and Cameron came bringing a bottle of Brandy which was her father's favorite.

Brig's and Bart were at the outdoor grill. The two young men joined them. They were going to cook on the grill while the women went through the boxes and decorated the house.

Katherine wanted the girls to pick items from Imogene's room that were special to them. Then she would choose some pictures, but the rest would be stored in a trunk with her flute in the attic.

"I want this house to be a new beginning for all of us. Only good memories for us to enjoy each other and our grand-children. The past will only be talked about once a year. We as a family I hope all agree, to go with Brigs and I, to the cemetery on her death date. To celebrate her life not her death. Now we will finish the unpacking, and then we will eat by the ocean."

"Well said, dear!" and Brigs raised his glass for a toast to his wife's speech. All raised their goblets and clinked, drank and began to chat.

The women completed their tasks, some with tears and some with laughter. The house was a skeleton this morning. When they sat to eat, it was warm and beautiful. The objects from their past were in their rightful places.

The ocean breeze cooled their overworked bodies. The moonlight shimmered over the water. As if Imogene and Anthony were looking down on them and blessing this gathering. They would never be forgotten.

The family enjoyed this feast and new memories were made. Katherine kissed Brigs, and told them all that they were welcome to spent the night, but no one could because of work schedules.

All hugs and kisses were exchanged after the outdoor area was cleaned, and they departed for their homes with today's good memories going with them.

Brigs and Katherine sat and watched the tide roll in and out.

They sat for hours without a word.

Just relaxing after a long day of emotional and physical hard work was over. They held hands and walked on the beach.

Brigs said, "This day was what we needed. Now let's go in and get some much needed rest. You are amazing! I love you more each day."

"And I love you!"

Phillip and Martina had the family in their thoughts that night. They decided not to go because the brothers needed that special time. Martina told Phillip that it was bringing up memories of Gabriella, and she didn't think she would be able to cope very well.

"These hormones are raging," and she growled at him.

He was smiling and said, "Let then rage all over me!" They had found out that she was pregnant again. It would be three months before they would know the sex of this baby.

Phillip said, "I can put her to bed if you want me to?" and began rubbing her tummy.

She said, "We'll see after you put your son in the bathtub while I do the dishes." She rubbed her hands all over his chest and bit his neck.

"Oh ... It's on!" he said to Martina. Quickly picking up his toddler and racing to the bathtub. Adam was flying through the air on the end of his father's arms saying, "Airplane dada!" and giggling.

After a long day at the law firm covering for his father

and uncle, Phillip always came home to his wife and child with new energy. They gave him new life.

Inside his heart he could not imagine life without them.

He said to Martina, "No day will I live without my family knowing how much I love them because tomorrow is not promised!"

"That I promise to you also, my Buttercup!" and they made mad passionate love and fell asleep holding on to each other.

Bart shared the previous day's happening with his son.

"That house was the best thing that Brigs did for Katherine and himself. I was skeptical when he said he was going to move out there, but son now I see why."

"Dad are you saying you want to move to the beach?" and Phillip curled his lip.

"No, heaven forbid! Can you see your mother with sand in her home. She cringes when I don't wipe my feet here. A grain of dirt in her house makes her crazy!" and he chuckled.

Phillip simply said, "Good!" and shuffled his morning briefs for court.

"Besides we have to be near our grandchildren. Yes, Martina told your mother that she is pregnant again and the woman has been on cloud nine."

Bart handed his son one of his Cuban cigars, "Congratu-lations!"

Phillip said, "Dad I don't smoke, you know that!"

"I know ... but the judge does and you may need to bribe him today!" and he frowned.

"That's funny! I don't like that look you are giving me. What do you know that I don't know?" Phillip asked.

"The man is guilty and you will get him off Scot -free," his father said.

"That's what I get paid to do and so do you. There is something else. What do you know that I don't?" Phillip was getting riled because his father never questioned his judgment before.

"He is brother to the man that killed Imogene. He is a drunk and may kill my grandchild in a wreck in the future that is, if he gets off today. You chew on that and decide. I am in rare form this morning. I'm going to work on some foreclosures and bite my tongue," and he walked to his office and closed the door.

At nine court was in session. The dockets were read and Larson's name was called.

"Your Honor may I approach the bench?" Phillip requested.

"I have to withdraw myself from this case because of a personal conflict. My former client has been given notice and needs a continuation to find himself another lawyer." Phillip waited for the judge's response.

"I have been informed of the situation by your father and understand fully," the judge stated.

He pounded his gavel, "Continuation granted. Mr. Larson you will need to find a lawyer before your next court appearance. Is that clear?"

Mr Larson was sneering at the judge but answered, "Yes!" He turned and gave Phillip an evil look saying, "I'll get you for this!" and walked out.

Phillip looked at his paralegal Jason and asked, "Did you him threaten me?"

Jason said, "Affirmative."

"Then get anyone else that may have heard it, their names and date and time. Record it for future reference. I may not need it, but I like to be prepared with this nut case on the loose," Phillip said.

Jason replied, "Will do, boss!"

Matt Larson was owner of the oil company whose oil tanker had exploded. He was wealthy and thought he could buy himself out of everything. He was not only a heavy drinker, he had another problem. He was known to dabble in cocaine for recreational purposes.

Following his large parties, Phillip's firm got plenty of business. From DUI s, drug abuse users and traffickers, just to name a few. These cases followed all of Larson's parties.

It made Phillip sick to his stomach to think Imogene had been killed due to the drunk driver of Larson's oil tanker. He was not injured. He jumped out of the truck after impact and had not a scratch on him. Didn't seem fair. "Thank goodness father reminded me," he said to himself.

In the past he would not have given it another thought to defend such a creep, but now that he had children of his own, it did matter.

He was going to speak to the DA and if she needed assistance, he would be glad to help. Brenda Faircloth was now the new DA. She had the best interest of the community in mind, and wanted a conviction for Larson real bad.

Phillip continued with the rest of his clients on the docket and went home to his loving family.

Martina couldn't figure out why her husband was brooding so tonight. Something was wrong and she was going to get to the bottom of it.

"Counselor their seems to be a problem. Do you want to talk to me or do I have to use my detective skills," she leaned against the sink while he was shaving.

She had dressed in her cocktail dress because they were going to a function at the country club, and Cynthia and Bart had the baby.

"It's nothing to concern your pretty little head about," he smiled and wiped the remainder of shaving cream off his neck. He knew she was fixing to inspect him. She like for him to look good when they went out.

"You can't fool me. Remember I know you personally," and she put her arms around his neck. In her heels, she was nose to nose with him.

"It's Matt Larson. I dropped his case. He's not a happy camper and has me on his list. You and Nancy keep your noses out of anything to do with him. Promise!" Phillip said.

"You got it mister! Glad you told me because his secretary called me this afternoon, and wanted to hire us to follow his wife. Seems she has been two timing Mr Larson, or is she just saying that. I'll tell her no dice tomorrow," Martina said frowning.

"Yep, he is already messing with the wrong person.

Me!" he was furious. He grabbed Martina and held her tight.

Martina said, "Buttercup, let's stay home tonight!"

"What and hide from that monster. No way!" swatting her on her butt cheek.

"Careful you know I am with child. MY baby likes to be rocked, but not spanked," licking her lips. She was going to keep him home tonight. She was on a mission.

She bent over and said looking over her shoulder, "Maybe ooh la la spanking is what I need."

He was behind her lifting her sexy dress, and there was no more thoughts of going out this night. Except to get the baby later, way later when they were completely sated.

PART FIVE

CHAPTER ONE

The horse was galloping around the last stretch at an unbelievable time. Cameron was beside himself with pride.

He had clocked FANATIC STRETCH at a time that matched the last derby record. The intense training had paid off.

Elizabeth was in her last trimester and could not get on the fence rail to watch. She stood leaning on it and smiling. She raised both hands as the horse crossed the finish line, "I knew it! I knew he would do it for you!" she was rubbing her belly and Cameron came to her.

"Are you okay honey?" he was concerned because she was grimacing.

"Feel of this! Then you will see what your son is doing to me!" and she made another face. She put his hand in the spot where the baby was kicking.

"Dang! That is a horse kicking in there ... No he is a kick- boxer for sure. Wow! That was a good one! Let me calm him," and he rubbed the spot until the baby was calm and no longer kicking.

"You can calm FS and our child. You are my hero!

Now go see about FS. I will be waiting for you. We need to go over to the house when you get through," Elizabeth said.

He nodded and off he went to rub the horse down and give him his treat which was always an apple. If Cameron forgot,

FS would kick the side of his stall like a spoiled brat.

Elizabeth was so excited because they were in their new house. They were working on the nursery. The house had been built on her father's property nearer to Brian's than her parents. That way Cameron had no problem getting to work on time, or getting home on time for dinner.

He could see when he got home how much work Elizabeth had done today. "It looks great. You have outdone yourself."

She had ordered the blue plaid bedding and bumper pads, and a rocking horse. She had been working on the solid blue curtains with her mother. She was forbidden to hang them herself, so tonight he promised to do it.

The crib was dark cherry wood, and had a matching chest of drawers. The top of an old desk she had as a child was just the height for a changing table. Her father had stained it the dark cherry and engraved it 'Beth's Stand'.

The women had gathered last week, and one was sewing a diaper bag hanger to coordinate with the bedding. Katherine had her handyman to install shelving, and a wooden wall plaque which she attached the diaper bag that held two dozen diapers. "You don't want to be bending over in the beginning."

Everything was coming together. They had not gone to get a chair yet because Elizabeth wanted Cameron to help. Also to see what he would be most comfortable in. "You will be rocking the baby as much as myself," she smiled.

"I'd like that. A real rocker not a prissy glider!" he stated firmly.

"Okay my cowboy wants a rocker to rock me and the baby in. It is fine with me!" Elizabeth grinned.

"Oh you wanna be rocked, do you?" he was grabbing her up and toting her to their bedroom.

"Put me down! We have work to do," she pouted and he did. Then she said, "You smell of horse. When I bathe you that might just change my mind." He started stripping down and she was helping him.

He had been working out so with FS that his muscles were larger, and his abdomen was showing a true six-pack. She was exploring every inch of him.

"When I have this baby and get my shape back, I'm going to have some of these," kissing his stomach and touching his abs.

"Stop or I won't have bathed," Cameron said.

"No need, I want to get dirty NOW!" She was undressed and lying on the baby's floor looking up at him. They made the most incredible love.

After both were out of breath, "Guess I showed you!" he said.

"Nah I planned it this way! Just to see if you would want me enough to do it anywhere. I'd said you still love me. As I get bigger, don't stop making it exciting!" Elizabeth teased.

She grabbed his hand and led him to their new sunken tub.

"As long as you don't get in this thing without me. You could slip and fall. Now down baby down baby," she sat down in the bubbly water that she had drawn before he got home.

"I promise to always have your hand when I do this and that and," Elizabeth was making him moan again.

"You are an enchantress, and I am in no way complaining."

"The race is coming up. May 2nd is opening night and the Derby is on the 6th. Candice do you have all your outfits lined up?" Colten asked.

He was anxious and she knew it. "Yes darling! I have all my bags packed and I have shopped for you, too. You do realize the man's outfits are a reflection on his wife. You will look so handsome and stylish," she wiggled up to him.

"I am not wearing no clown outfits," Colten was frowning.

"The movies stars do darling, and you are my movie star!" Candice was going to have to tie him down to get those key lime green slacks on him, and she laughed.

He grabbed her and lifted her into the air and marched to the bedroom. She had her red teddy on, and it was distracting his train of thought.

"This is serious business. I can't be distracted. You

do understand I have a fortune tied up in this horse, don't you?"

She nibbled his neck and smiled as she licked his lips.

"Yes you have told me that from day one so show me how much I am worth to you," he was peeling the lingerie off her slender body. As she was undressing him, unzipping and fondling, and pushing him onto the bed.

Where she climbed on him, he was ready and she rode like a cowgirl, and then stopped. "Oh my you are uptight, and I am so loving it."

He grabbed her buttocks, "Don't stop. Finish this race. I need you so bad!" and he was bucking her until she was making whimpering sounds as he flipped her.

"You are mine now! Take me, if you can?" she raised her hips to meet him at full steam. They had never done anything at leisure, it was always like a race with time to see who could get the other to climax first. This night, they were equal.

It was the same spontaneous coupling of pleasure. The same gratification for both. They knew that they were equally matched in every way. Strength of will and determination to satisfy their partner entirely.

"You are a billion dollar thoroughbred my precious Candice and you know it! I will never get tired of making you purr. You are in my very soul. I feel the life of me slipping away and pure ecstasy rejuvenates my body until I want you again."

"I know my love I feel you pulsing, and I am a good wife that wants it all! Every time you need me, I will be there. We are so lucky."

"Lucky Nell threw us together. Be still so I can breathe. Oh God you are amazing. You are blowing my mind."

He had her head in his hands as she was kissing and reviving his libido to the point of him slamming her to the wall to enter her. Waiting for her to breathe and she wrapped her long legs around him and held his head that was sucking her breast.

"I can't wait for you this time baby," Candice said and she was gasping and over the moon.

One more stroke and he was quivering in her body, "Oh baby! It is okay. I'm … I'm right behind you." Then they fell together on the bed.

"You're the best," she sucked his neck.

He said, "No you are the best!" and wiped the sweat from her forehead, glazing into her eyes and then he tucked her hair behind her ear.

"Now that I have your attention. I have booked the presidential suite at the Louisville Marriott Downtown and two hospitality suites. Does that sound good?"

"Heavenly, but two suites extra?" she had a puzzled expression on her face.

"One for Cameron and Elizabeth, and one for Brian and his two helpers. Oh my!" he stared at her. "You thought I was going to use them all for us?" he asked. She shrugged her shoulders and nodded her head yes.

"You do have a big appetite, but I don't want to draw attention to us. One will have to do, and it is a bigggg room. We will have many options. If we need more room, we will find every available space in that room. I will need you bad ... every day this tension is killing me. I never get this nervous about business. FANATIC STRETCH is our horse, honey!"

She was smiling at him and batting her eyelashes, "So he's now my horse, too! That is the first time you have included me. I am a happy woman. I may let you wear a pair of my thong panties for good luck. They'll look good with that PINK shirt that I got you," and she wiggled out of bed and ran to the bathroom in strides.

He was after her, and grabbed her. "You are kidding me. Right?" looking at a giggling model that was posing, and bending over, and shaking her head yes as she laughed.

"You are something else," he held her close.

"Yep! I am your wife and what I say goes. We use to dress identical remember when I met you," she reminded him.

"PINK SHIRT, really!" he gritted his teeth.

"Yes dear. You will be so stylish. I will probably have a HARD time looking at you," she had her nose in the air as she turned on the shower and stepped in.

"A HARD time is right. I am a stubborn man, but if you play your cards right, I will do anything you ask for this right here!" he patted her treasure. He was taking a shower with her and they would continue THIS on until the morning light.

Because she was flying out at six for a photo shoot in NYC again, their time was special between his business and her assignments.

He kissed her as she was leaving and said, "Sure glad you packed for us. I'll see you when you get home. Have a safe flight! I miss you already. We'll leave for Kentucky when you get home." He handed the cabbie her bag and kissed her before she got in.

She hated goodbyes so she would not say it. She just waved and blew him a kiss as he stood there in faded jeans with no shirt or shoes. Still he hadn't learned to dress as fast as she.

She was used to dressing in five minutes for anything that was thrown at her. She said to herself, he has always had time to spare, and do as he pleased.

She got on the plane and went to sleep, and then her phone rang. It was him, "Goodnight sweetheart," Colten said.

"Goodnight my love," and Candice hung up.

He stood there looking at his phone. "She is the only person that has ever hung up on me," he said out loud.

Martina called Nancy and told her what Phillip had said about Matt Larson.

"Oh my goodness … Curtis Curtis Come here quick! You got to hear this!" He came flying around the corner to the kitchen and she pointed to the chair beside her.

She cut the speaker on, "Now repeat that Martina what you just said, and do not leave out a word. Remember you told it to me five seconds ago. I will know if you forgot something!"

Curtis sat and he was waiting for an explosion because Nancy never talked back to Martina unless it was extremely important. He looked at the ceiling for divine guidance.

When she finished, Nancy said, "Don't worry honey.

Mr. Wonderful will take good care of Sugar for you. Won't you honey!" and she smiled like a little angel.

Curtis said into the speaker, "I am glad you brought it to my attention and I will have my guys keep a lookout for any misstep that man makes. They already want to nab him anyway, just relax little mama. What's Adam into tonight?"

Nancy said, "You two can chat another time I got to go to sleep and get to the office early and check it out for bombs. Goodnight Martina, see you!"

The next morning Martina was an hour late and she apologized.

"As usual, I am here doing the dirty work. All is clear so relax girlfriend, and prop your feet up. Look this pregnancy is worst than the last, your feet are already swollen. Toes look like little baby sausages! "Nancy started typing.

"I love you too. My BFF is testy this morning! I should not have told you but ... but ..."

Nancy stopped typing, "But what?"

Martina burst out crying.

Nancy said, "There goes them damn old hormones again. They like to have kill me your last pregnancy!" She got up and moseyed over to Martina and hugged her.

"Now Now Let it out!" Nancy was rubbing her back.

Martina got louder and was sniffling and wailing, "I don't know what I'd do if something happened to Phillip!" boohoo.

Nancy handed her a Kleenex, "Blow your nose and quit snotting on me. Everything is going to be alright,

Mr Wonderful is on the job now. If you hadn't called me, I'd be a mad sister! Especially if someone else told me first! You know how I am. I got to be the first to know everything!"

Martina had to laugh at Nancy because she was the first to know EVERYTHING. "Let's do some work, what you say?"

"Yep guess so that's what you pay me for ... I'd probably do it for free, but Curtis likes the paycheck I bring home," and she smiled at her friend.

Nancy had looked into the files and found Larson's folder and tucked it into her purse. Curtis would take a look at it tonight. She was going to help protect Sugar, if it killed her.

She typed faster, "If Martina got a hold to it and read it, she might have that baby too soon. She had compiled it last week when Larson's wife came to the office. Mrs Larson wanted her husband followed because she thought he was cheating on her. He is ... you dumb broad!" she was talking to herself and she had better look at what she typed.

She went to the shredder, "I messed up big time." She walked back mumbling, "I typed what I was thinking. Haven't done that in a long time!"

Martina was searching for Larson's file and could not find it. "Hmm have you seen ...?"

"Nope haven't seen it!" Nancy said snapping.

"I didn't say what, Nancy. What are you up to?" Martina had her hands on her hips.

"Typing that's what I do for a living," Nancy bit the inside of her bottom lip.

Curtis drove up and she grabbed her pocketbook, "That's Mr Wonderful out there. He has come to take me away. To lunch Martina TO LUNCH! I'll be back so do some work!" Out the door she went, and waved.

"Traitor!" Martina said to the empty office and she locked the door, and went into her office for a nap. She had to go to two houses to meet with clients this afternoon while Nancy is sitting behind that desk.

Nancy jumped in the police car and said, "Go! Go!"

Curtis sped off, "Have you got it?"

"Of course I do. It's in my shoulder bag. That girl is in big trouble, if she takes that Larson woman's case," shaking her head. "She's already looking for the folder."

"I'll stop by the restaurant and order and read it as they are preparing our food and you can take it back," Curtis said.

"I can't take it back. It'd be like feeding the gorilla at the zoo. He's going to break that glass and eat me eventually! You keep it and make copies for the trial!" she said.

"Now what are you talking about the trial? Sugar is going to be my lawyer, because if something happens to Martina. I'm going to kill that man, Police Officer!" and she stared at him with her eyes narrowing.

As he sat in his police uniform staring back at his wife, he said, "Good!" He began eating the plate of food the waitress had brought and set in front of him.

"You not eating?" Curtis knew not to discuss anything

in the restaurant because it could be overheard. "It's mighty good. Here eat my pie!" and placed it in front of her and gave her his spoon.

"Well if you insist. I'll force myself!" she started eating and moaning and the whole restaurant's patrons were looking at her.

"What? It's the best pie I have ever eaten people, "she moaned some more.

Curtis paid the bill and opened the back door of the squad car for her to get in.

She got in and took a toothpick out of her purse, "They know I ain't your prisoner!" and she giggled.

"Really?' Curtis asked.

"Yeah! I showed them my purse when you drove away. They think you are my chauffeur," and grinned into his rear view mirror. "I love you, Mr Wonderful!"

He dropped her off and blew her an air kiss. No way was he getting out of this car. He got a call and turned the blue light on.

"Show off!" she marched in and Martina stared at her.

"Guess the lunch, didn't go too well?" Martina said and rolled her eyes at Nancy.

"Why would say that! It was delicious chocolate cream pie!" and she smiled.

"I saw you get out of the backseat, Nancy!" saying with a big question and frown.

"Well I have all my desserts in the back seat of my husband's police car," she smiled and sat down saying to her self that ought to shut her up.

When in walks Phillip, "Got to steal her away, Nancy.

Mom's having a dental procedure and we got to pick Adam up," he was helping Martina and fussing over her.

"Sugar take her, she's yours!" and she went back to typing.

"What's wrong?" Martina said when she got in the car.

"Someone shot Matt Larson. Dad told me to take you and Adam to Brigs for a few days and stay out of the line of fire. Until he phones us, we are not to tell anyone!"

"I have to tell Nancy to close the office up NOW today!" Martina had to. Immediately she yelled at her friend.

"Nancy get out and get out now! I will call you tonight!" and she hung up.

Nancy flew out the door and got in her car when the office BLEW UP! She drove off in shock. She sat in front of her house for two hours when Curtis came home and found her.

Curtis heard it on the scanner and raced home as quick as he could after he saw Nancy's text. She let him know she was okay. He had to finish up the reports and make assignments to cover this tragedy. He held her tight. Real tight!

"I almost lost you! I will Never put you in the back seat again. I promise." Curtis was humble.

"I don't have a job. I don't have a office. So you can sit me anywhere you wanted me," she was humble, too.

"If Sugar had not came and got Martina, it could have been bad. If Martina had not second thought Sugar, I would be dead. She thinks fast and he had no clue," she finally cried into the Kleenex.

"I got to go back to work," Curtis said.

"You ain't going nowhere without me, Mr Wonderful. I'll sit in the back of that car until you get through. I told Bessie to take Michael in, and keep him there. Whoever did this knows I work for Martina, and I had access to that file," she was trembling.

"You are right. Get in the back and lay down," Curtis told her. "You are thinking like a cop now what else should I know," he was driving to the station slowly.

"That wife of Larson was a mean looking woman. My thought is she has hired a hit man. Just a woman's intuition.

To kill her husband, then she had to get rid of any evidence of turmoil in her marriage. The evidence is in that folder. Where is it?" she asked.

"In my desk locked up. I didn't have time to make a copy. That is good. It is the original. Her signature stands out loud and clear.

"You are going in with me and will not be out of my sight. Is that clear!" Curtis said.

"Yes sir, Captain Wonderful!" she replied.

CHAPTER TWO

The beach was a haven for Phillip, Martina, and Adam. Cynthia had to stay home for Bart, since he was holding the fort down. Brigs would go to the law office and help Bart, but Phillip was told to stay there out of sight.

Martina called Nancy and they talked for an hour. Nancy told her that Curtis had the original folder at the police station secure. "I'm in jail now!" Curtis and I may live here for awhile. Be safe my friend. Love you, Sister!" Nancy said.

"Love you too, Sister!" Martina said and hung up.

"Look at the news Buttercup!" and she went to play with Adam and rolled around on the floor with him. Katherine watched them having fun.

Then Phillip saw Martina's office blown up and he held his head and cried. Katherine got to him. Martina stayed on the floor with Adam to distract the child.

After he got himself together, he asked Katherine if she would play with Adam. She nodded. She was good with children and the little fellow ran after her to get a chocolate chip cookie. It was his favorite cookie.

Phillip took Martina onto the porch, and hugged her.

"I almost lost my wife and child today," and he bent and kissed her stomach.

"You were sent to save us. You are my world. Thank God nothing happened to you!" Martina said. They held each other in the moonlight staring into space while Katherine and Brigs played with their son. They could hear his laughter.

Elizabeth is in her eight month of pregnancy and she and Cameron are on their way to Churchill Downs. He had everything arranged for FANASTIC STRETCH to arrived the following day. There would be no day that the horse did not see Cameron. They had a lightweight jockey named Hosea that had been riding him every day also.

Cameron had trained them both to do what they need to do together to win this race for Colten Travis Bingham III.

He had met with Colten on arrival to the Louisville Marriott Downtown hotel and they were shown to the hospitality suite. Elizabeth was thrilled at the room and Cameron was anxious to get to the Paddock.

Cameron had asked Colten, if his wife would check on Elizabeth while he was at the race track. Elizabeth had decided to stay in the room and forgo all the walking. Plus, she didn't want to be a distraction for Cameron.

Elizabeth told him, "Go do your thing and I'll be here at the end of your day in your bed as I always am. I will be relaxing and I need that, I've worked so hard on our house. I need to rest before the baby comes. Now go!"

Out he went with Brian, Joe and his brother Clarence that worked at the stables. Hosea was to met them there.

FS was calming when he saw Cameron. The man said he was fit to be tied. "So glad you're here!"

Colten had joined them at the Paddock, and he told them all what a good job they had done. He told Cameron that his wife Candice was taking Elizabeth for dinner. They were doing a lot of girl talk and I left, he explained to calm Cameron.

Candice and Elizabeth had hit it off. They sat and talked about everything. Candice wanted to know about her pregnancy, "One day I hope to have Colten's baby, but right now my career won't allow time."

She didn't say it but her career would be nil if she lost her flat chest and gained a tummy. She had cowgirl clothes on today and Elizabeth felt comfortable with Candice.

"The big day is next month and Cameron has helped me get the nursery ready. You must come and see it. We are in our new house and have plenty of room so when back at home come on over. We live beside FANATIC STRETCH," and she laughed.

That's when Cameron and Colten came up behind the girls that were eating and giggling.

"I told you Cameron she was in good hands!" and he kissed the top of Candice's ponytail. My little cowgirl right here, makes everything alright," Colten said as he sat down. He was wearing a matching outfit.

"We're still in the honeymoon phase, and I hope it continues for another fifty years!" Candice stared into Colten's eyes.

Cameron kissed Elizabeth on the lips and sat holding

her hand, "Hungry? You gotta eat honey. He's been so busy lately I have to remind him," and she smiled at him.

He ordered his meal as did Colten, and they all talked about the impending race. The girls about the fashions that were being wore by others.

Cameron was so glad Elizabeth had someone to talk to because he was going to be with FS every minute from today.

On May 2nd and 3rd they had horse workouts. Cameron and Colten seemed to be inseparable. As were the girls.

Candice had been before to the races, so she had no qualms about going staying with Elizabeth. If she went anywhere ... people were snapping pictures and she had to be dressed to the nines.

When May 6th gets here, all women made a pack to dress accordingly, in a spring dress and large hats with personality.

Candice wore a pastel pink floral short designer creation with a pink Fascinator hat with feathers to the right of her side ponytail which cascaded down her shoulder. Her sandals were Italian in a straw colored leather that matched her clutch purse. She had a clear poncho attached to the handle on her clutch that had a four-leaf clover charm on the front of the poncho's one inch casing. She smiled at her Gucci symbol on her Square eyeglasses. Her only jewelry was a her huge 10 carat diamond ring and matching diamond eternity wedding band. She had tiny diamond studded earrings.

Everything she had on was an advertisement. Each had been given to her by a designer to wear because her picture would be everywhere. Every magazine would feature her attire.

"It's my business attire. I am ready darling," and she looked at her handsome tall husband standing with a smirk on his face. The embodiment of all he detested, but for her he donned the lime green slacks, and loafers with no socks. His shirt had the same pink in her dress paired with a ocean blue blazer and a straw fedora shaped hat. "Satisfied?"

"Yes you look good enough to eat! We must hurry! It took you too long to dress we cannot be late! I have to make an entrance," Candice smiled. He tried to kiss he,r but she ducked. "You will mess up my lip gloss by Covergirl," and laughed. She ran out the door to the limo, where he swatted her backside.

Turning to the paparazzi and he asked, "Did you 'all get that?" They all nodded and shouted questions. When in the car he said, "I DID as you asked, I didn't say a word! But I should have said that ass is mine!" and Colten grinned.

Candice puckered a kiss and pretended to kiss the air, "All yours!"

They were greeted at Gate 10 by the non-stop flashbulbs and were escorted to their suite in the grandstand by security.

She was given a cold Mint Julep which she did not drink and he had requested a bourbon and coke. They settled and could not get the butterflies out of their stomach.

He said, "This is it baby!"

She said, "Our horse is a winner even if he doesn't win the race!" and he smiled. "But he's going to!"

He got up and started pacing. She had to stand, and got a pair of binoculars and scope out FS's location. Then handed them to him, "Number 9 is my lucky number."

He took them. Hosea was calming FANATIC STRETCH who was fidgeting and snorting.

Cameron had done everything he could do to calm the horse He had whispered in his ear, and patted him as he always did without one ounce of variation. He stood beside Brian.

Brian said, "This is it!"

The National Anthem had been sung by Harry Connick, Jr.

They all had sung "My Old Kentucky Home!"

FINALLY .... YES! They were off and running! Candice could not watch. She went to the restroom, and prayed then eased back as Colten was shouting, "Come on Hosea … Let him go!"

Hosea did not until the last stretch, and he was gaining so quickly the other horses were tired, and he flew passed them to the finish line, and Colten grabbed her. She let him kiss her and kiss her. Then she pushed him, "Wake up it is not a dream. They will want you down there go!"

"I will … but you my lady are coming with me. He is our baby! Yours and mine." She quickly put on lip gloss, and put on her shades. Letting him lead her to Gate 18 where the owners were, and the Garland of Roses would be placed around the winning horse's neck.

Colten shouted, "Where is Cameron and Brian?' and he had his security guards to get them.

They were found and stood beside him and Candice. Cameron had tears in his eyes. Colten patted him on the back. "You did this. Proud of you!" Brian patted him, too!

Elizabeth was watching from the hotel and she had been jumping so she made herself sit and calm herself. The baby was kicking up a storm and she rubbed him as Cameron always did. She was so proud of him.

"Your daddy will be here in a few minutes little one. He just has to rub down FS first! That horse needs his attention right now! He's a winner just like you are!"

She had rewound the tape that she had made him for the last hour. She had watched it over and over.

She turned and Cameron was standing behind her. I'll rub my baby now, and he did over and over for the next hour.

"I am so proud of you. I wanted to be there under the Twin Spires ... AND I ... was in spirit!" she said holding his face.

"You were there. I felt you," and he placed her tiny hand on his heart and smiled.

"The crowd was unbelievable. People were pushing and shoving and if anyone had done that to you ..." he didn't finish only shook his head.

She kissed him, "I was right here taking care of our baby. This baby is more important to me. Next time your son and I will be there, I promise!"

He got on his knees and told the baby, "Did you hear that! She knows it will be a next time." Then to Elizabeth,

"This paycheck will mean a college fund for him, and I can relax and take more time with my family."

"Sounds good to me! We gotta Skype the family, I promised them." They did and drank sparkling apple cider after a toast to the owner Colten.

They lay in bed and watched the festivities on TV until they dropped off to sleep holding one another.

Colten and Candice had to stay behind to have pictures with the horse. The crowd was cheering as the Kentucky Derby Winning Horse was draped with a Garland of Roses. Pictures of them receiving the Kentucky Derby Trophy, he included his wife in everything.

The other accolades, Colten was not interested in. The only thing that interested him at this moment was getting Candice back to their hotel.

He was devouring her with his eyes.

"I am a mind reader, but pull that jacket down over my prize," and she giggled and kissed him not worrying about her lip gloss.

"You do that again and those photographers are going to have a REAL story to tell. I bet it hits the front page," he said.

"You are right. Let me IGNORE you!" and she sprinted off and fast paced it to the car.

He was on the chase for his thoroughbred wife was getting away. Her long legs were all he could see.

Into the limo that she had called for was waiting, she jumped inside. Two steps behind, he jumped in.

"How do you do that?" Colten asked.

"I have had to plan my getaways for ten years, Darling! It takes practice. I'll teach you!" Candice said.

"I'll teach you how to let others do it for you," he suggested.

"I got a better idea you stay you, and I'll stay me, and it will be more than exciting when we ... meet in the middle."

He said, "True! Remember May 6th was the greatest two minutes of horse racing. I intend to take twenty hours to race you around our room. I guarantee you will have Roses and maybe even a Trophy."

"Are you saying you want a baby?" she asked. He nodded.

FINALLY ... YES!

Cameron and Elizabeth walked pass the Do Not Disturb sign. He said, "We'll talk to them later. I want to follow FANATIC STRETCH home and get my baby in bed resting."

She asked, "Are you talking about me or the horse?" frowning at him.

"Both you and the baby! Brian will take care of the horse. You are my first priority!" he confirmed.

She said, "Good to hear it!" She was all smiles and laid her head on his shoulder. Looking out at the Kentucky mountains and she went to sleep while Cameron talked to the driver.

It was a long drive, but the RV had a bathroom and a pregnant woman needs to go every five minutes. She laughed, "I will be so glad to sit on a non-moving one. At least, I am too big to fall off."

"You are not too big. You are just right. The refrigerator is full, do you want something?" He asked. They had ham and cheese sandwiches that he fixed.

"You are going to be a good daddy. I can see you fixing him peanut butter and grape jelly sandwiches for breakfast when I am not around."

"And where might I ask will you be?" getting nose to nose with her to hear her answer better, and looking into her eyes.

"Why … I will be in his daddy's bed too tuckered out from nighttime activities to get up so early in the morning."

He smiled. "Good answer little mama," and kissed her freckled nose.

CHAPTER THREE

Martina was enjoying the beach with little Adam and Phillip was enjoying watching his family build a sand castle. He had been on the phone with his father, "This month has been a blessing for Martina. She looks well rested. I on the other hand am anxious. Has there been any progress?"

"The Private Investigator has all I need to have her arrested. Now sit tight, I'll call you back tonight!"

Martina asked, "What is that frown for?" and Adam let go of her hand and walked to his daddy.

"Dada Dada," Adam spit out sand.

"Wow! His first steps! If I had been at the office I would missed that. I got a picture with my phone. Look Martina and you are holding your stomach. As if in pain?"

He scooped Adam up and ran to Martina. "Why haven't you told me? Are you in labor? Holy Cow!"

"It's probably Braxton- Hicks contractions. Besides, relax I'll let you know when I need to go." She swatted his hand for help. "Let me see the picture. He ran to his daddy!"

"You have to go get checked out," he was gritting his

teeth because she had no doctor out here, and he knew she wasn't going back until that woman was in jail.

"Okay I will give the doctor a call and have her come out here. How does that sound?" Phillip grinned.

"Prefect! Good luck you are going to need it!" Martina said and waddled up the sand dune to the house.

By the time she laid down on the outside sofa, she was out of breath. Her pains were getting stronger, but thirty minutes apart.

"Tell Katherine to come here and you take Adam with you," she was talking slower.

He dialed the doctor and asked if she could come and she made arrangement to meet her at the nearest Emergent Care.

He dialed Katherine, "Can you come and take Adam for some fun. I am going to take Martina to get checked out. I think she is in labor."

He helped Martina into the Maserati and reclined the seat a little. "Relax honey. I am here!" he went around to give Adam to Katherine and took the baby's seat out encase they needed it before he got back.

"I'll call you," Phillip was on the coast highway and found where Dr. Malone said to met her.

Martina was not looking good and he was so glad, he had taken that picture of Adam's first steps. She gripped his hand and he knew then, this was it! His little girl was coming to see her daddy today! He was excited, but worried.

Once inside he explained the situation, and that the doctor was on her way to check her, "IT'S probably gas!" He didn't want them to get excited and they call an ambulance. Unless Dr,. Malone ordered it. No other doctor was going to touch his wife. For sure, not some quack that he didn't know.

Dr Malone came flying in, and told the personnel to get Martina in a room quick.

Phillip picked her up and took her to the room.

Martina was dilated five centimeters and Dr M was going to make arrangements. Phillip said, "Don't!" and she stopped.

"We cannot go back! Our lives are in danger. It is a long story but the ambulance, you, the hospital could be in danger. Her office got blown up on purpose. I beg you to get her in a hospital down here under another name. My little girl needs to be safe when she is born. Please doc!"

The doctor knew he was a lawyer and good at pleading a case. Looking at him and Martina that was shaking her head, "It is true!" and she screamed. The personnel came running.

She told them not to call an ambulance, "There is not time. I must deliver here," she told them what she needed.

Phillip was kissing Martina, "It's going to be alright. Dr Malone has magic in her bag."

Martina was breaking his hand, and looked at the doctor for help. "Please give her something."

"Do you want to delay this birth or get it over," she asked because she was now in sterile attire, and the staff was also.

Martina was screaming and Phillip was breathing the

hee hee woo woo hee hee woo woo LaMaze method He couldn't remember if he was doing it right, but continued to coach her to do it.

She finally did. "Come on baby, it helps to relax ...."

Dr. Malone said, "Push Martina Push!" and that is all Phillip remembered. He hit the floor.

When he awoke, there was a beautiful baby girl in Martina's arms. He said, "Hey little Eve!" the staff were oohing and aahing. Then doing the paperwork and calling a nearby pediatrician to come to the office, and check her out. Dr Malone explained this had to be done. All signatures must be legal and the birth record for the state records.

"Yes babies are born every day at home, but we want to make sure all are healthy. You had a bad time, last birth Martina. You may hemorrhage again, and may not. I want you to come back to the hospital with me. It's your choice."

Martina looked at Phillip and he went paled.

"I want to go home and Phillip's aunt will take care of me. She can call an ambulance, if she needs to. Phillip you have to take care of Adam, and Katherine will teach you to care for Eve, if I am not able. I need to sleep now," she was exhausted.

The doctor asked the staff, "Do you do any home care?" one said she did. Her name was Diane and she agreed to check on Martina every day. Take her vitals, if her pulse goes up, and her blood pressure starts dropping. Call an ambulance and call my number."

Phillip said, "Thank Dr. Malone. I will pay you extra next time, I see you!"

"Oh you will be getting my bill!" and she was out the door.

Martina was sleeping and he thank the LPN that was going to come to Katherine and Brigs's house. "You, too. I will pay extra to help my wife. You can quit your job and work for my wife full-time, if you want to. I'm not feeling well," and he sat down and rubbed the knot on the back of his head.

"I'll call my uncle. He and my father will get us home. Dear God, my mother will help!" and he began smiling.

His mother could do ANYTHING! Then he frowned, "Wonder if she knows what is going on. Wonder what Bart had told Cynthia?" Phillip needed to find out.

"Dad what does mother know because I need her help? You are a grandfather by the way. Eve has arrived!"

He stared out the window waiting for his father to take a breath. "Son, congrats. Your mother knows that something is amiss because her son has left town, but NO she does not know the severity of it. A warrant has been issued for Mrs Latham's arrest, but it seems she has left the country. Why don't you 'all come home and stay with us while Martina recoups. Mother can care for the babies?"

"As soon as that woman is behind bars, my family will be home. I can't take any chances with their lives. Tell mother about the situation and ask her to come help Aunt Katherine. One child I can handle, but two kids I am lost. Especially with the newborn because mother helped Martina with Adam. I was always working!" Phillip pleaded his case.

"Speaking of work, when might you be coming to help me?

This office doesn't run itself. I'll send your mother up tonight," he fumed. Then rethought, "Sorry I know you have been doing a lot on the computer and your briefs are spot on, but I miss my son."

"Then come with mother tonight and see the baby. I will bring her back when she tires of us. You can see your new granddaughter," he was persuading him big time.

"OK You have talked me into it. I'll tell Brigs!" Phillip's head had cleared and he was going to load them up.

Phillip went and bought an infant seat for the car. The facility would not let them leave without one. Diane the LPN followed them to the beach house so she would know how to get there tomorrow.

She also was going to take vitals on the mother and the baby twice tonight, and record it everyday. Dr Malone had insisted the LPN call her daily with this information.

The nurse carried the baby in, and Phillip carried Martina in and laid her on the sofa. The baby was ready to eat so the nurse helped Martina with her first breastfeeding. Martina had for a month had her bag packed with her breast pumps, bottles and care for her nipples. It went well but Martina needed fluids. Phillip got her water and juice, and Katherine got her food on a tray.

"You all are so good to me," and Martina started crying happy tears. Adam was kissing his mama and jumping. Phillip held him so he would not jump on the baby or Martina.

Finally his Mother and Father got there. He took Martina to the bedroom, and he laid beside her. They both went to sleep immediately.

Katherine told Cynthia, "They are exhausted. Now let's make a plan when we are going to feed the baby and Adam.

Bart and Brigs sat and talked. "Brother stay the night and we can drive together to the office tomorrow?" suggested Brigs.

"And miss out on having that big house all to myself. No, I got to go!" Bart said as he sneaked out.

"Katherine, I am going on with Bart! So my brother won't be alone tonight. Bye!" Brigs was out the door running.

Martina called Nancy the next day, "Yes... It was sudden. I passed out last night or I would have called you."

"I know you would tell me, if you were conscious. I got good NEWS. Curtis told me just a few minutes ago. That witch has been caught in Canada. They are extraditing her back to Los Angeles. We will have her arse in the slammer tomorrow night! Then I can go home," Nancy said.

"Where have you been?" Martina was nosy.

"Shacking up! What'd you think. I can do that because I'm not pregnant!" and she cackled. "Got me a job, too! Been typing and filing for the police department. Yep Curtis brings me in and takes me out! When are you going to rebuild and take me back where I belong?"

Nancy was making Martina laugh and she was holding tight to the pillow on her stomach.

"I have missed you my friend. We'll be home in the next week. Once Phillip know Mrs. Latham will never get out of that jail. She thinks all was blown up when she finds out it wasn't, it will be in a court of law!" Martina was so excited to tell her husband.

"You calm down and kiss Sugar for me. Talk to you tomorrow. Oh kiss Adam and Eve for Auntie Nancy, too!" she hung up. Phillip came in, and Martina kissed him real deep and his eyes started bulging. "Nancy said for me to give you a big kiss from her!" Martina admitted.

"And you do everything that woman tells you to do. I got to have a talk with her soon," and he moved his eyebrows up and down. She told him Mrs Latham was caught and being transfer to the LA jail. **FINALLY ... YES!**

CHAPTER FOUR

Emily and Eliot wanted to meet Cameron and Elizabeth at their house to welcome them back. It was the first time they had visited their new home. It was hard for Emily to think her parents no longer lived in the large house next door.

Emily told Eliot that this horse winning was so important to Elizabeth and there will be no one there for them since her parents had moved to the beach. "Let's go. Mama and Daddy are tied up with Martina and Phillip's baby. Someone has got to be there for my sister," Elizabeth said.

Eliot hugged his wife, "We will always be here for her and Cameron, like she will be when we have a baby!" he had been begging her, but her Ballet was taking over most of her time.

"When I am replaced by a younger ballerina, we will have a child. Okay until then we will practice, practice, practice our dance of love!" she kissed him passionately.

"I would not mind practicing while we wait," he grinned.

"They are too close and you know what the doc said

290

Eliot! You must take your time. Foreplay takes time. I am worth it aren't I?" she was working her magic on him and she was getting warm, too. "Maybe we could just walk around see what is inside at the old house," she grinned.

"Are you saying what I think you are saying?" Eliot took her by the hand and then they were running to the old house.

They made it to the porch swing and had amazing afternoon delight.

"I'm sorry I could not make it inside the house. Honey, you were just too ready. Doc would be proud. We can get there in record time, now." He was so proud of her. It had made him love her more than he thought possible. "I love you!" lifting her up to slide down him again.

"We had better start walking because I see a horse trailer coming down the road. They said they were following it," Emily said.

As the driver was turning in, Cameron told Elizabeth, "That looks like Eliot's truck."

"Yes and there is my sister hanging all over him," and she smiled. "Just like high school. Cameron they were sickening. That was before you showed me what love is. Those have always had it!" and Elizabeth laughed.

Eliot said, "Cameron that horse you are always talking about ... Is Number One! Congrats. We had to come over!"

Elizabeth was hugging Emily, and they were going into the house to see the nursery. Chattering away about the baby, not the horse.

"I got to go over and put the baby to bed. You want

to come?" Cameron waved Eliot on and they walked to the stables.

Cameron rubbed FANATIC STRETCH down and gave him an apple, patted him "Good night!" Then they walked back.

Eliot said, "Won't be long before you 'all have a little one to tuck in bed."

"Any day now. She is excited and I am scared. We are so far out. Wish we had neighbors. If ever you and Emily settle maybe you'll build out here near us, and have some kids for ours to play with." Cameron was tired and what he was really saying is I need some help out here.

Eliot said, "You know you are right I think Elizabeth needs her sister, and when the baby comes maybe she will want one. I want one now. My parents keep asking when they are going to be grandparents."

"I am hoping when we have our kid that her mother will come down that road to see our baby. It is tearing Elizabeth up that they don't come ever," Cameron was hoping Emily would tell Katherine.

Then he shrugged his shoulders and told Eliot come on in, and see the nursery.

Elizabeth thawed some stew out in the microwave and made cornbread. Emily made iced tea. They sat and talked and talked.

"We do have a spare bedroom, if you 'all want to spend the night you are more than welcome," Elizabeth said.

"Eliot?" Emily asked.

"We'd love to. You two girls need to talk anyway," he said.

Cameron went by Elizabeth, and pinched her buttocks and she grinned. "Doesn't change anything, take a nap," she said and he nodded.

They had taken pictures of the derby and Eliot was fascinated. "I'm going to take Emily there if that horse runs again."

"That horse is going to win many races," Cameron said.

When Eliot got into the bedroom, Emily was all bathed and putting lotion on her legs. He said, "You will never believe what Cameron said?"

"Probably what Elizabeth said. What did he say?" Emily asked.

"That we should build out here so you two would have each other. He is upset that your parents don't come."

"Ditto, I do love it out here, away from the maddening crowd. What did you say?" Emily asked.

"I would love it but it is up to you," Eliot was not going to rock the boat. He went and showered.

"I want to live by my sister," she said and he picked her up and kissed her everywhere.

"And what else?" he asked as he was licking her navel.

"And have a child to play with our nephews," Emily said.

"Nephews?" he turned his head sideways.

"They are going to reproduce like rabbits. Don't you hear them. Let's drown them out."

Eliot was plumb shocked, and then the second part

of that phrase hit him, and he didn't let her rethink what she had offered.

She soon was moaning and could care less what was happening in the next room.

Eliot said the next morning as they were leaving, "We are definitely moving to the country. You were a wild woman last night and I loved it!"

"Want a baby?" Emily asked. Eliot nodded. She said, "OK build me a house right there beside Sis!"

FINALLY … YES!

Colten and Candice jumped out of the helicopter onto the helipad. Candice wanted to go back to her NYC apartment for tonight.

Since she didn't drink, it was wise that they get out of the celebrating horde of drunks at the Churchill Downs. Colten barely drank any more after she told him it makes a man's wiener limp.

He had asked for kids. It didn't need to be limp, she pointed out. He was mindful that everything he said, she could quote it back. He had to have a clear mind to keep up with her.

He said to himself, "She is a health nut … A vegan and I love meat. She runs and I ride. She is going to be a great mother and teach their kids to eat healthy. I got to hit the gym whether I like it or not." He smiled.

He was just sitting there looking out the window deep in thought. She came down the staircase in a sheer Victoria Secret bustier set of white lace and straddled his legs and sat, putting her long arms around his neck.

Looking into his azure eyes she asked, "What makes my husband smile like that? I gotta. I gotta know?"

His hands had started roaming her assets and she was wiggling on his knees. She was getting hotter by the minute so he didn't answer. Just kept on making her move with him. When she couldn't wait any longer, he parted the clouds.

She was his to mold in any direction he chose.

Every time he told her, "Only you can make me smile!Before you, I never let myself feel anything, but sexual gratification. Now, I want more…more…oh yes much more!"

She listened as he begged for her to have his child. As they climaxed, she said "Yes, I want!"

"Want what?" he was withholding.

She was being tortured, "Give me Give it to me!

He asked holding her tightly on the verge, "Give you what?"

"Give me my child!" she whispered.

"I'll do my best!" he stated loudly.

That is when he could not hold back any longer. He was going slow because she wanted fast, and she was shaking with need. Her head had gone back and she was biting her lower lip.

"Come on Baby! You can do it!" Candice panted.

Colten rolled her off his knees, and pounded her slender body with his massive physique. It was the one time that he held back nothing. Closing his eyes, shivering as the waves overtook them both.

They lay spent on the white bear skin on the lavish living room floor, holding tight to every second of bliss.

They were drenched in sweat and she raised and propped her arm on his chest saying, "T he race is won. That's the one that swam up stream for us. Baby! I didn't take my pill this morning. I want our baby, too!"

FINALLY … YES!

to be continued

Printed in the United States
By Bookmasters